Gilgamesh

Joan London is the author of two prize-winning collections of stories published in Australia. *Gilgamesh*, her first novel, was shortlisted for the Miles Franklin award and was chosen as the *Age* Book of the Year for Fiction 2002. It is her first work to be published in the UK.

From the international reviews:

'A lyrical and thoughtful novel... Joan London discerns and explores the mythic longings, the invisible epic battles, that give depth to everyday lives. Her narrative spans a global trajectory and a rich and colourful cast of characters. Beautifully written and constructed, dreamlike yet believable, this a remarkable first novel.' Alev Adil, *Independent*

'An ambitious novel about the search for some spiritual remedy in a damaged world... London is an accomplished storyteller.' John Spurling, *Sunday Times*

'Edith's journey is epic... The providential strangers, war and exotic climes she encounters along the way are given a rare and beguiling immediacy that is due to London's sparse prose.' Lilian Pizzichini, *Financial Times*

'Vivid... London tells an engrossing tale.' *Sunday Herald*

'A beautifully written meditation on life and loss.' *Harpers & Queen*

'A masterful work... London's writing is beautifully breathtaking, immersing readers in a war-torn world.' *Good Book Guide*

'A beautiful novel of faith and fortitude… London's writing is poetic and her heroine quietly formidable.' *Metro*

'A pleasure to read… London's prose is a seamlessly shifting blend of poetry, pathos and humor.' Elizabeth Ward, *Washington Post*

'A compelling debut… The epic scope of the novel is complemented by an extraordinary sensitivity to detail… The settings glow with a dream like intensity, evoking both the allure of adventure and the ambivalent embrace of home.' Amanda Heller, *Boston Globe*

'Compelling… a remarkable study of a young woman's most literal rite of passage, growing up.' Judith M. Redding, *Baltimore Sun*

'An epic tale from a writer of considerable distinction.' *Sydney Morning Herald*

'Wonderfully economical prose, alternatively bristling and resonating with suggestiveness.' Stephanie Trigg, *Australian Book Review*

Gilgamesh

Joan London

ATLANTIC BOOKS
LONDON

First published in 2001 by Picador, an imprint of
Pan Macmillan Australia Pty Limited, St Martin's Tower,
31 Market Street, Sydney.

First published in Great Britain in 2003 by Atlantic Books,
an imprint of Grove Atlantic Ltd.

This paperback edition published by Atlantic Books in 2004.

1 3 5 7 9 8 6 4 2

A CIP catalogue record for this book is available
from the British Library.

1 84354 183 1

Printed in Great Britain by Mackays of Chatham

Atlantic Books
An imprint of Grove Atlantic Ltd
Ormond House
26–27 Boswell Street
London WC1N 3JZ

To Geoffrey

Acknowledgements

Above all I wish to thank Drusilla Modjeska whose great generosity and inspiring narrative vision were crucial to this book.

Special thanks also to Susan Hampton for her acute and skilful editorial work.

And thanks to Charlie Mann, John and Julie Lewis, Cisca Spencer and Jack London.

I am grateful to the Eleanor Dark Foundation for a Varuna Fellowship during the early stages of this book.

The lines from *The Epic of Gilgamesh* are from the translation by Andrew George (Allen Lane, The Penguin Press, London, 1999).

Contents

The Clearing

Frank met Ada when she came to the hospital to visit the soldiers.

It didn't suit her. She was supposed to chat and join in sing-songs and pour tea. But she was clumsy and offhand and didn't smile enough. She lacked the sense of charity that lit the faces of the other young women. That afternoon they were all wearing a white gardenia pinned to their coats and, as they entered, a nun-like sweetness filled the vast draughts of the room.

It was a convalescent hospital south of London, a gloomy country house requisitioned for the duration, where the soldiers, patched-up, jumpy, bitter, tottered and prowled like ancient temperamental guests. Frank shared a room with another Australian, an artilleryman from Melbourne, who wept like a baby in his sleep. Frank suffered from insomnia so it didn't disturb him too much. He didn't tell the doctors about the insomnia. Some were kind, but for some reason he found himself infuriated by kindness. He craved isolation. In isolation he would cure himself.

They were days away from Armistice. On the afternoon that Ada came, Frank had expected to be discharged, on the train to London. His leg was officially healed: he'd been waiting all week for the order. Only boredom made him come downstairs for tea.

They should really never have met.

They were singing around the piano, 'Over There' and 'He's Coming Home' and 'We'll Gather Lilacs'. The young women sang in fervid sopranos, harmonising with the men. Most of them, Frank thought, would have lost someone, husband, sweetheart, brother, in these past years. He noticed that Ada had left the group and was looking out a window. He went and stood beside her.

'A bit painful, this old stuff.'

'I never learnt the words.'

Outside was a tennis court, with the nets rolled up. Beyond it black-limbed trees held back the mist.

'What are you going to do when it's over?' He couldn't help looking at her gardenia, desperately lopsided, which was about to slide off the generous slope of her bosom.

'I don't know. Much the same I expect.' She had a flat, composed way of speaking, at odds with her appearance. Her dark hair was so bushy that she had to clutch her hat when she turned to him. She had fiercely sprouting eyebrows, dead white skin, a little silken moustache. She wasn't old, but like him, like all of them, she was no longer young. He had the odd sensation that she was the only real person in the room.

'What would you *like* to do?'

'Oh I see, you are joking. Well, I would like to go far away to a country where there will never be another war.'

'That's where I'm going!'

'There is no such country!' The gardenia dropped and she was stooping down to it. Her hat fell off, and her hair uncoiled. Everything about her seemed ready to erupt. He'd never known a woman so precarious.

'There is,' he said, crouching down beside her as she scrabbled for hairpins. 'Come home with me.'

He found her odd, mysterious. She had been orphaned very young, grew up living alone with her older brother. Frank thought this might be the key to her: no one had taught her to be nice. Her brother had died early in the war, at Ypres. She lived with her sister-in-law and little nephew in the top half of a house in Cricklewood. The sister-in-law, Irina, was a White Russian. There were Russian lodgers in the bottom half of the house. It was an unconventional set-up, to say the least.

They had visitors at all hours of the day. Whenever Frank called, there would be a strange hat or cane or pair of galoshes by the stand in the hall. The visitors, men and women, were always Russian. He sat among them in the dark parlour and drank cup after cup of black tea from the brass samovar on the table. They were a lively crowd who soon forgot to speak English in front of him. Ada said little but did not seem out of place. Sometimes she played trains on the floor with her chubby nephew, her hair uncoiling down her creamy neck. Frank, a poetry reader, thought of petals falling. She hardly ever looked his way.

She only seemed to come alive off-stage, with Irina. He heard them laughing in the kitchen, or calling out to one another down the hall. Irina called her *Ar*da, in the Russian way. Ardour. He didn't trust Irina. She was the opposite of Ada, tiny, worldly, elegant in her widow's weeds. She spoke excellent English, having lived in London since 1910. The others had only recently arrived from that debacle in Russia. She was in mourning not only for her English husband, but for her younger brother left behind in Russia, killed on the Russian front. Sorrow gave her a hard edge. There was a shrewd gleam in her eyes when she talked to Frank. He judged her to be clever and domineering, not his sort of woman.

She even dragged Ada off to the Orthodox Church with her. He found this out one Sunday when he visited, and for once there was nobody at home. One of the lodgers let him in, and insisted that he wait. Suddenly Ada ran in alone, in hat and coat, pink-cheeked from the cold. It was ridiculous, she said, standing by the door, as if continuing a conversation, as if she'd known he would be there, she didn't understand a word of the service, she only liked the chants. She wasn't religious, she added shyly, she was a free-thinker like her brother. This pleased Frank, because though raised strictly Methodist he had become an atheist during the war. And then still standing there, she burst out that she was tired of the gossip in the émigré community, everyone knowing your business, she was tired of it all, she wanted to go away and make a life for herself.

Then suddenly she stopped. They had never been alone together before. She started to move towards him. They fell on one another.

There is no wedding photograph, but a few months later, in the spring, someone took a snap of them in front of the house in Cricklewood. They are leaning against a railing, their hips both slightly crooked to the left. Both are hatless. Frank, in cricket whites and pullover, has his hands in his pockets. This is as complacent as he will ever look. Ada rests one hand on his shoulder. Her pose is languid. Already she is pregnant with the first of their two daughters. They aren't smiling but stare evenly at the camera. They look shy and proud and private. Is it the haze of a London spring that gives a dreaminess to the scene? They are proud of their dreams. They are going to take up land in Australia. Fresh air, honest toil, taking orders from no man. Because Frank can't lose the habit of God looking over his shoulder, he feels that the War spared him for this. He has no money but he will find a way. Meanwhile he has promised Ada plants and animals she has never seen before, light so clear you seem to swim in it.

They feel bold and superior, like revolutionaries. They have both just turned thirty. Their passage out is booked.

Frank joined a government scheme to open up the wilds of south-western Australia. Land, parcelled into blocks, was given to a group of twenty or thirty settlers who would initially work together to clear each home block and build each other a house. Every man was made a loan by the Agricultural Bank to get him started, repayable over thirty years. Of course, if all went well for you, you could end up owning your own land much sooner, in a matter of five or six years. The scheme was called Group Settlement.

In Frank's group were other ex-soldiers, English and Australian. There was an ex-butcher, ex-blacksmith, ex-grocer, even an ex-sea captain. All of them had a passion to own their own land. Each farm was 160 acres. They were drawn by ballot. This made Frank nervous. He had a Methodist's revulsion for gambling: he trusted only his own will.

By the time they came to live on their own block their daughters were nearly school age. A son was born but died soon afterwards, while they were still camping in a hut, waiting for their house to be built. 'We will put this behind us,' Frank said to Ada, to stave off his own panic. 'We won't speak of it again.' He dreaded her weeping. She could go quite wildly out of control. He spoke softly. One of the Settlement women was outside at the fire, cooking dinner for them. The hut had a dirt floor and whitewashed hessian walls. He took her hand. Ada kept her eyes closed. 'We have two fine girls.'

Their block was the outermost, cut off from the other farms by a belt of national forest. An afterthought, tacked on at the last minute over some government drawing board. It ran just beyond the dunes of the coast into bushy hillsides ridged with granite boulders and limestone caves. Close to the beach the soil became white with limestone. Only the wattles and melaleucas kept it from blowing into sand. Even at its furthest boundary, deep in the forest, you could hear the echo of the sea. It was the least arable of the blocks, but the most picturesque.

Their nearest neighbour was an old wooden hotel, the Sea House, built high on the escarpment to catch views over the forest to the ocean. On still afternoons Frank and Ada could sometimes hear the *tock* of a tennis ball and scraps of laughter from drifting guests. It was only half a mile away through the bush, but it was another world, isolated from the district, far away from the life and death struggles of the settlers. Frank despised the guests—city clerks on honeymoon—but Ada liked to take the girls with her and sit in the gardens, like a governess on a nature ramble. It was the only place with any romance in this country, she said.

The district was called Nunderup, but until 1927 it didn't appear on any map because there was nothing there. Then by petitions and subscriptions the settlers managed to erect a wooden hall up the road from the Sea House, for meetings and dances and concerts and the occasional picture show. The milk truck stopped there and the bus to Busselton. This was the Nunderup Hall.

Frank and Ada, or the Clarks as they were known in the district, didn't go to the dances or the pictures. They didn't go to any church service either. They didn't socialise with the other families in the area, the Lewises, McKays, Wards, Robertsons and Rileys. Nobody saw Ada for years at a time. When the girls went to school she turned up once or twice at the end-of-year prize-giving concerts but she didn't help the other women with the supper. She sat in an empty row of seats, her lips flecked with saliva, nervous as a student who has failed a test. Her girls left the other children and sat on either side of her.

Frank came to meetings in the hall as the Depression worsened and more and more farmers couldn't repay their loans. He spoke about being indentured slaves to the government, paying blood money to open up the country for them. He was a stirring speaker, Clarkie, he used to be a schoolteacher before the War.

He built the shed across the seasons of a year. He cut the trees down one spring when he was clearing the hill paddock. With a wedge borrowed from Bert McKay he cut them into slabs: it was a case of finding the right grain, and in the end, like skinning a rabbit, he got the hang of it. He dragged the slabs back to the home block while he still had the horse and chains. All summer they lay drying in the yellow grass. In autumn when the ground had softened, he dug a three-sided trench and stood the slabs up in it, side by side. He cut saplings for beams and poles and laid in a little hoard of corrugated iron. He hoped to roof the space before the winter rains.

But every day there was so much else to do, and nobody to help. He was methodical in everything he did, but slow and clumsy, teaching himself as he went. Some of the other men in the group had farming experience, or had worked with their hands in former life. Practical types. Some had already built a herd up, were picking up a nice little cream cheque each month. A bit of capital helped of course. Time and again before he took the next step he'd have to stop and hire himself out. A month picking potatoes down at Albany. A week here, a week there helping others to seed, in return for the loan of a team and plough. The ten cows he was entitled to from the government (to be paid for later of course) had never thrived. The two most adventurous had broken out and fallen down a gully. Another died calving. He thought he would go into pigs. But first he needed a shelter for them.

He'd never built anything on his own before. He didn't like to ask the other men for one more thing, even advice. Late at night he sat up in the kitchen working out how to do it, drawing diagrams on the backs of Agricultural Bank envelopes.

Sometimes when he sat at the table and saw the lamplight pooled over his scraps of paper, he thought that this was the only terrain he could ever really work. Beyond the light were his books ranged along the top shelf of the dresser. Shakespeare, Wordsworth, Tennyson, Scott, Stevenson and Dickens. He didn't have time to read them now, but he felt their presence. It crossed his mind that this was where he was really most at home, in the idea of things.

Winter was well and truly over before he came to finish the shed, perched on the roof, hammering in the last nails. It was spring again, and still no pigs wallowed in the boggy earth of the clearing. He'd been working all day on the roof, it was late now, almost dark. He was always late. Across the clearing Ada and the girls sat watching from the verandah steps. There was a sense of ceremony in their waiting. All winter long the roofless shed had sat like a small ruined monument in their landscape. Even now it didn't look quite like other piggeries. Even they could see that. It was too high, too tottery, like one of their skinny cows. None of them spoke.

Out of the corner of his eye Frank could see them on the steps. Their pale female faces, pale pinafores glowed in the half light. Maybe this was what made him lose concentration for a moment. Sitting there like a row of birds with their beaks open! He was dog-tired, stiff, sunburnt, from crouching all day up here. He took a swipe at the final nail and mysteriously—there were many mysteries in the course of Frank's carpentry—smashed straight down on his thumb.

He dropped the hammer with a clatter, and fell foward, the whole structure swaying a little beneath him. He raised his head and howled *God!* The dog barked crazily at the foot of the ladder. He sat still, clutching his hand, his eyes closed. The little girls thought he was crying, and stole towards him as he descended the ladder. Ada came to meet him with a teatowel she had grabbed. Something in her face made him wheel away from her and stride off into the bush, grabbing the axe as he went. The dog sloped after him, its ears flat.

'*Another pair of hands.*' That's what he said to himself as he slashed his way, one handed, through the bush. To share the burden a little. He might get somewhere then. If only he had a mate, a partner. A son. He thought of the Robertson brothers, bachelors, with ninety acres cleared. Or Violet McKay, as good as a man, who swung her last born in a basket from a tree and with the rest of her tribe brought the harvest in. Took charge of the dairy, served up hot scones with freshly churned butter if you so much as set foot on the place.

What *did* Ada do? Mooned about. There were certainly no scones for tea. Ada rested like a lady in the afternoons. After the boy, she seemed like half an invalid. Headaches. Women troubles. He'd never known a woman could be so much at the mercy of her cycle. She seemed to spend her mornings doing the washing, stirring away at the great iron tub under the trees, hair flying, grim, perplexed. She was always trying to keep the girls clean. She fed the chooks, collected the eggs. Kept the stove stoked with the wood he chopped. She could never get the hang of the axe. She never left the clearing, she was afraid of the bush. She was afraid of snakes, fire, the dark, of getting lost. Afraid of bloody everything. Kept the girls close to her, made them nervous and fanciful. They'd be useless like her if he didn't take a hand to them soon.

Who me? she said, that one time when he asked her to catch the mare. It escaped, and was lamed. Now the cart stood rotting in the clearing. No point in going over that. It boiled down to this: *she couldn't take the life.* It was a common enough story in the district.

He held his hand in the creek and after a while the pain subsided and the sound of the water soothed him. Then the guilt started. He was dismayed at his disloyalty. At the savagery of his thoughts.

After a while the girls followed their mother inside. They stoked the fire for her while she lit the lamp. They ate the stew made from the rabbits their father trapped. Their mother ate nothing, just drank cup after cup of black tea. The moon hadn't risen yet and outside was a thick darkness. Ada stacked their plates but didn't go out onto the verandah to wash them. The girls knew that she never went outside at night if their father wasn't here. They washed their faces at the kitchen table in the enamel basin filled with water from the kettle. Ada put out the lamp to save kerosene and took the girls with her to sleep in the big bed. The wind rattled the little house.

They heard his tread on the verandah and the dog noisily lapping up water. They could sleep then.

He always came back.

Only once he nearly left them.

One Sunday at the height of summer they walked down the powdery track through the dunes to the ocean. It was too hot to work, too hot to rest in the house. Even Ada was driven out. Frank had to piggy-back the girls across the burning white sand of the beach. Ada wrapped herself up in towels like an Arab woman, swathing even her face, and crouched well clear of the water's reach. The endlessness of the horizon reduced her to misery. But Frank in the water became rough and playful, rising like a walrus out of the depths to catch at the girls, water and mucus running down his moustache. Afterwards he went for a swim by himself, a vigorous breaststroke, feeling the sting of all his cuts and bites healing in the salt water.

But this Sunday he swam out too far and was caught and carried further out by an unseen current. He stopped swimming, and trod water, facing the shore. He raised his arm once or twice, casually, as if to say hello. But there was nobody to save him, no party of Sea House holiday makers, no passing boat on that blank horizon. Ada threw off her coverings and ran up and down the beach. The dog chased her, barking. The little girls stood in the shallows and watched him. He kept on bobbing, as if he were riding a bicycle, watching them back. They thought they could see his face. He wasn't agitated, he was alert and thoughtful. It was as if he was deciding something. He trod water, making up his mind. The girls didn't take their eyes from him. They knew that if they did they wouldn't see him again. Suddenly the wind started up, a wave came in his direction, then another and another, and with what strength he had left he was able to catch a ride into the shallows.

He waded out of the water towards them, a little defiant smile on his face, as if to say *What, were you worried? Don't I always come back?*

In the end they survived because of the Sea House.

In 1930 the old hotel burnt down to the ground and was sold for a song to an English couple, the Tehoes. Some people, it seemed, still had money. The Tehoes built another hotel, a great brick and timber two-storey English manor house. Frank and Ada could see the chimneys and the dormer windows winking through the tops of the trees. Frank did some labouring on the construction, though by then the work was almost too much for him. There was hardly any part of his body, ribs, legs, back, hands, that hadn't been injured by war or labour.

Reg Tehoe opened a public bar, liked to yarn with the locals if any of them could spare the money for a beer. By this stage of the Depression few could. Prices for crops hardly covered cartage costs. The bank kept their cream cheques to pay off their debts. By 1933, more than half of the settlers had walked off their blocks. They couldn't sell, couldn't pay their interest and the bank foreclosed their loans.

Frank sold eggs to the Sea House and firewood and a few fresh vegetables. But Madge Tehoe had plans. Riding trails to the sea, holiday cottages. She eyed off Frank's block. Every few months she offered to buy another few acres from him, virgin bush or the sour sandy paddocks he had so painstakingly cleared. By '35 all that was left was the house and clearing. Their livestock was reduced to the chooks and the dog. Frank never did get his pigs.

They survived, though Frank's health was broken and Ada didn't speak any more.

Frank told the girls that he believed their mother was homesick. He decided to take her back to England. They would all go, he said, things couldn't be worse in England, and Irina could jolly well put them up. All these years she'd lived like a queen in the house in London, the house of Ada's parents. The girls could have a decent education at last, he told Ada. All that remained was to sell off the home block to Madge, and they could buy their passage to Southampton.

Then he fell sick. He lay all day on the old couch, tended by the women. He was too tired even to read. Now that there was no more work to do, now that the great adventure was over, he wanted to ask Ada to forgive him. He wanted to say to her that he had thought he was one type of man when really he was another. But Ada stood and looked out a window, from a place too far for him to reach. The doctor, Bly, came, walked up the track from the Sea House carrying his bag. He'd been a medical officer at the Somme, where Frank had fought. They had some good conversations, if short because the doctor was so busy. The best conversations Frank had had in years.

The doctor told Frank there would be morphine when the time came.

There had to be some point to it, Frank thought, as Ada stood looking out the window. Her hands were swollen and worn, she'd given up wearing her wedding ring. Her hair was still thick black and untidy. He could still, so easily, be proud of her. There had to be some point to the force that had drawn them together. What? What was it? he asked one of his daughters who was sitting beside him. This was something he might talk over with Bly when he next called. Perhaps it worked itself out in the following generations. His daughter bent over him, wiped his face.

It isn't over yet, he told her.

Visitors

Strangers ride into town.

Here they come, in a cloud of dust, bumping over the gravel on the road to Nunderup.

There were two of them, two young men, dressed alike in black narrow-brimmed hats and black coats, longer and blacker than those Australians wore. They looked like emissaries or the members of a religious sect, but in fact they'd simply used the same Arab tailor to outfit themselves for this journey, in haste and without knowing what to expect. They were hot. Their coats were powdered with red dust.

They were riding in the cab of an old Ford utility with a local carrier called Bickford. Behind them they could hear their suitcases sliding around with the milk cans, and the incessant barking of Bickford's spidery black dog.

Where had they come from? The cab was filled with the foreign smell of them, Bickford knew it, he had served in Egypt in the AIF. It was in the food, the soap, the skin of the women, something spicy and sweetish that got into your sweat, your shit. Close up they were young, mid-twenties. Officer age and class. One was wiry, dark as a Gyppo, the other fat, spoke like a Pom. What had brought them here? They weren't the type to work in the timber mills. Out of the corner of his eye Bickford watched the fat one wipe the sweat from his hands with his neckscarf. Soft hands like that on a man turned his stomach.

All things come in twos, thought Bickford. *Fat and thin, old and young, dark and fair. Good years and bad years, hot summers and cold winters. Crook and well, happy and blue. Peace and war. Married and single.* His whole life could be fitted into it. Sometimes when he was on the road he could swear he saw everything in pairs, *bush and paddock, horse and buggy, man and dog.* Sometimes it clicked in his head and wouldn't stop. They passed a wooden shack with a fallen chimney and a flock of crows roosting on the roof. Bickford spat out the window. His place. Had to walk off it in '32. Going on for five years now. *Success and ruin. Heaven and hell.*

The sun had gone down. Clearings were darkening around giant dead trees. The fat passenger, shouting above the din of the cab, asked Bickford if he knew a family called Clark in the area. Bickford said nothing for a mile or two, trying to put two and two together. At least he knew they weren't from the Bank.

'Old Clarkie, he passed away last year,' he shouted back at last.

Leopold was suddenly weary. He shut his eyes for a moment. He had been here before, a long time ago, he was re-entering a scene. The rattling cab, the barking dog, some horror being revealed as the light faded on an empty road. The same landscape he could swear, the blocked-out horizon, the stricken trees, the desultory cows. The end of the world. He must have dreamt this, or he was dreaming now.

But Aram was here, wedged beside him. Leopold opened his eyes and studied his friend's profile. He had spent every day of the past year with Aram. Everything they saw or did was shared. Sometimes he wondered if the world he saw was the one reflected in Aram's dark gaze.

In the dream however he had been alone.

What did they think when they were deposited with their suitcases in the driveway of the Sea House? In this light the apparition of an English manor house rising out of the wilderness was almost surreal. They stood looking around them at the tennis courts and rose beds and terraced lawns, while beyond, like a country to be conquered, lay miles of uninhabited bush.

Bickford took his tobacco pouch from the pocket of his army shirt and started rolling a cigarette. The fat one tried to offer him five shillings for the ride, but Bickford shook his head.

Laurel and Hardy, thought Bickford as he watched them set off down the driveway. *Jekyll and Hyde.* He lit his cigarette and headed for the bar. He wouldn't have said no to a beer if they'd offered to shout him one, but they were foreigners and didn't know the way to do things here.

The black dog lay down to wait outside the bar.

An English countrywoman, authentic in every detail, brogues, tweeds, pearls, right down to the spaniel yapping at her heels, gave them directions to the Clark farm with raised eyebrows, faintly amused. 'I wouldn't call it a *farm* exactly,' she said, 'not these days.' She waved down at the valley. 'If you meet young Edith on the track, tell her to hurry up. She waits on tables here.' What was her accent? Not county, not English at all. Australian genteel? She had a good-looking girl's face gone puffy, and girlish shoulder-length blonde hair. She studied the cut of their coats in the twilight, her head to one side. 'You can always stay here, you know,' she said. 'It's off-season, we've plenty of rooms.'

'They won't last two nights down there,' Madge told Reg over pre-dinner sherry.

The dark one especially was rather attractive.

Down the brick stairway they went, following the gravel path, into the Honeymoon Gardens, famous throughout the South West, though they did not know that. They thought they were walking into an oasis. The air was fragrant and damp beneath great white-trunked eucalypts. Birds swooped into the spray of sprinklers hissing over banks of lawn. There was a whirring sound, then a throaty staccato. Leopold held up his finger. This was one of the wonders he had promised Aram, the Australian laughing bird.

At the bottom of the garden, following the woman's directions, they turned right, crossed a wooden footbridge and found a rough track that wound its way up through shadowy bush. Suddenly light and wind burst into their faces, they had emerged at the top of a massive escarpment. They clutched their hats. A great silver ocean lay before them. There was no sign of any human presence. They seemed to be standing between sky and water.

Edith was late. She ran with the skirt of her baggy black uniform bunched up in one hand, a pair of shoes in the other. This was both to save shoe leather and for speed—she was faster barefoot. She was nearly seventeen but away from other people and for lack of more adult diversions she still pretended she was running first in a race, leaping the ruts with breathtaking skill ...

She looked up and saw them. Two men, strangers, about to descend the track she was climbing. Two black silhouettes, one fat, one thin, against the iridescent sky. Had they seen her? She stood still.

The fat one was leading, one hand splashing about to counterbalance his suitcase. And strangely, though Edith had never met him and had no warning of this visit, she knew at once who he was. The other one moved as smoothly as if he were descending a staircase, looking around him. He saw her first. He tapped the shoulder of the fat one, who looked up at her and waved.

Edith never knew why she did what she did next. It was a reflex action, like a worshipper entering a church, or a peasant in the presence of kings. She crouched down and put on her shoes.

Soup had been served when at last she ran into the dining room. 'I know, I know, you have *overseas* visitors,' Madge Tehoe hissed. 'But I shall have to dock your pay for this, Edith, Mr Tehoe will insist.' She stood back to look at Edith, her evening face all sharp and gleaming. 'And who might they be, these young men, may I ask?'

There weren't many diners, four tables, but she was forced to stand at the sideboard watching over them until they were done. All the long evening, as they leisurely chewed and turned their glasses in their fingers and slowly slowly wiped their mouths on their napkins, Edith wondered what the visitors would be doing. She saw them standing around the lamp on the kitchen table, huge and exotic in their black clothes. Holding their black hats, bowing towards Frances and her mother.

'Aunt Ada? I am Irina's son, Leopold.'

She saw Leopold kissing her mother's hand.

They were lying in the girls' narrow iron bedsteads. Frances said that she and Edith would sleep with their mother. Leopold apologised once again for arriving without warning. The girls' room opened off the kitchen, and smelt of the fried eggs which Frances had made for them, her forehead glinting with nervous sweat. As they ate, old Aunt Ada came and went, came and went, until Frances took her off to bed.

Leopold thought of Ada as old, although her long, loosely-plaited hair was still dark, and she was younger than his mother. Ada had an old woman's air of anxious preoccupation, her hands clenched, her eyes shallow and troubled. She kept offering them cake, jam, vodka, none of which appeared. All they could see was a pan of dripping and half a loaf of bread on the table. The visitors drank tea from thick china mugs, but Frances drank from an old condensed milk tin with a beaten-down edge. Leopold fancied a slice or two of fried bread sprinkled with salt, but did not like to ask in case they should run short. He assured his aunt that he had eaten his fill. 'My mother was always telling me not to overeat,' he said cheerfully. But Ada did not seem interested in Irina.

Was this the Ada of those letters, witty and rueful, that had once entertained them each Christmas with stories of 'the bush'? How long had it been since she had last written? Nor was there a trace of the Ada of his earliest memories, a presence around which his mother was always happy, a presence which he remembered as light, playful, sensual.

Her daughters were such serious girls. Mute, stiff, thin, their hair pinned back and plaited like schoolgirls, their faces childishly bare.

He reminded himself that they were recently bereaved.

There were chinks between the rough boards of the walls of the bedroom. The flame of the candle that Frances had set down on a set of shelves twisted and flickered in the draughts. On closer inspection the shelves were made of empty kerosene boxes placed one on top of another. The calico curtain was stamped *Dingo Flour*. What had he expected? A whitewashed cottage, green fields, flitches of bacon hanging from sturdy rafters? Kangaroos coming to be fed at the back door, wasn't that what his aunt had written?

He was appalled by the bareness and roughness, appalled for these poor female relatives of his.

To hide his shock, and his shivers in the draughty room, he'd made some joke to Frances about snakes under the bed. But she replied seriously that the snakes were hibernating at this time of the year.

Wise snakes. He was glad of his coat to put over the thin grey blankets. In the other bed Aram already lay sheathed beneath his coat, its sleeves trailing on the floor. Probably asleep. In all the strange beds they had slept in, Aram always slid into an instant, elegant slumber. So quiet you wouldn't know if he were asleep or thinking in the darkness. Perhaps, thought Leopold, as he tried to stop his coat sliding off from his bulk, adaptability had something to do with being lean. He blew the candle out.

The bush advanced. A herd of creatures seemed to be moving around the house, chewing and thudding, bumping against the thin walls. The house strained and creaked like a woman in corsets, and something, rats were they? scuttled in the roof. He must tell the girls in the morning. Far away he could hear the crack of the surf. The air was cold. He pulled his scarf out from the pocket of his coat and wrapped it around his ears. He told himself that this visit would be good for his health, like a stay in a sanatorium.

As he was about to fall asleep he had an image of the younger girl, Edith, leading them to the house. He saw her bounding in and out of the shadows across the clearing, Aram following, while he, tortoise-like, brought up the rear.

Their door was shut, but there was that foreign smell again as Edith tiptoed past their room. The whole house smelt different. She pulled off the black dress, lay down on one side of her mother. On the other side lay Frances. By her stillness Edith knew she was awake.

'Did they tell you why they've come?'

'No. Ssh.'

The two girls lay for a long time on their backs looking up at the ceiling.

They said it was a last-minute decision. They had been travelling together through the Middle East. They met some sailors in a restaurant in Aden, who invited them to take a berth on their ship to Australia. They had a little money left, and no immediate obligations, and they said why not. Leopold had always wanted to meet the antipodean branch of the family.

Ada was still sleeping. They were eating lumpy porridge at the kitchen table. Leopold declared himself bowled over by Australian golden syrup. Steam rose off the clearing in the bright sunshine. The dog thumped its tail, the daughters shyly smiled. They all went to drink their tea sitting on the edge of the verandah and the visitors, as young men always seemed to do, talked about themselves.

They had met in Iraq, where Leopold was working on an archaeological dig, not far from Baghdad, on the Euphrates. Aram was working for the expedition as a driver. He was Armenian, born in Turkey, where his parents had died when he was very young. He had grown up in an orphanage in Syria. He was driving a taxi in Aleppo when Leopold's professor hired him to drive the team to the dig. He stayed on. Leopold and he became friends. When the expedition finished they decided to travel. In Aram's taxi they drove all across Mesopotamia, visiting other sites, ancient cities, Ur, Larsa, Nineveh, Uruk, buried beneath the sands.

They buried themselves in the ancient world. Because, of course, the whole modern world was about to erupt. That, they said, was what was waiting for them at the end of their travels.

The girls listened with their bare feet swinging off the verandah. Leopold said that he admired their hardiness, and envied the *au naturel* mode. He was going to get his feet into training, he declared. He took his shoes off, rolled his trousers up and picked his way up and down the clearing. His stumpy little feet were fishbelly white, like prisoners he said, shut away for years from the light of day. He hobbled, wincing, while Aram and the girls laughed on the verandah.

It was a long time before Edith understood the gallantry of his performance.

Hens scratched in a little scrappy orchard. The sky was deep blue. Beyond the moment of their laughter the huge silence of the bush surrounded them. It was going to be all right, Leopold thought.

Frances and Edith avoided each other's eye as they laughed at their cousin. Many years ago their Aunt Irina had sent a photograph of herself and Leopold in her Christmas letter. Leopold as a schoolboy. Fat, shiny-cheeked, in long shorts and a striped cap, holding on to a bicycle. How Frances and Edith had loved to laugh at him. Haw haw haw, they laughed, the way the big boys jeered at sissies at school. They pointed out to one another his fat white knees, his straining buttons, his air of stolid cheer. Irina's letters were always full of news of him, how clever he was (though poor at sports), his prizes, his scholarships to grammar school and university where he studied archaeology.

In rare moments of unity and out of hearing of their mother, Frances and Edith sometimes played a game called Fat Leopold. This is Fat Leopold running with a wobbly bottom. Fat Leopold flopping round on a horse. Getting stuck on a fence. Talking posh—'Oh I say, poor show old chap.' Goody-goody Leopold bending over, ripping the seat of his shorts with a farting sound.

These games were savage, vengeful and unfair. What had he ever done to them, except to be a boy, doted upon, richer and cleverer than they could ever be, living at the centre of the world instead of its extremity?

Meanwhile, what did their mother write about them? What could she write? That they attended a one-roomed school where the teacher was boarded with whichever family in the district could offer a bed. The teachers, mostly young, left as soon as possible. That there were times of the year, burning-off or harvest, or if the creeks ran over, when the school was empty. That after Eighth Standard her daughters gave up school, because their father needed help and she, Ada, couldn't bear to be without them?

Aunt Irina's Christmas letter was a ritual of their childhood. It always arrived early. She took no risks with the time it might take to reach them in the wilds of the Australian bush. Each day in early December Ada made a pilgrimage to their mailbox, a kerosene tin hammered to a stump beside the Nunderup road. In the same mailbox Ada would leave her letter to Irina to be collected, with ninepence for the stamps.

Irina's letter *was* Christmas for Ada. She used to wave it as she walked home across the clearing, through the yellow summer grass. She read it without moving on the verandah, her daughters hanging over her shoulders. Irina's racing black script looked like a voice in a foreign language, all rapid with waving hands. For many hours their mother would say nothing, just pace, in a trance. Over the days she would read it to them. It was ordinary enough, the ice on the pond, the feuds at Church, her success at cards. The queues of the unemployed. How hard it was for a widow to make ends meet (she always wrote that). What Leopold achieved.

But for some years now their mother had not seemed interested in Irina's letters. She would read a few lines and lie down on the couch. When they asked her what the news was, she said 'The usual' and turned away her head. Irina's last letters had remained unopened.

When their father died, the girls had asked each other whether they should write and tell Irina.

'Mumma will, when she is better,' Frances said.

Even though it had been many years now since Ada had sat flushed and determined at the kitchen table, swatting at early summer flies, penning her letter, laughing softly to herself.

Reg Tehoe paid for the funeral and attended himself. Dr Bly sent apologies, he'd been called to an urgent case. A few farmers, old settlers who were still in the district, came back to the house afterwards and their wives brought scones and cakes. The women helped Frances and Edith to pour the tea. Ada stayed in bed throughout. The women exchanged looks. *She couldn't take the life*. They ran their fingers over surfaces, clicked their tongues. The men strolled around the clearing in their Sunday suits and pointed out to one another how run-down everything was. 'Poor old Clarkie,' they said, 'he never had any luck.' They offered the girls help, but Frances and Edith said they could cope. The women kissed them and the men touched their hats. Nobody expected them to last.

The girls became preoccupied with looking after Ada. She never seemed to come back into her life. She left little piles of kindling on the steps, shifted the lids on the pots, like mementoes of old tasks. Because she could not seem to concentrate on the food in front of her, they started helping her to eat. They started helping her to dress. On the first warm day after their father's death they sat her on the edge of the verandah and washed her long black hair.

They did not speak of her condition, it seemed disloyal. They supposed that it would pass. They expected that one day, one of the spring days she loved, she would wake up and be her old self again. Besides, what else was there for them to do? They had always looked after their mother.

The summer after their father died was endless. A haze lay over the bush. The fruit trees, unpruned, shrivelled up in the orchard. Some tattered female rags were flung to bleach over bushes. Ada trailed around the clearing, her hair down her back, calling the chooks in, the one job she loved. The two girls were sitting on the verandah one afternoon when a groundsman from the Sea House appeared. He offered to plough the firebreaks around the clearing. Their place was a danger to other property, he said.

'Thank you,' chorused the sisters and heard their voices, young and shrill, echoing across the clearing.

They didn't speak of this incident, as they never spoke of anything of importance to each other. But each was shocked. What had happened to them? They had been close to drifting back to Nature, like their mother and the house and clearing. They had stopped talking, they had almost stopped thinking. It was obvious that action was called for. But what?

The next day Madge Tehoe left a message in their mailbox, offering one of them a job as a waitress. She called it 'summer help'.

'Dad wouldn't like it,' said Frances. He had called Madge 'The Lady of the Manor'.

So it was Edith who went.

The visitors liked to escort Edith to or from her shifts at the Sea House. She noticed that there was always a competition between them, about who was first or best or right. Aram was stronger and more deft, Leopold had more knowledge. At the same time the competition was a joke, and the real loser was the one who took it seriously. They teased and jostled each other all along the track.

She wondered if Leopold ever ran out of things to say. He was capable of discussing every moment of the day as it passed. Odd things made him curious. 'Could you walk this track blindfold, Edith?' or 'What does it take to know a piece of land?' He listened carefully to her answers. Before he came it was as if she'd never learnt to speak.

They made themselves at home at the Sea House, playing tennis or reading the newspapers left in the deckchairs. At night they drank beer in the bar with the locals, and played pool with the guests. Sometimes they were invited to make a bridge four with the Tehoes. Aram was very quick at cards. One night Leopold came home alone with Edith, leaving Aram to finish a particularly intense game of two-handed rummy with Madge.

Edith in cap and apron served the Sunday roast while, outside, her visitors' tennis ball bounced like a popping cork. She could hear Leopold calling out scores in the best Wimbledon manner. They bobbed in and out of vision through the diamond-shaped window panes. Edith dropped a potato she was serving, the way she had been trained, between a spoon and fork. Of course at that moment Madge Tehoe swept past.

'Eyes on the job, please, Edith. *You* can't afford to be a lady of leisure, I'm afraid.'

Later as Edith was washing up Madge dumped a large stale sponge cake onto her tray.

'For your guests' tea. You might like to make a trifle or something.' She was strolling outside to the sunshine, carrying a book and a cream straw hat and a frosted glass.

As Edith set off home across the lawn, the cake wrapped in her apron, she heard Madge's voice rising up from the depths of a deckchair. *'Of course, Reg could never live in the city. He's a countryman through and through.'* Edith could see her legs crossed in shiny brown stockings, and cigarette smoke coiling up from beneath the brim of her hat.

'Edith! Don't think you can steal away like that!' Leopold suddenly sprang up from the deckchair next to Madge. Then Aram popped up next to him and, folding the Sea House newspapers, they took their leave of Madge with hasty little bows.

Down the garden stairway they swept, one on either side of her. 'Good afternoon,' they said, bowing to the guests they met. The men had to salute back to them, and raise their hats to Edith in her black servant's dress.

'What is this?' Aram fingered Edith's parcel.

'It's a cake. Mrs Tehoe gave it to me.'

Aram unwrapped it.

'A little past its prime, wouldn't you say?' Leopold said. Aram picked it up and spun it straight into the arms of a nearby laurel bush.

Edith was too shocked to speak. Waste, the worst of sins. At the very least they could have fed it to the chooks. And what if somebody told Madge?

Then suddenly she started laughing, and waving her apron, she ran lightly down the steps.

'When are you and Frances going to join us at tennis?' Leopold said when he caught up with her. 'Then we can play mixed doubles.'

'We don't know how to.'

'I will teach you,' Aram said.

Edith said nothing. For a start, she was a Clark, she was *help* and you didn't see *help* on the courts. She hoped they would take her silence for a lack of interest. Because of course in the end it was always a matter of shoe leather. She and Frances shared one pair of shoes.

Madge informed Edith that since the May holidays were upon them, facilities were now reserved for guests only. 'Summer is over,' she said. Her cheeks each bore a spot of rouge as if already bitten by winter frosts. She looked down at Edith, haughty, swathed in a mohair shawl.

The visitors still sometimes waited for Edith after a night shift, smoking and talking in the little bar. One night they arranged a ride to Bunbury with genial Reg in the Rover the next morning. They came home late and a little drunk from their excursion, swinging sugar sacks from their shoulders. They had bought bacon, raisins, port wine, bananas, rice and lentils, flour, oil, cinnamon and cloves. Chocolates for the girls, and for Ada a pair of lambskin slippers.

The girls had never seen men cook before. Leopold was patient, stirring and tasting, his podgy hands strangely delicate. Aram was quick and precise. He made Armenian bread, yeastless loaves flat and round as plates. He made rice spiced with lemon, lentils stewed in oil, vegetables charred over the stove. Leopold made omelettes, bacon sandwiches, beetroot soup called *borsch*, *coq au vin*. Aram selected the hen and wrung its neck when Ada was asleep. But after it had spent the afternoon stewing in the iron pot, she sucked its bones along with the rest of them, wiped its juices up with bread.

Each meal Edith had to restrain herself from licking her fingers, holding out her plate for second helpings. She could feel herself growing. She ate as if at any moment this food would be taken away from her and there would be no more.

The visitors changed. They rarely left the clearing, except for walks. Like the women of the house they went early to bed and slept away the cold dark rattling nights. In the bright mornings they splashed themselves with water from the tank by the verandah, shouting with pain, and shaved in a little mirror they'd nailed onto the verandah post. They chopped firewood, comparing biceps, and proclaimed that rural life was developing their strength.

They liked to sit on the verandah, smoking and talking in the autumn sun with the girls. Leopold was fascinated by Group Settlement. Was it a socialist experiment? And if not, had it fulfilled its capitalist aims? Had the failed settlers been radicalised after their treatment by the government? And were there native peoples that the experiment had displaced?

The girls didn't know. They had never thought of these questions, in fact they did not really understand their terms. Frances blushed and licked her lips, trying to find words. 'Our father was too busy to worry about politics,' she said. 'And we've hardly ever seen natives here.'

But she sounded uneasy. For, Edith thought, wasn't everything their father did in some way *against*, the government, the city, the upper classes? The angry way he used to rattle the pages of the newspaper . . . was that political? And didn't she, didn't all of them sense something in the bush, a presence they didn't understand? That made them suspect they didn't really know this land at all. Was this what made Ada so afraid?

Once when she was a child out walking with Ada they came on an Aboriginal family on the track. 'Don't speak, don't look at them,' Ada had whispered, clutching her arm. Ada was afraid of them, as she was afraid of the gaunt-faced men who came to the door asking for a bit of tea or flour. But Frank insisted that she always send the girls out with anything she could spare. 'At least we have a roof over our heads, Ada.'

Edith cursed herself for her laziness, for not reading books as her father had urged. Their father would have been ashamed of them. They were ignorant farm girls.

She wanted to get away. She wanted to learn about the world.

A rustling started up in the grapevine that clustered thick as a wall down one side of the verandah. It was Ada picking the last few muscats, nearly brown now, sweet as sherry, popping them in her mouth. She grazed and hummed and spat out pips, like an invisible giant bird.

In the afternoons the men slept again in their sun-warmed room. The house creaked and snapped in the warmth, like the thinnest membrane between them and nature. They slept to the ocean's distant roar and the cries of cockatoos passing overhead. When they woke their faces were creased and vulnerable. They felt safe, safer than they had ever felt before.

Perhaps this is our Paradise, Leopold thought as he lay on his bed, Frank's old copy of Stevenson's *In the South Seas* open on his stomach. He heard a girl's bare feet padding in the kitchen. Gaugin's Tahiti, Stevenson's Samoa . . .

In this light, the bare floorboards, the rough wooden walls, the fluttering threadbare curtains were austerely beautiful. He was beginning to say this word often to himself.

They tramped in every direction. Sometimes Edith and Frances went with them. To the middle of the forest, a secret place of ferns and creeks and limestone caves. To hidden beaches beyond the rocky headland, accessible only at low tide. Through the olive-green scrub along the escarpment, the wind too strong to speak. A hawk circled, crows called. A silvery prehistoric reptile, unblinking, lay in their path and refused to move.

'This country is so ancient, you can't think of it as belonging to any farmer,' Leopold said.

'You wouldn't say that if you saw my father clearing it,' said Frances. 'He had nothing but a crosscut saw and a broken-down horse and us girls to help him. When he burnt this hill off the whole sky was lit up. Now the Tehoes own it. There'll be holiday houses here one day.'

Frances's forehead burned, she looked all tight and angular. Loyalty racked her, she felt she had to defend every stone they stumbled over, every blackened stump with its crown of regrowth.

They walked home in silence. A large male undershirt waved on the line. The little shaving mirror winked from its nail. The dog was watching over a woman in an old green hat as she trailed round the yard calling in the chooks, making the clucking sounds that all her childhood Edith had thought of as Russian.

Edith could not sleep at night. The kapok mattress sagged and the daughters fell into a trough beside their mother. Edith didn't like to be so close to Frances. It had started when they were very young. They couldn't bear to share a bath, hold hands, eat a piece of bread if the other had touched it. They were like negative magnetic poles. Even now, the sound of Frances's breath irritated Edith.

She made a bed for herself on the sitting room couch where her father used to lie under the window. She lay beneath his old army greatcoat. It was warm from the fire and she could see the stars through the window. The coat smelt of sweat and earth and gamey meat, like the pelt of an animal.

This was where the visitors sat at night, stretching out their legs, talking, butting their cigarettes into the fire. She could smell the meals they cooked, slow-fried onions, thick stewed tomatoes, fresh bread, soothing homely smells.

Men filled a house, she thought, and yet these ones trod gently, stood back for the women, calling them all by name. *Edith*, they said, *Frances*, *Aunt Ada*, *Madame*, a gleam of alertness in their eyes.

She thought of small courtesies from Aram, turned them over one by one in her mind. A plate passed to her first, a smile, a tap on her arm, all the more thrilling because he spoke so little. Signs of secret favour. She was reminded of a game she and Frances used to play, pretending to be trackers, leaving signs through the bush for the other to follow, a broken branch, a pile of stones, a twig pointing a certain way. Their purpose, of course, had been to trick each other. Where did this trail lead?

She woke each morning with a start, a leaf tapping at the window, *something is waiting for you* ... She lay listening out for sounds of the men. She thought she'd hardly slept and yet she felt washed smooth as a morning beach. She tiptoed past the men's door, crouched in the bush to pee as she collected kindling for the stove. At last they came into the kitchen, yawning, rubbing their hands by the fire, and the house filled with their good humour.

Everything about them had become familiar. She could time the day by the growth of their beards, Aram's dark bloom spreading up his cheeks, Leopold's cornfield stubble, shadowed in the folds of his chin. Aram looked dapper at any hour. He attended to himself, filed his nails, trimmed his thick black hair, darned his socks sitting cross-legged on his bed like an Oriental man. She hadn't known that men cared about such things. In the orphanage you learnt to look after yourself, he said. That was why he finished his meals before anyone else. And why he was always watching, always on the alert. Wherever he was he positioned himself. He always sat facing the door.

While Leopold could talk to you for hours over breakfast, crumpled pajama top falling open over little fatty breasts, puffy eyes all warm at the sight of you, all alight from the morning's ideas.

One warm day on the beach the men had stripped off and run into the water. Only their undershorts covered the last unknown inches of them. Every other part of them she knew by heart. She started pulling up her dress to join them, but Frances scowled at her with such horror that she remembered her sagging, much-washed singlet and drawers and subsided, paddling in the shallows. Poverty always subdued her. When the men, shivering, came rushing out again, their shorts clung all pouchy to them and she and Frances looked away.

She had seen Aram rise up out of the iron tub on the verandah, his satiny shoulders, his tight boylike buttocks, his whiplash spine.

They were strangers and yet she felt close to them, so close she could sense wherever they were and what they were doing. As if now that they ate the same food, breathed the same air, they were part of her. All the habits and needs of their bodies had become familiar.

An outdoor lavatory with a rural vista was his idea of heaven, Leopold said, heading off with a book under his arm.

This was what husbands and wives know about each other, she thought.

Edith was the last to sleep, the first to wake, the watchman of the house, and yet she was not tired. Sometimes deep into the night, her eyes wide open, she felt she could rattle the cutlery in the drawer, make the water jump from the jug, like a witch in a fairytale. She could almost think it was this force that caused the men to sigh and groan and turn in their sleep.

In the dining hall at the Sea House she watched the honeymooners with a new intensity. She saw lovers everywhere. Some were restless and lonely together, others sated, at peace. Some were stiffly discreet, as if they had something to hide. One couple shocked the older guests by lying on the lawn in the sun, kissing one another with a slow, airy compulsion. She envied them, studied them for their secret.

She caught sight of herself in the dining hall mirror and saw that her eyes shone and her cheeks were pink. She could swear she was taller. It seemed to her that the guests noticed her more. A party left a tip for 'the pretty little waitress'.

Sometimes at home when they were all sitting at the table Frances shot her a look. The sort of look she used to give her in the schoolyard if Edith tried to giggle with the others or did handstands with her skirt around her head. The look said: *I know what you really want.*

Frances had become offhand with the visitors. Edith might be getting carried away by them but she'd have them know that she, Frances, was not.

Ada preferred to eat her meals at a little work table under her bedroom window. If the girls didn't sit with her she could spend an hour gazing at the light in the trees, crumbling a piece of bread.

Some nights she agreed to join them by the fire. The visitors instantly stood and helped her into a chair. Ada became flushed and gracious, called for vodka, clapped her hands and said they must have music, her daughters must dance, her daughters had not done enough dancing, poor girls. She squeezed Leopold's hands and tears shone in her eyes. 'There is no romance in this country,' she said.

The girls sat struck with embarrassment for their mother. They knew how she'd be talked of in the district. *Off with the fairies. A few kangaroos loose in the top paddock.* Two fingers tapping the head. Who could understand her like they did? Who could know how much she was still there? But the young men suavely responded to Ada without so much as exchanging a glance. Ada's hair came unpinned and her eyes went glittery. She threw her hands around and said some Russian words, called the men *Sergei, Vassily, Franzi.* The girls knew that she was back in the room with the lace curtains and the samovar on the table. She was happy here, she was at home at last. But was she making a fool of herself? Should they persuade her to go to bed?

But here Leopold and Aram were their most charming, most at ease.

Perhaps, Edith thought, they had sat at many tables like this, with women fussing over them, demanding their attention. Perhaps they expected all older women to go a little crazy.

Perhaps they understood, better than anyone, why she had despaired.

On the morning they were to leave, Leopold knocked on Ada's door, entered, closed it after him.

'What did you talk about?' Edith asked as she walked with them to the Nunderup Hall where they would catch the bus. Everything along the track seemed still and unreal. She had to make herself speak.

'That's between my aunt and me.' For once Leopold had no words.

But as he was about to climb aboard the rattling bus he said: 'She asked me to look after you. She meant it. So look out.' His lips were white. He kissed her on the mouth and climbed aboard without looking back, ceding to Aram the last farewell.

In their last days the rain had set in. Everything felt damp in the house, sticky damp, like salt spray. The shaving mirror misted over, blankets felt gritty, razors rusted up. The sea grew wild, giant waves broke in blasts against the rocks. It sounded as if war had broken out, the visitors said. In the raw grey light of the kitchen, while the rain drummed on the roof, they started to talk about the desert again, about being *hot*, about all the places they wanted to return to, the tower of Babylon and the site of the royal libraries of Nineveh. This was where the fragments of clay tablets inscribed with the Gilgamesh epic had first been found.

'What's "Gilgamesh"?'

'The world's oldest known work of poetry. Gilgamesh was the king of Uruk in the land of Sumer. He was supposed to have lived about three thousand years BC.'

Leopold went into his room and came out with a book that he had carried with him all the way from England, a long slim book bound in brown cloth with *The Epic of Gilgamesh* stamped on its spine.

'A recent translation,' he said, turning its coarse yellow pages. 'A heroic piece of work. Please, read it if you're interested.'

Leopold and Aram spoke of Gilgamesh as if they knew him. Young King Gilgamesh became too big for his boots so the gods sent a wild man, Enkidu, to challenge him. They fought, proved to be an equal match, and became great friends. They set off into the world on heroic quests together.

'Then what happened?' asked Edith. They were thinking about travelling off together again, she could tell.

'The two of them became so arrogant together that the gods decreed Enkidu must die and go to the Underworld.'

'You talk as if you believe in all these old pagan gods,' said Frances.

'Why not?' said Leopold.

Frances licked her lips before speaking. 'Because there is but one God.'

Edith had never heard her mention God before.

'Isn't that just another story we tell ourselves? I thought your father was an atheist.'

'Not underneath. Not in the end.'

Leopold was untidy, he left a trail of cups, books, cigarettes around the house. But Edith noticed that he did not leave *The Epic of Gilgamesh* lying on the kitchen table. He took it back into his room.

The visitors had a fencing contest during a break in the rain. They circled each other in the clearing, brandishing bush poles taken from the pile of timber that had once been Frank Clark's piggery.

'Behold King Gilga-tosh and the Wild Man,' said Frances. Edith was dismayed at the scorn in her voice. 'They act as if this whole place is their playground. I wonder what our father would have said.'

'He would have liked them! They would have talked about books. He would have liked some men around the place.'

'They're not men, you know, they're boys.'

Frances was digging and replanting the vegetable garden, refusing all offers of help. She wore her father's boots and his old oilskin cape, and from the back she looked like a smaller, ghostly version of him. She sounded like him too, lone and angry, as she stamped the sods off her boots on the verandah steps. She went straight in to sit with her mother in the bedroom. When the rains started, Ada had taken to her bed.

Leopold read and wrote for long hours at the kitchen table. He refused to come on walks when the rain stopped. He said he'd fallen way behind with his Arabic. But Edith was beginning to understand that he stayed home out of supreme good manners. It would be too rude to leave Frances behind, slaving with a spade, and Ada lying alone in her dark room. He kept the fire stoked all day in the sitting room in an attempt to entice Ada out.

He tried to engage Frances in conversation. 'You would make a very good teacher, Frances, have you thought of that? Perhaps you could train as a monitor at the local school?' But Frances stared at him and said she didn't want to be a teacher. All her life there had been only one thing she wanted to do and that was farm. Leopold went thoughtful. He realised he was surprised that this plain shy cousin was not more receptive to him. It wasn't often that anyone resisted his attentiveness. He respected her for it.

Edith heard the visitors deciding their departure date. She told herself it was unreasonable to feel hurt. They never had been going to stay forever. They had only speculated about it once, on the beach, on a particularly balmy autumn day.

They discussed their plans. Leopold was going to find his way back to London, to see his mother and, he groaned, find a proper job. Aram had decided to make a new life in Armenia, his motherland.

'You know where is Armenia, Edith?'

All these weeks she hadn't dared to ask, or admit that she'd never even heard of it. He drew a map for her on the back of a brown paper bag. 'Here is Russia. Here's the Black Sea.' Armenia was a tiny circle in the south of Russia, bordered by Turkey and Persia. He circled it again and again with his pencil. It was Soviet Armenia now, ruled by Moscow, but it had a culture of its own that went back thousands of years. It had been the fate of this tiny country in the Caucasus mountains to be overrun by Mongols, Turks, Persians, now by the Communists, but it remained the oldest Christian state in the world.

For Armenians, Armenia was the motherland, as perhaps England was for Australians?

'*I* don't want to go to England,' Frances said. Her father had always told them that England was class-ridden, cramped and soggy.

If they had asked Edith what her plans were, she would have said: *Take me with you.* It was a vision that flashed into her head at odd moments, wringing out the dishrag, say, or hurrying along the Sea House track. She saw her own profile at a train window, looking out at some darkening unknown landscape. Someone was with her. Who?

But nobody asked about her plans.

Besides, compared to the others she knew she longed for shallow things, plucked eyebrows, high heels, waved hair. Ice-cream, the boogie-woogie, a pink satin quilted dressing-gown. A big hot cinema smelling of sweat and hair oil and chocolate.

In the end only Aram and Edith were left to go for walks. Whenever the rain stopped they hurried to a favourite place, the look-out, where half a dozen man-high boulders stood at the top of the escarpment, like the rampart of a ruined fort. If you climbed the boulders you had a view both of the ocean and of the miles of bush beyond the bay. If you crouched at the boulders' base you were sheltered from the wind and could talk.

At first they were shy. They had never been by themselves before. They scrambled up the boulders without looking at one another. But one day after gazing at the landscape for a while Aram slid down and started to speak. This land made him think of Armenia, he said, Armenia without mountains. The terrain of his homeland was also wild, ancient and barren, or so he had been told. I have a sickness for my country, he said, though I have never seen it.

The sun broke out against the boulder behind him and filled his high-boned face with light. He did not take his eyes away from Edith's. He spoke English the way Edith ran along a track, leaping from one safe place to another. He'd picked it up from a thousand conversations with Leopold. He also spoke Armenian, Arabic and French, learnt in the orphanage.

'How did your parents die?'

That was the question she had been wanting to ask him most of all. The question you never asked. You didn't talk about the dead.

He shook a cigarette out of a crumpled packet. His parents had been killed in the Massacres in Turkey in 1915. They had lived in the town of Diyarbakir, on the Tigris, in eastern Turkey, where generations of his father's family had traded in spices. When he was three years old Turkish gendarmes had come, taken his father to the city square and hanged him. He and his mother were marched in a convoy of women and children across the desert to Syria. By the time they reached the Euphrates, his mother, like most of the convoy, was dead. Some Syrian Christians rescued him and took him to Aleppo. I don't remember this, he said. I don't remember my mother. I don't remember any of it.

What you must understand, he said, is that more than a million Armenians were slaughtered in the Turkish Massacres, and nobody came to their aid.

For Armenians to be strong they must have a strong homeland. They must be prepared to fight for their independence.

He was not familiar to her now, but a sombre foreign man. The weeks he'd spent here were not important to him, she saw that now. All this time he'd really been thinking of something else.

The sun had disappeared behind bruise-coloured clouds. It was hushed, about to pour again. He kissed her on the forehead and took her hand. They set off down the track, silent as if returning from a ceremony. By the time they reached the clearing it was dark with rain. There was a round white blur in the kitchen window. Leopold was watching out for them.

On their last night in Nunderup there was a dance in the Hall. Leopold and Aram saw the poster in the Sea House bar. Frances said their family never went to those things, thanks, she would stay with her mother. But Edith, who these days seemed as detached and free as a traveller herself, said why not? She wound her plaits into a crown on top of her head. She wore the shoes. She didn't need anything else.

Leopold started to feel uneasy as they approached the hall. How many weeks had he been shut away from the world? In the yard were trucks, utilities, buggies, spilling children. Horses stamped and tossed together beneath the peppermint trees. At the steps of the porch, blending into the darkness, a crowd of young men, farmers' sons, were handing round a bottle, their faces following Edith as they stood back to let her pass. He knew from talking to Reg that the lads were penniless, the land could not support them and in the cities there were no jobs. They were waiting for something to happen. War. He could hear muted whistles, murmured jeers.

The hall was lit by hurricane lamps. Couples of all ages shuffled through sawdust strewn across the floor. On the stage a woman in a hat was thumping out *The Pride of Erin* on a piano, her hands firm and capable as if she were kneading bread. An old man in a bow tie timidly dabbed at some drums. The clarinetist had paused to tip the spit out of his instrument. Aram and Edith slipped into the circle of dancers like swimmers into a river. Children threaded their way between the couples, or sat on the edge of the stage.

Between dances the men and women parted ways. By the door was a table with jugs of beer where the men stood talking. Farmers in oldfashioned high-buttoned jackets, necks too strong for ties, faces toughened and reddened, prematurely old. Frank Clark would have looked like this, Leopold thought. But nowhere could he see a woman like Ada. The women gathered round the trestle tables where a supper was being laid, rows of mugs, sandwiches and cakes. The cream cakes looked especially good. All the women helped. Country women. The girls had shy healthy faces, walked round-shouldered and rollicking, like boys. One hitched up a stocking as she crossed the room. The older women talked with arms crossed, chins tucked into weatherbeaten necks. Mouths pressed together, a dry twist to their eyebrows. Indicated those they talked of with a nod of their heads.

Nods came their way. Not only at the Clarks' visitors in their black suits, but at the little Clark girl, looking up at Aram, beneath her crown of hair.

A strange terror struck Leopold as the piano thumped and the couples swept past him. He was back in the bleakness, the menace of the dream on the road when he first came here. He was watching his own fate. He felt breathless. Why had he come to this event? He had wanted to see a little more of these people before he left their country forever, hear their music, see the men and women together.

But in this dream everybody looked hardened and narrow-minded, xenophobic, graceless to the point of denial of all beauty. *There is no romance in this country.*

'Are you ready to go home?' he whispered to Aram and Edith, as he mopped his forehead with his handkerchief. But they shook their heads, smiling kindly at him. As they danced away, Edith had her arm curved around Aram's shoulder, the way a woman's arms curve to hold. *Too late, too late!* He couldn't stay here a minute longer. He waved to them, pocketed his handkerchief and left.

He lay on his bed in the darkness, waiting for them.

When he and Aram joked together they called each other brother, in the Arab way. Brother, everything I have is yours. Language, knowledge, shaving water. Family hospitality. Beautiful cousins. Trust me, brother.

He thought of little Edith, leggy, shining eyed, her country girl independence, her heartbreaking adoration. Who would not want to touch her? Or did he see her too through Aram's eyes?

He felt an ache of possessiveness, he wasn't sure for whom.

He was the fat man peering through windows, Aram the man of action. Together they made a whole man, or so they used to joke.

What did he really know of Aram?

He only knew him as a traveller. Who took what he needed but needed little. Water, a bedroll, tobacco. The occasional woman. Wheeling off into a lit doorway, a little private coolness between them afterwards. That was the one thing they didn't share.

He travelled light, like a warrior. He didn't take what he couldn't carry.

Leopold heard the dog pattering a welcome on the verandah. The back door creaked open. A whisper, a long silence. Their breath, raw and vivid, filled the house.

Up through the Honeymoon Gardens rushes Edith, dwarfed inside her father's oilskin cape. The lawns are awash with strips of bark like pink-brown flesh ripped from the eucalypts by winter squalls. No guests wander in this washed-out twilight. Inside the back hall she hangs up the cape, wipes her feet on the inside hem of her dress, puts on her shoes. She glides into the dining room with her eyes down, like a nun who musn't be tempted by all she can't have—roasted meat, curls of butter, treacle tart. But from the moment she enters she keeps her eye out for scraps to slip into her pocket, because if there are too few guests Madge will send her home straightaway.

Everything has gone back to how it was.

'I have been very patient,' Madge Tehoe says. 'But I hope you'll be able to keep your mind on the job now your visitors have gone.' She has reverted to the amused tone she seems to keep just for Edith, as for a naughty child whose innocent front doesn't fool her for a moment. She tells Edith she has decided that she *will* keep her on during winter, as if Edith has begged her for this privilege. In fact Edith knows that the relentless rain and wind make city waitresses moody and nervous as horses, make them suddenly remember urgent family business and pack in time for the next bus out. And that she, silent Edith, farm-girl Edith, moves quickly and can think for herself. Besides, she can't leave, she has nowhere else to go.

Edith files away Madge's words and tone to imitate to Aram and Leopold. They love Madge stories. She knows that far from her mind now being cleared, a blank space for Madge's bidding, it has never been so occupied. Because she's having a sort of conversation with the visitors all the time in her head.

She feels their eyes on her, as if they're peering in through the diamond-shaped panes, watching her serve. They watch her mop up the water that the bishop has spilt, the very important Bishop of the South West with a napkin tucked into his dog collar as he gnaws on a drumstick. Madge apologises to him for Edith's carelessness, and nobody bothers to protest that the jug slipped out of the bishop's greasy fingers as he reached to take it, not even the man of God himself. Shameless Madge doesn't acknowledge her treachery by so much as a wink. But Edith can hear Leopold's voice. *What does it matter? You're not going to be here forever* . . . Their voices seem real, the rest of the world is dreamlike. Or rather, she feels like a visitor herself here now, a citizen from some far-off, superior country.

They're with her whenever she's outside. She can hear their quick voices, sense the density of their bodies beside her. She still makes room for them on the track. But now at last she's telling the stories, her voice strong and certain, telling them everything, speaking her mind. She almost enjoys them more now than she did when they were here in the flesh!

Strange that it's always the three of them. She inhabits the early, happier days of the visit, the perilous, lighthearted energy between two men and a woman.

Sometimes a moment opens and she sees that she is muttering alone on a dark track, her smile glittering and frozen, frozen in time, back to a moment of eternal youth. She gasps and the moment closes. She's afraid. She's afraid she will go mad.

She can't remember Aram's face.

One night she runs into the bar to buy some cigarettes for a guest, and on impulse, in that smoky, masculine atmosphere, buys herself a packet of Capstans, ten for sixpence, and slips it in her pocket. What a comfort this little packet is, like a piece of the past. For weeks she had seen these blue and white packets everywhere, lying on the kitchen table, peeping out of a shirt pocket, crumpled empty in the fire. After work she lights up in the darkness of the Sea House porch. The smoke fills her head, she coughs, but she can hear them cheer and egg her on, and she puffs again, she's going to get the hang of this. Who would know if they saw her shivering and coughing out there alone that she does it for the company?

Smoking marks the change in her. Everything about her feels different.

Not at home though. There the silence signals the visitors' absence minute by minute. Only the sound of chewing and swallowing, the winter coughs, the moans of sleep. The house seems darker as if the men's bodies had given off light. Ada knows that something is missing, she won't take her hat off inside or out, she paces up and down the verandah as if she is waiting to leave. Frances still sleeps with her. Edith sleeps in her old room, in either bed, alternate nights. She can't bear to wash the sheets.

Nobody speaks. There is something self-righteous about Frances's silence as she goes about her chores. Edith feels that if she speaks she will lose her real, inner life, she must stay remote from Ada and Frances or they will drag her back with them again. To escape the house she checks the mailbox every day. There has been one letter, a note sent from Fremantle, addressed to Ada, thanking her for her hospitality, and, of course, that of her daughters. In Leopold's hand, but signed by both. Edith doesn't really expect another letter—nothing was ever promised—but once she sets off up the track to the mailbox, the voices return to her, and she feels jaunty and excited again.

She will go to them. At night she lies awake and replays the vision over and over, gathering detail. Now in a high fur collar with her hair rolled up she is smoking a cigarette in a station café with misted windows. Now she is wearing a large hat with a veil, like a lady explorer. Camels are passing. Didn't they speak of taking her to the desert? Something is going to happen, she can tell. Her body is in a strange state of excitement, she's a little queasy all the time, she's tired but can't sleep.

One night deep down in the drum of her belly she feels a tiny beat, and she knows.

She has known all along.

She slumps down into a heavy sleep at last. There are no more voices. The visitors have finally left.

Edith slept a great deal. Whenever she tried to think about what she should do, she fell asleep. All she did was sleep and stumble off to work at the Sea House. Winter was passing and still the loose black dress fitted her and the big white apron covered her changing body. At home she wore her father's old stretched pullover. That was all she could think of to do, keep the secret to herself.

One day Madge grabbed Edith by the arm as she was clearing tables and turned her towards the light of the window.

'Let me have a look at you,' she said. 'Heavens, you're *blooming*, girl.'

Edith's sleepy face flushed with terror.

'Have you an admirer, Edith?' Madge herself was jaunty and good-humoured these days, as noted by her staff. A retired English major had come to stay. His wife had caught a cold and Madge, exuberantly tweedy, took him for scenic walks with the dog.

'No.' Edith was too afraid to pull her arm away.

'No, you don't look happy enough,' Madge said, losing interest, tapping Edith's shoulder to dismiss her back to work.

Reprieve, and yet Edith was queerly disappointed. There were some women in the district, women with red raw hands and six children and half a dozen new-born calves, who would only have had to take one look at her to know. Edith knew this. Call yourself a woman, Madge?

Did she half want to be found out?

Perhaps it, the child, had a very obedient nature? It kept itself small and low according to Edith's will. Or perhaps what she carried was not human, but a tadpole or a swirling ball of worms, conceived when she drank from the creek? Once she dreamt there was no baby, it was all a mistake, it was nothing but wind, because she had gorged herself on raw onions and potatoes in Frances's vegetable plot. Frances hovered in the dream, glaring, furious at the trick she had played.

Once when there was an absence of kicks for several days, she thought the baby had died. She thought of the stillborn calf she had seen, bloodied and perfect, delivered with all the drama and bellows of a normal birth. Perhaps she could run away and give birth alone in the bush somewhere, bite the cord with her teeth, bury the tiny body, and it would all be over. If she could will the child not to grow, perhaps she had willed it not to live?

She was sitting at the table with Ada and Frances when she felt a foot race across her belly, like a sail across the sea. It was hard to believe that no one could see it. She put her hand over it, under the table, as if to say, *Ssh. I know you're back.* In spite of herself she was relieved.

She started walking, to try to clear her mind. She paced, not in her old leaping style, but steadily, down the tracks of her childhood. A hawk spied on her from high above, and she saw herself through its eyes, circled by ocean and forest, a female mammal bearing her young.

She no longer thought about Aram and Leopold. Who were they? What sort of men were they? It made her too tired, she would have to lie down in the bush and sleep. She understood the boys she had gone to school with better than them, at least she knew how those boys thought. *Up the duff. Knocked up. A bun in the oven.*

Once the name Gilgamesh came to her mind as she was walking, and she remembered Leopold's story of the young king and his friend setting out to conquer the world. She remembered how Leopold and Aram had joked about him, as if he were still alive, as if he were their hero. No doubt Gilgamesh and his friend also left behind a child or two in their travels.

One of them dies, she remembered. Which one? What happened next?

One thing she saw very clearly. She had been a fool to think of herself as one of them. She had no part in the adventure. Women had no freedom to go adventuring.

She started to avoid men. The more solid she became the more she made herself into a shadow. If Reg Tehoe came into the kitchen, or a gardener crossed her path, she disappeared. It was quite easy for men not to notice you. All you had to do was not notice them. The men at her tables, young and old, smelt of tobacco and alcohol and meaty sweat. Their necks and backs and shoulders were hard as walls. They had tremendous appetites. They ate up everything that was put in front of them. When they had finished they threw their napkins down, leaned back, talked more loudly, pleased with themselves.

For them she could never be more than someone who filled their water jug before they asked for it. A server. She had never understood this before.

Spring came. Winds blew away the heavy rains and tossed the gleaming trees. Dandelions crept in a bright wave across the clearing, and arum lilies sprang up beside the rushing creek. The evenings were delicate and melancholy. It was a year now since Frank Clark had died.

One night Ada, straightening her knife and fork on the table like a dinner guest, turned to Edith and discreetly, in formal tones, as if starting a conversation with a neighbour's daughter, enquired:

'And when is your baby due?'

'In the summer,' Edith said.

'You must be thankful for that. It's too cold in winter here for a baby. I was always glad I didn't have a little baby here in the winter.'

Frances kept standing at the stove, her back turned.

'And do you have your things ready?'

'No.'

'I will look through what I have,' said Ada, graciously. But she kept looking into Edith's eyes as if she were trying to tell her something. 'And the doctor? What does he say?'

'I haven't seen him yet.'

'Oh my dear, you must.' She wagged her finger at Edith. 'It's not just for yourself now, you know.'

Edith flung her head down on the table and cried.

Frances brought the pot from the stove.

'I'm glad our father isn't alive,' she said.

The lies that Edith had prepared—a secret marriage, a husband who had gone to look for work up north—deserted her when she sat facing Dr Bly across his desk. She'd forgotten about faces like this, faces of men like Dr Bly or her father, so careworn and dignified and grim. No chance of hiding from those sad, shrewd eyes. The world worked because of men like this. Yet she felt for him as she had for her father, a queer sort of pity.

He seemed to know at once she was unmarried.

'Tell me, Miss Clark,' he said, as he washed his hands, 'are you a lonely girl? In my experience it is usually the lonely girls who get themselves into this sort of pickle, eh?'

Edith couldn't say if she was lonely or not. She could not answer him, though she knew she should, when he was trying to be kind.

'There's always the Home of the Good Shepherd in Perth, you know. An adoption could be arranged.'

Edith found herself shaking her head. For if she didn't feel lonely, who had been with her all these long months?

'Have you thought about how society will regard you and this child?'

You didn't have to think about it, you knew. It seemed you'd always known, even as a little girl. It was the fall over the edge. It was the darkness beyond. It was the worst thing that could ever happen to you, next to death.

But more and more Edith did not believe people could see her. She was no more than a tree or stone in the landscape. Outside the surgery window petals fell non-stop from an almond tree, their soundlessness a message. *Stay silent. Promise nothing.*

Dr Bly said that in view of her youth and small pelvis, the isolation of her home and the state of her mother's health, he would arrange for her to go to Matron Linley's in Busselton for the delivery and lying-in. That she mustn't worry about the cost, Matron was a friend of his.

'I had a lot of time for your father,' he said, head down, writing in his pad.

He didn't deserve this, poor old Frank.

Somewhere on the track back home, as darkness fell, Edith lay down, shut her eyes, lost consciousness. When she woke it was dark, before the moon had risen and she lay and listened to the rustles of the bush around her. *You haven't done anything wrong,* she heard a voice say. Who spoke? It wasn't a voice she recognised. Could it be, repaying her for her loyalty, the voice of the child? Or was it her own, startling, thought?

On the appointed day, calculated on his desk calendar by Dr Bly, Edith set off across the yellow summer grass of the clearing to catch the bus to Busselton and Matron Linley's. It was seven in the morning, not yet hot, but she walked slowly, as if she carried a stone between her legs. Frances stood watching her from the verandah, the closest she could come to saying goodbye. A few weeks ago Frances had gone to Torville and bought flannelette for napkins, to save Edith from prying eyes. She had delivered a message to the Sea House that Edith was sick with tonsillitis and would not be back to work for the time being, doctor's orders. It was kind of Frances to do this as she hated to lie. She never spoke the word 'birth', as if it was obscene.

Edith hoped nobody from the Sea House would see her now, especially as she was wearing her black uniform, it was all that would fit her. She covered it over with a shirt of her father's, and pulled her straw hat low over her face. All that she carried with her was stuffed into a raffia shopping bag. She also wore Ada's long outgrown gold wedding ring with some wool wrapped round the back of it to make it fit. She stood at the far side of the Nunderup Hall until she heard the bus. She was lucky—there were only schoolchildren getting on, no sharp-eyed farmer's wife. She sat at the back, invisible, while the children shouted and flirted and conspired.

All the way along the road to Torville the bus passed mailboxes with the names she could chant from her childhood, *Lewis, McKay, Ward, Robertson and Riley*. Her father had made their mailbox out of a kerosene tin, as he made everything they used. He had painted CLARK across it in whitewash that was too sloppy so that each letter ran like a tear. When he nailed it to the stump at the end of their track, he would have hit his thumb or torn a nail. He always did.

She remembered how he used to swipe his fingers across a pan of dripping, and rub the fat into his suffering hands.

In these last days she thought about her father constantly.

They said he never had any luck. But what was luck? He used to rage at her and Frances, tell them they would starve if they didn't hop to, look smart. You will only have yourselves to blame, he shouted, as they stood squinting up at him. He didn't believe in luck. Luck was what you made of your life.

Yet in the end he had lain patient and gentle all day on the couch, as if resigned to what life had brought him.

She felt his resignation, his exhaustion had taken root in her.

She'd forgotten that it was bumpier at the back of the bus. She cupped her hands over her belly to protect it. Did luck get handed down?

Matron Linley's was on a flat stretch of road on the outskirts of town. As Edith trudged towards it she saw far ahead of her an Aboriginal woman walking softly through the dust, carrying a baby and holding the hand of a little child. I wonder where she had *her* baby, Edith thought suddenly, I wonder if she was afraid.

The flat brown earth seemed to open out around the woman and the sky above her seemed immense, burning blue and cloudless.

The hospital was built of stone, with an iron roof and wide verandahs all around. It had probably been a farmhouse once for an early settler. A cow still grazed in a dusty paddock beside it. There were no other houses in sight. This gave the impression of quarantine. Out the front was a yellow lawn and some old peppermint trees. Smoke uncoiled from a chimney, and white sheets flapped on a line. It looked too quiet, too innocent, like a witch's house.

Matron Linley herself met Edith at the door.

'Goodness, you're small, lass,' she said. 'I hope you've got your dates right. We're overbooked as it is.'

Edith's head swam after the brightness outside as she stood in the dark hall. It smelt of carbolic and something sweetish, medicinal, a strange unnatural smell. The hall was lined with closed doors. Very faintly, as if from far away, came a mewling cry.

Matron Linley wore a veil, a grand affair of folds of stiffened voile, to frame her handsome face. This was a surprise. Sea blue eyes, clear as a nun's. White clean-pored skin. A calm low voice. Surely a good witch. Edith followed her onto a side verandah, partitioned off with canvas blinds. A solitary high iron bed faced out onto the paddock. A magpie sat on the verandah rail.

Matron turned and paused, and the light fell full on her face. Even the little creamy middle-aged pouch beneath her chin was adorable, and the gold watch pinned above her full bosom.

'We call this the Overflow Room. Nice and cool at night! Put your bag down and come and have a cup of tea, lass. Then perhaps you could give a hand with lunch. I'm afraid it's all hands to the wheel round here for the present time.' Being pretty gave her even more authority. She knew God was on her side. You felt grateful for her smile, it was a pleasure just to see those shapely lips curve. Edith tried to smile back.

Besides Matron there was another nurse, who rode a bicycle to work, a thin freckled woman with round shoulders called Sally Baker. She never sat down, or ate or even drank a cup of tea. Baker! Matron called, and Sally's feet went flying up the hall. There was also a cook, a huge woman called Doris, who seemed indifferent to everything around her. She called Matron 'The Widder'. A lanky young man in working clothes came in for lunch. Doris dolloped corned beef and mashed potatoes onto a plate and handed it to Edith. 'Widder's son,' she said with a nod in his direction. The young man winked at Edith as she set his plate before him. He had pimples on his chin and Matron's blue eyes. One day he would be flashily handsome. He was about the same age as Edith. Something about the way he looked at her made her flesh crawl, filled her with shame. She took her plate and sat on the back steps.

After lunch a hushed commotion started up in the shadowy part of the house, frantic footsteps, telephone calls, a wailing voice. Matron's son went outside to smoke by the woodshed. Doris lay back in a wicker chair with a newspaper over her head. Edith found her bed on the verandah and lay watching the afternoon breeze ripple through the yellow grass. When she woke the sweetish smell was very strong and she could hear the thin afternoon wails of hungry babies.

Edith washed and dried the breakfast dishes, Widder's orders, said Doris. She ran a mop up and down the hall. It was a dark house, shadowy from the peppermint trees. Doors opened and closed on secrets, straps and pulleys, chamber pots, bloodied sheets. There were five other patients, Edith counted as she helped set out the trays. Sometimes one or two of them sat whispering in dressing-gowns on the verandah, or shuffled to the bathroom holding sponge bags and tin washbowls. None seemed to be expected to put their hands to the wheel. It was hard to tell from their swollen bodies who had or had not given birth. Matron addressed each one of them as 'Mother'. She scolded them for walking. They were supposed to lie in bed, bound up, for two weeks.

In the evening husbands came and sat on chairs beside the mothers. Edith could hear snatches of conversation through the French doors which opened onto the verandah.

Johnson's got his transfer, that leaves us underhanded.

Did you bring in the wash? Did the children eat their tea?

Later a little woman with a high voice and fine silvery hair, popped her head around the canvas partition and asked Edith if her husband was coming. Edith said he was away. That's probably best, the little woman said. Best not to have to bother about them. She gave a tinkling laugh, but her glance flickered over Edith's left hand. She said her name was Mrs Taylor, Margery. She had Three under Five, three girls, so she was keeping her fingers crossed for Number Four. Edith said that she was Mrs Clark, Edith and that this was her First.

'Isn't Matron *wonderful*?' Mrs Taylor said. 'I just put myself in her hands.'

Three days passed, and still Edith's baby was not born. Matron set her to sweep all the verandahs and help with the wash. Edith wished Matron would smile at her. She wondered if the child did not like Matron and was lying low and would never be born here. Late in the afternoon as she sat on the back steps watching Lance Linley in the distance tinkering with his motorbike, Matron suddenly appeared with a brown glass bottle and a tablespoon. 'Open wide, lass,' she said, and pushed the spoon into Edith's mouth. 'Castor oil. I've told Doctor we need your bed.' She scraped a drop up off Edith's chin and tipped it in. 'Now we'll see some action.'

A long high wail wafted down the hall from the Labour Room. Edith thought she recognised little Mrs Taylor's soprano tones.

'I think we've had a false alarm,' Matron said. She was without her veil, in a hairnet, beneath which were tight-coiled snail curls. Her uniform was buttoned over her nightdress. She certainly wasn't smiling. Without her veil she looked smaller and angrier. The baby seemed to have changed its mind. Sally Baker yawned as she took Edith's pulse, because she had just ridden her bicycle through Busselton's dark streets.

'I'm sorry,' Edith gasped to Sally Baker, who said that there was nothing to be sorry about, babies always chose their own time.

Matron said that since there was nothing doing she would try to catch some beauty sleep.

'Don't leave me,' Edith heard herself wail, clutching Sally Baker's hand, as surely all the mothers did. For as soon as Matron's footsteps had faded down the hall, the child started to make its way again. Sally held Edith's hand and said she had the pulse of an athlete, she was a strong farm girl, like her, Sally Baker, and that she was going to be fine. Every time Edith opened her eyes she saw that Sally Baker was watching her very steadily, as if she was willing her onward through the waves. Her flat freckled face, just beyond the circle of light, was spare and delicate and concentrated, like a lover's. Sally Baker had no lover or child, but she understood pain.

A bell rang, Doctor Bly was here after all, and Matron in her veil, they were leaning over her together, putting a cloth over her nose and mouth. *A whiff of Twilight Sleep, Edith,* said Dr Bly, and she was overwhelmed by the sweetish smell. *Reluctant little cove,* he was saying, and from a long way off she saw something skinned and soapy held up like a rabbit, getting spanked for being her child.

⁂

Mrs Taylor called her baby Raymond because she'd always thought the name refined. She couldn't stop calling out to Edith in her bed on the verandah. Little Raymond was beautiful, everybody said he was, his little ears lay flat against his head. Their boys were almost twins, perhaps they would be friends, share birthday parties! Her silvery laugh rang out again and again.

Edith couldn't say her baby was beautiful. He had a thatch of black hair and a big nose and sallow skin. More than anything she felt surprise. She had thought of him as a spirit that had taken root in her, an old wise spirit, and here he was in this helpless, primitive form. She had no name prepared for him.

She couldn't call him Frank, she wasn't sure her father would have appreciated it, in the circumstances. Frances certainly wouldn't. She thought of his middle name, James. A quiet, dignified name tucked in between Francis and Clark. A name to lie low in. But she wasn't sure this child looked like a James.

The next day Mrs Taylor's milk came in and she cried and said she wasn't used to boys, it didn't seem right, you know, to give him the breast, and come to think of it she had never really felt at home with men.

Edith couldn't answer because by then her baby, whatever his name was, had started to scream.

Matron had never known a child to scream like him, and she had known a few screamers in her time. Some of the Mothers were finding it hard to get their sleep. She said she thought he was a hungry baby, and should go straight onto the bottle. She would come back when she had a minute and bind Edith's breasts.

'As a matter of fact, lass,' she said, lowering her voice, leaning down so close to Edith that her veil seemed to make a private room for them, 'there's been an expression of interest from a lady—I'm not naming any names, she lives in the area—all I can say is, it would be a *very* good home.' Her breath had a perfumed, toilet smell. Her clear calm eyes surveyed Edith. Eyes that knew everything, like Dr Bly's. Eyes that had right on their side. Any moment now she, silly little Edith, would give in and do the right thing. She had to, now she was a mother.

'You've made a terrible mistake, lass, but you can still give your son a chance in life.'

She doesn't call me Mother, Edith thought.

'Doctor has been very kind to you, but don't think life won't make you pay.'

A strange memory crossed Edith's mind. She was being wheeled out the door of the Labour Room. Matron was bending over the delivery table to gather up the sheets and Dr Bly reached out his hand and jabbed his finger between her ample buttocks. The picture was so vivid that Edith shut her eyes so Matron would not see what she knew.

Surely not! Not the good doctor, her father's friend! Could this just be an effect of Twilight Sleep?

'Think it over,' Matron was saying. 'The lady is going to pop in for a look-see tomorrow.'

Edith's baby screamed so hard that Matron turned away and picked him up. 'Come on, young man,' she said, 'you're going back to the Nursery.' Off she stalked with the red-faced bundle. '*Nobody* will want you if you scream like that,' Edith heard her say.

From her bed on the verandah Edith saw Bickford's Ford coming along the road. Surprising the pang of recognition it gave her, like a messenger from a long lost world. It was slowing down outside Matron Linley's, it was turning up the drive. Sure enough, when she peered around the canvas partition, there was Bickford having a smoke with Lance under a tree.

Bickford wasn't a talker, she remembered. He would be here for the length of his smoke. She had five minutes. She pulled her hospital gown off and stuffed it under the pillow. She pulled her black dress on, loose now over the slack bandaged flesh of her belly. She had to lace her shoes tightly, they were so big. Her legs were rubbery, and her hands were shaking. In the kitchen she could hear the clatter of the afternoon tea trays. She climbed down through the verandah rail into the yellow grass and made her way to the front door ducking low along the side of the house. No one was sitting on the verandah. The screen door was unlatched. The Nursery was on the right, its door closed. What would she do if Matron was in there? The room was dim, three babies slept in a row of wicker cribs. A long muslin curtain sucked in and out of the window as if in the peaceful current of their breath. No Mother about. Her baby was the darkest, already startlingly familiar to her. She unwrapped his hospital blanket, picked him up and wrapped him in her father's shirt. Such a long walk, across the hall, across the verandah, across the yellow lawn. She felt so light she could blow away, except for the bundle she carried. Bickford's black dog started barking at her as she approached the Ford. Bickford, his trouser bottoms flapping high above his boots, made his unhurried way down the driveway.

'Mr Bickford.' Her voice was weak, as if she hadn't used it for a long time. 'Could you please give me a ride?'

Bickford came to open the door for her. She and her bundle climbed inside.

Bickford didn't speak or look at her all the way to the Sea House. There was just the rattle of the truck and the dog barking and the bush in the late afternoon light. It seemed to be welcoming her back after a long absence. She hardly knew how to hold a baby yet, but she sat up straight and gripped him tight. She didn't know if he was asleep or not in all this noise, but he was quiet. She would have liked to turn and watch out of the cab window to see if anyone was in pursuit, Matron, say, veil flying, behind Lance on his motor bike. Very gently, because of the *Font-A-Nelle* that Matron had spelled out, she blew away the red dust that powdered his feathery skull.

At the top of the Sea House driveway, Bickford pulled up, jumped out of the cab and came around to open her door.

'Thet your bebby?' She had never heard his voice before.

'Yes.'

'Boy or gel?' He gently pushed the shirt from the baby's face with a sausage finger.

'Boy.'

'Mother and son,' said Bickford. There was a movement in his moustache and he produced a brown-toothed smile. For some reason the fact that she was now two seemed to give him great pleasure and just as unaccountably Edith was cheered.

'What name?'

'James,' said Edith, uncertainly.

Bickford bent down over him. 'Gidday, Jim,' he said.

It was only as he drove off that she realised he didn't have any deliveries for the Sea House.

Bickford, unlikely saviour.

Bickford and Sally Baker.

That was the first of her and Jim's escapes.

'Now let me have a look at this baby.' Madge Tehoe peered down at Jim who was lying on a rug in the autumn sun that splashed across the verandah. 'Hello there,' she said after a pause, with a stiff lipsticked smile. Jim did not look like a baby, more like a miniature youth going through an ugly stage. Strands of long black hair fell over his solemn face. His nose was big and his dark eyes seemed glitteringly aware. His arms were long and skinny and he had red pimples in a rash over his cheeks.

'It must be the cow's milk,' Edith said. 'I'm trying to wean him.'

'I'm not a baby person,' Madge said, straightening up with relief, 'but I'd say that's an old soul there.'

Jim started to wail. 'Ssh,' Edith said sternly. Her face was thinner than Madge remembered. Jim kept wailing. Edith picked him up, swung him on her hip in an experienced manner. She kept him wide, hoping he wouldn't grab at her blouse and nuzzle like a little cub in front of Madge. Although, funny, she didn't feel so daunted by Madge now. As if in spite of everything, Jim was a weapon in her arms, a source of power. 'Look at the doggies, Jim.' The Clark dog and Madge's spaniel were sniffing tail to tail, shyly like well-bred strangers.

'Dear girl,' Madge said, 'you *know* you could have come to me. Never mind, never mind, we've put that all behind us.' An amber-coloured feather with streaks of salmon pink was tucked into the band of Madge's brown velour hat. Edith had an impulse to reach across and pluck at it. It seemed so long since she had seen something pretty. Out of the corner of her eye she could see Frances crouching in the vegetable patch, her back assiduously turned. She wasn't going to stop work for the lady of the manor.

'I'm not the knitting type,' Madge went on, 'but you've been on my mind and I'd like to help. The Tehoes have *always* helped the Clarks, you know that. I'm not narrow-minded, never have been. I'm offering you a job. Not front-of-house, of course, we couldn't have that. Backstairs. I've been left in the lurch again without a word of notice. Housemaid, two pound ten a week and I'll throw in lunch. Starting as soon as possible. That is, if you can leave the child with your sister and—and your mother . . .'

Ada had come to stand like a shadow at the kitchen door in her battered lambskin slippers. The dogs were suddenly growling and tumbling over the grass. Jim screamed and fumbled at Edith's blouse.

'He will be weaned,' said Edith, in her new, stern voice.

Perhaps it was better for a boy without a father not to be too much with his mother, who might spoil him and make him soft, as Frances said she did? Each morning Edith tiptoed out and left sleeping Jim wedged around with pillows in her bed. She lit the fire in the kitchen before she went so Frances could warm his milk at once when he woke. At first he used to scream when he found she was gone but after a week or two Frances reported that he had stopped all that silly business. When he cried and climbed all over Edith after she came home, Frances said that he'd been as good as gold for *her*, it was only with Edith that he turned into such a sissy.

'My dear,' said Ada, as Jim held out his arms to weary Edith, 'is that *your* baby?' Sometimes Ada held him and hummed and brushed her hand across his head. But she could not be relied on. Once Frances came in to find that Ada had laid him down like a stone on the floor and gone her own way, to call in the chooks.

Still, he grew, fattened up on cow's milk. His first word was 'dog', and it was Frances who heard it, a personal triumph. As Leopold had noted, she had a strong pedagogic streak. She pointed round the clearing, and waited for him to repeat, 'tree', 'sky', 'dog'. She carried him as little as possible, to toughen him up. He crawled early. In the mornings she tethered him to the verandah with a rope until she finished her chores. 'Dog! Dog!' cried Jim.

It was dark when Edith left Jim behind, dark when she came home. She watched the light of the day wax and wane through the Sea House windows. She had been brought out of hiding into the harsh light of the world. On her first day she would have skipped lunch in the kitchen but she was too hungry. At half-past eleven she sat at the end of the great table with Gwen, the other upstairs maid, and ate a cold mutton sandwich, while the kitchen staff bustled around them preparing the guests' lunch.

'So you're back,' said Mavis Staines, the cook. 'Skinny as ever.' Edith felt the waitresses' curious eyes on her, and a sort of mocking current in the room. She had the sensation that she was sitting there stripped naked, the object of everybody's lewdest speculation. She sat chewing, studying the knots and whorls on the wooden table. She found it hard to swallow. Gwen was as young and shy as she was, and thought to be a little slow. Nobody spoke to them. They ate in silence and avoided catching anyone's eye.

But a few days later Ronnie Tehoe started to sit with them, to make their aquaintance while he took what he called his 'elevenses'.

Ronnie Tehoe was Reg's younger brother, recently arrived from England. He was everything Reg was not, slight with small feet and sloping shoulders, a quiff of fair hair and fine English skin. He was here to see Australia and to be Madge's right-hand man for the length of his stay. His light steps bustled up and down the corridors, his bright eyes peeked in and out of rooms and cupboards. He was as domestically observant as a woman. Already he knew all the staff and guests, and everything that was going on above and below stairs.

He observed for instance that Edith always took two biscuits with her tea but ate one, slipping the other into her apron pocket. Once she caught him watching her.

'For the birds on the way home,' she said. She was businesslike in the way she lied these days. She made it a rule not to mention Jim.

'Ah, I knew you were a Child of Nature!' said Ronnie, winking at her. 'From the moment I laid eyes on you.' He acted as if he had special knowledge about everyone, which in her case he probably did. Nobody ever told him to mind his own business. Somehow it was flattering when his eyes fell upon you. Besides, he was in cahoots with Madge.

He called Gwen the Child of God.

Gwen lived for her job. She had pale floppy hair and shiny shins and a distracted thin-skinned face across which colour flooded and retreated like tides. 'Mud tracks on the stairs!' she would gasp at Edith as she flew past with a mop, or 'Hot water for the Bridal Suite!' She confided to Edith that she'd spent her last day off cleaning the western windows. She couldn't live with herself, the way they looked. She paused only to write reminder notes to herself which she shoved into her apron pocket. Madge had a special way of talking to Gwen, in an exhausted half-whisper. Gwen listened, her face crumpled in sympathy, then raced away to do her bidding. The rest of the staff despised her a little. Did Madge pay her extra for all the extra work she did?

'You are an angel come from heaven,' Ronnie told Gwen, whose colour became so fiery that tears came to her eyes.

Gwen lived in a little one-roomed cabin attached to the Sea House garage. She took Edith there at morning tea to show her. It had whitewashed walls and a polished timber floor. Its window overlooked the hills above the creek with their ridges of limestone.

Before the job at the Sea House, Gwen used to live with her brother and his family in one of the timber towns. She had slept all winter on the verandah on a stretcher bed. Now the morning sun poured through the window onto her white cotton bedspread, and Gwen patted the pool of warmth. One day Mrs Tehoe was going to let her have a kitten, she said. The room had a chair and table and a small chest of drawers and some hooks on the wall for Gwen's hat and coat and spare uniform. It was a room for one person only. On the window sill was a pot of lily-of-the-valley, green spears and white childlike bells that you could almost see breathing.

Gwen had no sense of the taint surrounding Edith, no curiosity about her. She only thought about the Sea House, and what Madge might think or want. She was as devoted as a nun. Being with her was restful, as it is with the pure at heart. Edith lay back on the white coverlet, sighed and closed her eyes. Gwen's room sent a pang into her stomach that took her by surprise. Gwen's room, where nobody wanted anything more of you, where there was nothing more to want.

There was a hush upstairs. Couples came out of their rooms whispering as they locked their doors. The rooms held silent clues to their lives, spilt powder, crumpled nightclothes, intimate tumbled beds. This was Edith's domain. She mopped and polished and changed the linen. She laid fires in winter and in summer set up mosquito nets. She cleaned shoes and turned back beds and delivered breakfast trays. She also snooped a little, inspected clothes in wardrobes, thumbed through diaries, ate from bowls of fruit. When she was sure the occupants were safely in the dining room she tried on coats and kimonos and puffed herself with shell-pink powder. She never could resist a hat. She liked to pee in their lavatories, using the special roll of paper, treating herself to a chain flush.

She looked at herself in the three-faced mirrors from all angles. For the first time in her life she could see the back of her head. Her childish plait dismayed her more than ever. Her face looked different, tighter, set. Did she look like a mother? When she worked she forgot about Jim.

She loved the light in these rooms, infinitely changeable, closer to the heavens. She didn't have to look out the windows to know how the clouds were moving across the sun. The light changed like moods which she could feel through her fingertips.

'Whatever happened to those visitors of yours?' Madge said when Edith was collecting her pay in the office. 'Your cousin and his friend, the Albanian. Adam?'

'Aram. He's Armenian.'

'Yes, Armenian. Heavens, where *is* that?' She raised her eyebrows at Edith. 'He was quite the man.' She took a cigarette from a box on her desk and tapped it up and down. 'Where are they now?'

'England. Aram is staying with Leopold.' Edith was backing towards the door. Did she used to lie so easily? Did she used to lie at all? Once there had been nothing to lie for.

'They were always pretty thick, weren't they? Are they coming back here?'

'I don't think so. They have to get on with their careers.'

Madge lit her cigarette with a silver lighter. 'That must be very disappointing for you.'

'No,' Edith said, opening the door behind her, 'why should it be?'

Their eyes met and locked for a moment and Edith remembered the old competition between them. Competition! Yes, that's what it had been.

Edith rushed into the bar and left money for a packet of Capstans on the counter. It was cold going down into the Honeymoon Gardens, and smoke was coiling up from smouldering piles of raked leaves.

Madge knew. She must have guessed, looking at Jim. In every way that Aram was beautiful, Jim was not, but he certainly didn't look like any Australian baby she had seen.

He was quite the man. When Madge had said that, Edith in a flash had a vision of Aram, arms and legs outstretched, strung naked between them. *Quaite the man*, she whispered, imitating Madge's genteel vowels. What had Madge known of Aram? He had only ever laughed at her.

But who knows the strange ways of a man? She thought of noble Dr Bly's playful hand.

Edith, walking fast through the bush, felt her easily moving bones, her small empty breasts, her lightness regained. Her body had healed. She felt strong, ready for something. She was yearning for Aram again.

He was back. Resurrected, detached from Leopold, shy, watchful, beside her in the darkness of the track. She heard his voice, his hesitating English. She reconstructed his hands and lips, resuscitated his touch. Remembered tenderness that she had once banished from her mind. She remade him into her lover.

And with the lover came the anger. Again and again she enacted it, finding him, standing before him, confronting him with Jim.

And then of course he would hold his arms out to them, and they would have a home at last.

Where did the idea come from, to go to Armenia? Such a preposterous idea, in a place where most of Edith's generation, the children of the settlers, had never even been to Perth, in times so straitened that you would choose to walk five miles to save a sixpenny fare. Where those like Ada, who had come here from other countries, were never able to go back.

Who had even heard of Armenia? Was there really such a place? You might as well say you were going to Woop Woop or Timbuctoo or the Great Inland Sea. You grew out of such ideas. You put your head down and got on with it, accepted your lot, stayed put.

This was the voice that Edith heard in the night as she and Jim lay small and frail together in the darkness. But in the morning as she sped up the track, she traced that voice, so reasonable, so powerful, back, back to the hospital bed at Matron Linley's, to the moment when she'd been about to give up, to give in. She had only just saved herself and Jim by running away. She had to save them again.

The letter lay waiting for her in the mailbox. Here it was at last, *The Misses Clark*, in Leopold's flowing black script. Even their humble address, *Lot 44, Nunderup*, looked elegant in that writing.

Dear Frances and Edith, he wrote. The paper was a sheet of ordinary foolscap, as if he had picked it up off the top of a pile on his desk, and written on it quickly among all his other writing tasks, his translations and studies. The script had the flourish of speed.

> *My very dear long lost cousins, in retrospect the time in your company and your spectacularly remote land was the island in the whirlpool. These are troubled times in this part of the world. My days of irresponsible youth are well and truly over. I have a job with the Government, there being a shortage these days of frivolous archaeological expeditions. My job is, roughly, to do with maps, which will make you laugh, knowing my sense of direction. And Aram has heeded the call and gone home to the Motherland. I myself for the time being am living with my mother (who is well and sends her greetings etc), but later I may be required to set off for parts unknown.*
>
> *I often think of you both and it seems to me that you are women of exceptional qualities. For the time being of course, like all of us, you have responsibilities. But one day you will not. Let me say to you this: Take your life into your hands. Work, travel, study: you are more than equal to the challenge.*
>
> *I wish only to assure you that I am ever at your service.*
>
> *My fondest regards to your mother. Until we meet again,*
> *Your cousin, Leopold.*

The letter lay on the kitchen table, where it would soon be splashed with soup.

'Nice of him,' Frances said. 'Dashes off a little advice to the colonial cousins after he's ruined their lives.'

'He hasn't ruined our lives.'

'Well look at us.' On one side of the table Frances was cutting up Ada's bread into bite-sized pieces. On the other Edith was feeding soup to Jim on her knee. As she spoke to Frances the soup went too fast down his throat and he spluttered and howled. Edith rose and walked around the room patting him. He cried on drearily as if it was a matter of principle.

'Has he been like this all day?'

'Of course not. He only tries it on with you.'

Edith took Jim out onto the verandah. Relief made the stars look brighter. Word at last from the outside world! This was how prisoners must feel, she thought. She hadn't realised how much of a desertion Leopold's silence had seemed to her.

For all his even-handedness, she couldn't help feeling that the letter was really speaking just to her.

Ronnie Tehoe was a traveller. He had been travelling since he was sixteen. He was working in a hotel in Brighton when he met a yachtsman who offered him a job with a millionaire's crew in the Caribbean. From there he went to Alaska with a sealing company, and then on to Japan in a cargo ship. He sailed down the China Sea, through the Malacca Strait to Madras, and then travelled overland till he caught another ship from Constantinople to Marseille. When he arrived back in Brighton he had been away five years. That was first of his voyages.

Everybody in the kitchen listened to his stories, of ice floes, typhoons, Saddhus, mountain passes, camel trains. They had never heard such stories. They had never met a traveller in Nunderup before. They didn't know whether to believe him, or whether he was making fools of them all.

'All well and good if you have money,' said Mavis Staines.

'It's not so terribly expensive,' Ronnie said. 'That's what people don't understand. I stop somewhere and work and then I buy a cheap passage on a cargo ship. I once had a job as Second Entertainment Officer on a transatlantic liner, but it's not an experience I'd care to repeat. I like the cargo ships. You go to out-of-the-way ports, and you go where the sailors go, the cheap cafés and hotels, and then you link up with other ships. It's a sort of trail. Your money goes a long way. When it runs out, you find work.'

'What sort of work?'

Ronnie threw out his arms. 'I've worked in hotels all over the world. You don't have to stay at home! You don't have to wither on the bough! You can go anywhere you want. You don't have to grow old. How old do you think I am?'

'Thirty?' ventured Gwen.

'I'm nearly forty. Five years younger than Reg.' They all peered. He was lean and compact and restless. His teeth were white, his eyes clear. There was barely a boyish fuzz on his cheeks.

'It's a way of life,' he said. 'Every day a holiday.'

'Some of us have got mouths to feed,' said one of the yardsmen.

'Ah, there you have it. The traveller must be prepared to leave behind all responsibilities. A true traveller takes care to avoid them.'

'A girl in every port, eh!' said the yardsman, a grin spreading on his face.

Ronnie didn't deign to reply.

Later upstairs as he was counting out sheets for Edith from the linen room, he said: 'Don't think that there's some leafy Tehoe estate back in England. Father was a drunk. Reg and I grew up in cheap hotels. We had to leave school when Father couldn't pay the fees. Hotels are all we know. The money in this place is all *hers*, if you want to know. But he's got the accent. They were made for one another. Poor old Reg.'

Ronnie seemed to seek out Edith. She sensed that he didn't judge her, no shade crossed his eyes when he spoke to her, to remind her that she was a fallen woman. He seemed rather intrigued by her. She felt excited by his interest. She tried to imagine briefly what it would be like to love him, to feel his small muscly arms around her, and his smooth cheek against hers, but she could not. The excitement was for something else, the old travelling dreams, the sense of the world lying wide open before you.

'You say you can go anywhere you want,' she said. 'How would you get to Armenia?'

'Armenia?' said Ronnie, smoothly as a ticket seller, 'From here? For yourself? Single or return?' He winked.

'Oh, just in theory.'

'In theory, nobody wants to go to Armenia. You do know it's a territory of the Soviet Socialist Republic? Lord knows how one would ever acquire a visa.'

'Can you get in without a visa?'

'In theory no. In practice, my dear Edith, as we both know, you can *get in* anywhere.' A little later he said: 'But you'd have to have a passport of course.'

Armenia had become a landscape superimposed over the hills and valleys around her. Armenia was certain marked glowing places, like the path down the escarpment where she had first seen Aram. The full moon was Armenian, and so were the Honeymoon Gardens when no one else was there. The look-out was a citadel to Armenianness. The spire of the Anglican church on the outskirts of Torville was very Armenian, because as you saw it from the bus it seemed to promise something ancient and spiritual, not Torville's flat municipal streets. The delicate morning light was Armenian, and when Ronnie Tehoe made them all laugh at the kitchen table, that was Armenian. Spirits were higher in Armenia. The people were proud and reserved but they had generous, hospitable hearts.

Ronnie popped his head out of the Sitting Room and beckoned Edith. He was waiting for her with the big old atlas opened at the World, Political. He traced a route with his finger, from Fremantle to Southampton, from London overland to Istanbul, across the Black Sea to Georgia and down through the Caucasus mountains into Yerevan, Armenia's capital. Armenia was so small that its name overran its borders. Australia was one of the pink patches on the map, while Armenia was Soviet green.

'The first step would be to find out when a cargo ship was going to England,' Ronnie said. 'Announcements are in the shipping news at the back of *The West.*'

'How much money would you need?' If she could get to London, there would be Leopold. He would come with her to find Aram. He'd promised Ada to be *at her service.*

'Fifty pounds for starters,' Ronnie said. His eyes challenged her.

If it hadn't been for the twenty pound note left stuffed into a pocket of a guest's tweed coat, Edith most likely would never have seriously considered making the journey. The coat was left hanging in the back hall to dry from a sudden shower of rain while its owner rushed late into the Dining Room for lunch. It was still hanging there at the end of the day as Edith put on her old cape. She saw the tip of the note peeping out with a shoved-in handkerchief—the owner must be careless, she thought. It was still there next morning. The coat belonged to the large man with the reddish beard who drove the Armstrong Siddeley that everyone admired. And then the car left and the coat was still there. The yardsman who had cleaned the car for him reported a generous farewell tip. The big man was going back to Scotland, he said. So he was generous and careless and rich, and not coming back. The sort of person who could afford to forget his coat, afford to forget twenty pounds, afford to lose it. Moreover, if he should write, the coat was left downstairs, and the upstairs maid would not be under particular suspicion. Edith told herself that if the coat was still there at the beginning of next week, it would be a sign.

She took the twenty pounds. She hid it in her childish hiding place, a toffee tin tucked into the stumps of the verandah.

She sent off for passport forms.

Of course she had more need of the money than the man with the red beard. She had a son to save.

Did all thieves think they had a special need?

She wasn't a real thief, she told herself. She would give it up as soon as she had fifty pounds.

Do all people cheat when there is something they must have?

No. Not Frances. Not her father. But look what had happened to him.

It became, so quickly, a habit of mind. It was like a sport. She enjoyed it. She found out she was good at it.

There was a pair of silk stockings left at the bottom of a wardrobe. They were dirty, with a hole in one toe, not likely to be reclaimed. Edith mended and washed them and hung them to dry out of Frances's sight behind a bush. She gained a white cambric blouse, good as new after bleaching in the sun, in the same way. The knickers, pink and ivory satin, pale-blue cotton, she took out of various suitcases. Nobody was likely to report the theft of a pair of knickers to the office. She kept her eye out for a woollen bodice and a suspender belt.

Madge herself gave Edith a pair of unclaimed walking shoes that had been left on the porch.

She kept these things in her father's old Globite case.

Tipping was not official at the Sea House, but often enough money was slipped into a hand, left on a table or beside a bed. These tips were supposed to be taken to the kitchen to be pooled. Edith, who was quick and never had to be asked twice and looked, with her plaits and stick-thin legs in black stockings, urchin young and touching, received her fair share of tips, more than the more-deserving Gwen. She made sure that Ronnie or Mrs Staines were around when she dutifully deposited her coins in the jar in the kitchen, and that they fell with a convincing ring. Most of the coins she kept, silenced in her handkerchief.

She'd never noticed how much money people left lying around before. Not only tips, which, swift and efficient, she hunted down as soon as guests booked out. But pennies, threepences, little mounds of shilling pieces, rolled around in chair backs, drawers, under cushions, in the dust beneath the beds. Small change was the flotsam of the world. Edith made sure at least twice a day that she walked past the telephone in the hall, where there was often a few coins. She handed some of them in of course, in case Madge had set a trap. It kept her very busy, all the calculations she had to make. Would that gentleman miss a shilling from his bedside pile of small change? Did that lady know there was a sixpence floating free at the bottom of her evening bag?

Once a five pound note was left in a hatbox in a vacated room, but she suspected the woman, and took it down to Madge. Just as she had handed it over Madge was called out to register a guest, and she left the note sitting on the desk. As Edith walked out the draught blew it to the floor. Edith took it and left the door open. If Madge remembered it she would think it had blown down the hall. She could hardly challenge Edith, who had brought it to her in the first place. But she would have to be careful after this. Madge was shrewd. In her new sharpness, Edith judged Madge and Ronnie to have, like her, the criminal cast of mind. They would soon sense a thief in the house.

Madge paid her in coin. At home she put her pay, along with Frances's egg money, in the old crock on the mantelpiece. When she or Frances needed to buy anything they stood tiptoe and delved their hands in for what they wanted. Each week she put fewer and fewer coins in the jar.

By the time Jim had cut three teeth, she had saved up thirty-five pounds.

Growing reckless, she took a little navy blue topper coat and a pair of woollen leggings from a tiny girl called Lavinia with Shirley Temple curls. Lavinia wouldn't miss them, sitting like a princess in the special highchair in the Dining Room, everyone cooing over her. Besides her mother had never even taken the coat and leggings out of the bottom of the suitcase, it was far too warm. Now they had a new home in the Globite case.

She spent two pounds sending off to Perth for her and Jim's birth certificates, and another ten shillings taking Jim into Bunbury, to a stuffy little photographic studio.

'Mr Tehoe is a Justice of the Peace, isn't he?' Edith asked Ronnie.

'He is. Why?'

'I have some forms that a JP must sign.'

'Show 'em here. A passport application, eh? Nice photo. Going somewhere?'

'It's just in case,' Edith mumbled.

'Good idea. Everyone should have a passport. What if Australia is invaded by Hitler and you all have to run away?'

'They say there isn't going to be war now.'

'There is, my darling, believe me.' His face tried to be serious. Perhaps Ronnie felt a pang of responsibility for her. Perhaps he'd never thought his seeds would fall on such fertile ground. 'And in case of war, you know, Nunderup would be the safest place of all.'

Edith stared stubbornly at the floor. I will have to hurry, she thought, if there's to be a war.

'Still, what is war when you are young and in love! I'll pop these under Reggie's nose after the fourth whisky. Mum's the word, eh Edith? Leave it to me.'

As summer came on Edith helped out in the beer garden and discovered that when people had been drinking they didn't count their change. And if you were quick you could run your hands under the tables when you collected glasses. Coins fell out of loose beach-coat pockets into the grass. Her riskiest coup, however, was reaching inside the window of a car parked in the driveway by the beer garden. It was dark, she was on her way home. There were seven pounds ten in the glove-box. This time there was a hue and cry at the Sea House, but the gardens were full of strangers. By then the money was safely stowed in Edith's toffee tin.

'Armenia,' she said to Jim in the darkness of their room. 'Armenia.' There was no one else she could say the word to. She liked the symmetry of the word, the way it started as it ended, with an 'a'. She thought it had an optimistic sound.

'Mumma,' she said to Ada one day when they were sitting peacefully on the verandah, 'what do you do if you have one thought that won't go away?'

'Catch the horse,' said Ada. 'Rein it in, lead it to the home paddock.' Did Ada, with her hat permanently on her head, have a place she too thought of night and day?

Armenia. Edith dared herself to write it on frosty windows, on steamy mirrors, on the crisp sand high on the beach. She left a trail of clues if anyone had been interested. *Armenia.* Whispered, it sounded like the end of a prayer.

'The *Touchpole* is due the second of February', Ronnie read out from *The West* at morning tea. 'Let's see, this paper's three days' old. That means the good old ship is here now, berthed in Fremantle. She's docked for repairs.'

'What sort of ship?' Edith asked.

'Cargo. About twenty years old. 5,000 tons. Registered in Colombo. Makes the Indian Ocean run. Colombo, Fremantle, Capetown. Then on to the Canaries and Southampton.'

'The First Mate,' Ronnie drawled on loudly, as if this was of interest for the whole kitchen, 'is a very good friend of mine. Natty Crawford. Natty would do anything for me. Just have to mention my name. Any friend of mine is a friend of Natty's.

'Matter of fact I owe old Nat a letter. I'll drop him a line in the next few days. I'll ask him about places for passengers, just in case any of you lot are interested. I'd take off myself except I promised to stay for the Easter rush. Maybe next time round.' Ronnie drained his tea and closed the paper. 'Shabby old bumboat, the *Touchpole*. I'd say she'll be in dock for a couple of weeks.'

In the district it was said that Edith had left a note on the kitchen table for her sister, telling her that she had taken Jim to

Perth for a few days. At least that was what Frances told Madge. Madge carried on as best she could, but after two weeks had to hire another maid. Ronnie swore to himself that he wouldn't tell but one night when Madge needed to be entertained and he was sure that the *Touchpole* had well and truly sailed, he told her that Edith had gone to Armenia.

'I don't believe you,' Madge said. 'Where *is* Armenia again?' All the same she checked out her jewellery before she went to bed. Her brown velour hat had gone missing, but she thought she must have mislaid it. Word got around, but nobody really believed that Edith had gone to Armenia. Wherever on earth that was. More likely she had taken up with some fancy man she'd met in the hotel. She was a ruined girl. They supposed she would never come back. It was as if she were dead.

Flight

The track had never seemed so long. She had to swap Jim and the suitcase from arm to arm. Jim hadn't had breakfast but was not crying, enchanted at the novelty of the journey and the singing of the magpies. She saw nothing, heard nothing, just plodded on. It was as if she was dragging them all behind her, the two sleeping women in the dark bedroom, the dog chained so it wouldn't follow, even her father buried in the earth.

There was a woman waiting among the school kids on the steps of the Hall, with a sun hat and shopping basket and a goodnatured ruddy face. The type who couldn't resist a baby. Edith stood by the road and pretended to be preoccupied with Jim.

Sure enough the woman called out. 'Peek-a-boo! Who's a big boy?' Jim jiggled disloyally over Edith's shoulder. 'How old is he?' the woman called.

'Nearly a year.' But the bus was rounding the corner, Edith picked up her suitcase and didn't look around. She spread out on the bus seat so the friendly woman would not sit next to them, and looked steadily out the window. *Yes I saw her, the little Clark girl, the one with the baby. Come to think of it she did have a suitcase, but I never dreamt . . .*

The countryside had the shimmering emptiness of mid summer.

There was a damp circle on her knee where Jim was sitting, and wet circles beneath her arms. The shoes which Madge had given her were dusty and the white cambric blouse, so carefully laundered in readiness for this journey, was crumpled and smeared by Jim's hands.

On the rack above her was the small brown Globite suitcase. She had packed it late last night and placed it ready behind the wash tub on the verandah. In it were their garnered travel clothes and two bottles full of milk, and a paper bag of the Sea House biscuits she had saved. She couldn't help feeling proud of the fifty-two pounds ten rolled into a pair of satin bloomers. It just went to show that there was money still around, Depression or not. There was also her brand new passport and her mother's wedding ring and Leopold's letter. And right at the top—it had been a last-minute decision in the back hall yesterday as she hung up her apron—Madge Tehoe's brown velour hat.

She could never come back.

They had to wait all morning in the Bunbury station for the train to Perth that afternoon. On her own Edith would have liked to explore the streets of Bunbury, but Jim was too heavy for that. They sat side by side on a bench up the far end of the platform and ate biscuits, and Jim crowed as the trains came and went. Then he grew tired and bored and nothing would settle him. He even pushed away his bottle. Had the milk turned sour in the heat? Edith walked him up and down the platform. She hated him drawing attention like this. She left her suitcase with the stationmaster and set off up the road that ran alongside the tracks. The hot sun made Jim cry even louder. All at once Edith deposited him in the shade of a little thorny tree, and continued alone along the road. Oh how lightly she walked, into the cooling sea breezes of Bunbury! Lighter and lighter, as if she could never turn back. Jim gave a terrified scream. She wheeled around and ran to him. What had she been trying to do, test him? Test herself? Sorry, sorry, she cried as she held him and rubbed his wet cheek with hers. How could she have been so disloyal?

Didn't he always do the crying for both of them?

She changed his nappy in the long yellow grass, the flies buzzing around them. She washed the nappy in the basin of the Ladies washroom and hung it to dry over an old fence. Jim slept on her lap on the platform bench, while she stared sombrely ahead. So this was how it was going to be. Nobody to leave him with, not even for a minute. Never to be one moment by herself.

Just before the train rolled in there was a burst of music from the ticket office. Edith saw that a young woman had started work and was swaying in time beside a big black wireless. *In The Mood*, a voice was singing, a male voice, smooth and happy, with a big slow happy band behind it, that made you want to dance. The music and the woman's bolero dress and rolled-up hair and swaying padded shoulders made Edith feel happy. This was it, this was what it meant to be young and of your time. It was so much in the mood of her vision long ago with Aram and Leopold that she took it as an omen, and climbed aboard the train with a feeling bordering on elation, because her old life was coming to an end.

They were both subdued as they took the train from Perth to Fremantle. The suburbs spread out in the twilight across the sandy plain. Each house had its gate and path, its dried-out lawn, its beds of rose bushes and canna lilies, its tidy umbrella tree beside the porch. Perth! How she and Frances had once longed to come here, to the fabled Royal Show.

Edith took her passport out of the Globite in readiness. The photograph was dismaying. She had pinned her hair up for the occasion and, alas, a rogue strand fell down her young thin neck. She looked like a schoolgirl trying to be grown-up. While Jim, squeezed immobile at her shoulder, his chins belligerent, his black eyes distrustful, looked like a little old man. But the passport, in black and gold, was reassuring. The Governor-General himself declared that Edith May Clark and James Francis were British Subjects by birth, and requested that they be allowed to pass freely, and be afforded every assistance, in the name of His Britannic Majesty.

They were rumbling across a bridge and suddenly before them was a great harbour with towering cranes and ships, and beyond it, the sparkle of the open sea.

As she mounted the gangplank up the vast iron grey flank of the *Touchpole*, Edith's straw hat blew off. She had no spare hand to grab it. She watched it circle slowly down onto the water between the ship and wharf.

Time for the velour hat, she thought, stepping on deck, now that she had left Australia.

Natty Crawford himself showed her to her cabin. 'If you don't mind me asking,' he said, in a Cockney accent, 'how old are you?'

'Twenty,' said Edith, though in her passport, which he had thumbed through, she was not yet nineteen.

'And the nipper? He won't be sick? He's well-behaved?'

Although he was tanned and well built like a working man, there was something dandified about Natty, with his navy blue gaberdine jacket, his white shoes, finely shaved cheeks and crinkly slicked-back hair.

'I'll be honest with you,' he said as Edith put Jim and the Globite suitcase down on the bunk. The cabin was dim, deep down in the ship. The porthole was not far above the water. If she stretched her arms out she could just about touch each wall. 'If R.T. hadn't pleaded your case, I would never have let you on board.' He doesn't like me, Edith thought. His eyes were hard and unfriendly, without one flicker of gallantry. 'A ship like this is no place for a woman. Especially if she's young. Stirs things up.' He ran his hand through his hair. 'I'd prefer you to lie low, if you understand my meaning. Probably best if you take your meals in the cabin. Cookie will look after you.'

The fare was fifteen pounds. There were no other passengers.

The *Touchpole* sailed that evening, but Edith was too intimidated to go on deck for a last glimpse of her native shore. She felt queasy as she and Jim fell asleep, and by the time she woke up the next morning to the sway and throb of the ship, she felt very sick indeed.

Cookie said it was very rare, but he thought it did happen. 'Young chap signed on once at Southampton and never lived to see Bombay. Threw up day and night like you. Seasickness. No other cause we could see.' He stood among the nappies strung up across the cabin as Edith tried a spoonful of his soup. He had a glum pugnacious face and smelt of hot fat, but he was the only person she'd seen for days on end. The only one to ask if anyone ever died of this.

She put the bowl down and laid her head back on her sour pillow. At the end of the bunk, Cookie was tickling Jim. Perhaps she was delirious, but she thought she heard Jim laughing. She'd never heard him laugh before. 'Come on, guv,' Cookie said, holding out his arms. 'We'll leave your ma in peace.'

How did this stranger woo shy Jim away from her? Days and nights were one in the dark cabin. Sometimes Jim was with her, sometimes he was not. She only knew it was night when Jim was there asleep.

She woke once with a start, sensing his absence. It was pitch black outside the porthole. She leaned forward, patting the emptiness at the end of the bunk. Up the corridors and stairs she stumbled, to the galley, which was empty, its surfaces swept clean. On the far side of the galley there was a strip of light beneath a door. She opened it. All around a table sat men in singlets, smoking and slapping down cards. Jim was sitting on Cookie's knee, licking Cookie's stumpy finger which was crusted with sugar. He looked peculiarly content, and fatter than she remembered. She opened her mouth to claim him but her throat was too parched to speak. Of course! she thought, it's all a dream. She fell down in a faint.

The worst part of her weeks on the bunk were the dreams. She dreamt she and Frances were sliding on the wet lurching deck of the *Touchpole*, trying to save Ada from drowning. She dreamt she saw her father get on to a train that disappeared with a whoosh into a tunnel underground. She lay shivering and retching, like one accursed, punished for her desertion of them. She knew now this journey could only end in doom. There was nothing to distract her from this darkness, no light of sky, no birds, no sweet air. How foolish she had been ever to think that there was anything more she needed.

She wondered if she was dying. She made herself get up and rummage in the Globite for Leopold's letter. She scribbled across the envelope that if she should die on this voyage, she wanted Jim to be put into the care of her cousin Leopold, at the above address.

After the Cape of Good Hope, Capetown offered three days' respite. Cookie advised fresh air. Edith was able to dress and feebly wash nappies and hang them out to dry between lifeboats. The sky was blue and raw, like in Australia, only bluer and higher. She stretched out on the deck beneath the nappies and tethered Jim to her with a piece of rope. The glare hurt her eyes. She would have liked to return to the dark cabin but Jim needed to be outside. Cookie invited her and Jim to ride into Capetown but she refused. She knew that once she touched dry land she would never leave it again.

'Look, Jim, palm trees! Flying fish, dolphins!' They had crossed the Gulf of Guinea and it was smoother sailing now. There was a tracery of tropical coastline and, at night, new constellations of stars. Jim walked on deck with her, holding her hand. During all the weeks she had languished in the cabin, Jim had learnt to walk and clap his hands and say 'Ta' and 'Bye-bye'. When someone waved a finger in front of him, he swayed in time like a cockatoo. Cookie had cut his hair off and fed him man-sized meals. He even looked a little like a miniature pudgy Cookie. He no longer screamed. Wherever he went there was laughter. Edith, pitifully weak and thin, was ignored.

Jim had his first birthday as they approached the Canary Islands. Cookie iced a cake. Edith offered to help, but could not find her way around the galley.

'Didn't they teach you nowt in Or-stralia?' Cookie elbowed her out of the way. Natty Crawford sang Happy Birthday over the ship's PA. Jim was returned to her later in the cabin, smelling of tobacco and brandy. He seemed like a little stranger, remote, rough, a man's boy. When she tried to make him go to bed his temples throbbed with anger at her, at her female fussiness and fears.

Once she woke to see Cookie lit by moonlight in the cabin, his head among the nappies. His hand was at his crotch, moving rhythmically up and down. Who would come for her if she called out? She lay still, closed her eyes. She heard him sigh beneath his breath, and the click of the door. He hadn't been looking at her but at the other end of the bunk, at Jim.

For the rest of the journey she kept her door locked. When Cookie came to take Jim with him to the galley, she said that she would keep him with her now. Cookie turned without a word. He didn't bring food to them any more, but there were only two days left. She went into the galley at night and foraged for cheese and bread and powdered milk.

In Southampton all the crew were busy, rushing to go ashore. Men stood aside for them in the narrow corridors as they made their way up the ship. Edith's silk stockings gathered round her ankles, her skirt dipped beneath her coat. Even her head had lost weight, Madge's hat sank down below her ears. Natty Crawford shook her hand at the top of the gangway and pinched Jim's cheek. Edith lifted up Jim and descended into England's damp grey air. She felt herself picked white and hollow as a bone. Not forgiven, but beyond retribution now. Jim waved bye-bye over her shoulder, but nobody was looking any more.

What Edith hadn't expected, had never taken into account, was that Irina would be beautiful. Neither her parents nor Leopold had ever said that she was. Her father always gave a little snort at any mention of Irina, as if to say *he* had her measure. In the photograph of Fat Leopold she had been a background figure, dark, matronly, sharp-faced. Now her hair was silver, swept into a turret at the crown of her head. She was fullchested as a dove, and walked with her head held high and her shoulders back. Her skin was velvety and pale and crinkly like the back of an old rose petal. No older woman's skin in Nunderup had ever looked like that. Her alert brown eyes were almost triangular over her high cheekbones. She still spoke English with a faint accent, and her manner wasn't English, she was far too intimate and dramatic.

Irina had thrown her arms around Edith in the hall and hugged and kissed her as she had never been hugged and kissed, even as a child. *Edith*, she said, as if she were setting the name alive. Tenderly she had held Jim and helped Edith remove her damp coat. She uncrowned her of the velour hat, its proud brim sadly drooping from the showers of an English spring. 'Now let me have a look at you,' she said. 'Edith, Edith, what has happened to you?'

'Aunt Irina, where is Leopold?'

Irina clutched the soft folds of her neck. 'My darling, Leopold is not here.'

⁂

Jim sat next to Edith beside the fire, holding his own cup, draining it of milk. After their bath he was soft and fragrant like an open flower, his hair brushed back from his temples, a good little mother's boy again. They had floated for hours in Irina's great porcelain tub while outside across the rooftops the dim northern twilight turned to night. Their clothes looked like rags in a pile on the floor, stiff with sea salt. In their bare feet they stole across the polished boards and little jewel-coloured rugs of Irina's floors. Irina's eyes were very bright as she studied them.

'Did you know, Edith, I left behind a little brother in Russia?'

'Yes, I think Mumma mentioned it.'

'His name was Dmitri. That means Jim in English. Did your mother tell you that?'

Edith shook her head. 'What happened to him?'

'He was called up for the army and he couldn't stand it. He walked off into thc snow.' Irina lit a thin black cigarette. 'Are you married, Edith?'

'No,' said Edith. After the *Touchpole* she was beyond telling lies. Besides she knew would never get away with lies before these shrewd eyes. Why was everything so familiar? She had a sense of coming home, so strong that she was surprised to feel a prickling behind her eyes. 'But I will be, when I find Aram Sinanien.' This was to avoid the next question, the biological question, which Irina, with her un-Anglo-Saxon directness, would not hesitate to ask.

'Leopold's driver? The Armenian?' Irina's eyes darted to Jim for a moment. 'Oh Edith!'

'I'm going to Armenia. I hoped Leopold would help me find him.'

'Leopold has gone to the Middle East.' Irina's voice dropped to a whisper. 'For the government. Even I don't know where he is.'

Edith kept on eating. For tea there was poppyseed cake sliced into black-edged scrolls. It tasted female and delicate after Cookie's fare. She and Jim picked at every last crumb on the table.

'Darling, you are not going anywhere,' Irina said, 'until we've put some meat on those bones.'

She put them to bed in Leopold's room, under a great white feather quilt. Jim wet the bed in the early hours of the morning. He had drunk so much milk that Pushkin, Irina's cat, woke them by mewing, outraged at his empty saucer.

Irina still lived in the top storey of the house that Ernest Stubbs had left her. She had survived by renting the rooms on the ground floor. Irina's boarders were old men now, bent and silver-haired. Russians! The passionate, soulful people in Ada's stories of her past. Sometimes old Vassily beckoned to Edith as she passed by his door. He had a sweet for Jim. His room was crammed with books and newspapers stacked up on the floor. Sometimes from the upstairs window she saw Mr Osipov in his black coat and beret, bent over his walking stick, creep his way past the hedges in the grey English light. 'Off to the Russian Officers' Club,' said Irina. 'You should have heard the gossip about us once.' She sighed. 'We're way past scandal now.'

It hadn't been a luxurious living, especially with a son to educate, as Irina was quick to point out. But she was frugal and diligent and managed to live with style. In the mornings she lay in bed with Pushkin and drank tea and attended to letters. She wrote a long weekly letter to Leopold, though she had received only one note from him. The mail seemed to take a long time. The letters were sent to and from an address in London. 'It is hush-hush,' Irina said with a finger across her lips. 'It is because he has the gift for languages. That's why they came to see him here.'

In the afternoons she set off in her long grey coat and fox-fur stole, and little mauve netted hat speared at an angle into her silver turret, to play cards with friends. Sometimes she came home lit by a small deadly smile, a spray of violets pinned to her coat, and something nice for tea, macaroons, or a bit of fish.

'I have a feeling, Edith, that you would be quick at cards,' she mused. 'You know, there are worse ways to make a little extra when you're on your own with a child.'

Some afternoons Irina's lady friends came to tea. Edith and Jim were presented to Madame Sofia Rustikova, Madame Olga Porter, Madame Anya Nikoleyvna Black, to be kissed and exclaimed over and admired. The samovar bubbled on the table. Steam coiled from their cups about their sharp, proud old faces. Soon they were talking Russian. The voices rose to a hubbub as Edith led Jim out.

'Questions, questions.' Irina rolled her eyes at Edith in the kitchen as she set out the cake. 'I've told them you are going to join your husband in France.'

I am going to join my husband. Edith said this over to herself. The very word 'husband' warmed her. From now on this is what she would say if she were asked. She felt grateful to Irina, and proud of her, the most youthful and beautiful of the women around the table.

'It would be better if you don't mention Armenia,' Irina said in a low voice.

'Why not?'

'They will become upset. They are always upset if somebody talks of going to the so-called Soviet Republic. There will be talk.'

'I don't care. I'm used to talk.'

'Listen, Edith, nobody goes where you are talking of going. And most certainly, nobody comes back.'

Everything was as her mother had said it was, the visitors, laughter, smoke. In these rooms Ada and Irina had kept house together and Ada had helped with baby Leopold. After she and Frank were married they'd lived here for a while before they came to Australia. Frances was born here.

By the stipulations of her parents' will, it was Ada's house too. And if the house were sold, a share of the proceeds was to go to Ada and any children she might have. Ada used to tell her daughters this would be their dowry. At one time Frank was all for writing to Irina and insisting she sell the house. He said their only chance to get the farm working was to have a little capital. But Ada would not let him, she said the house was Irina's living.

'Irina would survive,' said Frank with a snort. 'She does very nicely. A lot better than we do. Madame Irina could survive anywhere.'

These were the rooms in which Ada had lived and slept for the English part of her life. They were high above the green-tipped chestnut trees, faced by a row of houses identical to theirs. She'd been protected here behind the hedges and the lace curtains. The light was pearly, orderly like the world of a book. Was this what Ada kept her hat on for, to return to? The girl Ada would never have dreamt that one day she would wander round a lonely clearing in an old green hat and broken-down lambskin slippers. Perhaps Edith had made the journey for her.

Irina was very fond of Ada. 'Ar-da was a sensitive soul. She had *dusha*, your mother, you know, soul. When Ernest died we became very close. How she used to make me laugh! She was very gentle but every now and then she would be taken over by a sort of wildness.' She gave Edith a speculative look.

Every teatime Irina had a new reason to dissuade Edith from making her journey. 'Your mother made a journey too and she never came back. To make a life in a new country is very hard. Believe me, I know what I am saying, Edith. I myself left Petersburg in 1910.

'Her letters from Australia were so funny, but I read between the lines. It was a terrible life for a woman like her, terrible. Her letters became shorter and shorter. I knew that she was going under.'

Why had Ada 'gone under'? Was it so terrible in Australia? What had Leopold told his mother? Edith felt the colonial's suspicion of being patronised. She thought of the violence of its weather, the savage brightness of the air. Here everything seemed muted, stilled. Cabs and buses passed silently beneath the windows. People passed each other in the street without greeting. It made Jim seem noisy. His footsteps clattered on the wooden boards as he chased the cat. He shrieked as Pushkin spat at him. He tugged at Edith's hand, impatient to go out.

'He is a creature of the wilds,' Irina said. 'But then Leopold was a little old man from the day he was born.'

Edith, looking down at Jim, suddenly remembered that Ada had lost her baby son.

'Think of your mother, Edith,' Irina said with a theatrical sigh each teatime. 'All she has been through. How she must worry about you.'

Edith wrote a short letter to Frances and Ada. She said she hoped they were both well and that she thought often of them. Irina was being very kind. Jim could walk now and said many words. She said they were going to Armenia and she would write from there.

⁂

When Jim sat quiet beside Edith, bathed and happy because it was teatime, Irina liked to sit back and survey him. 'You know, Edith, he reminds me of Leopold.'

'Why?'

'His spirit is similar. He is devoted to you, as Leopold was to me. But be warned. One day he will leave you. He will hardly say goodbye.'

'Stay here with me, Edith,' she said. 'I know what it is to bring up a son alone. We will send him to a good English school. He's a clever little boy, like Leopold, I can tell. We'll make him into a real English gentleman.'

'Leopold said he led a Russian life with you. He said that he never felt English.'

'Yes, it is true, the English never let you feel one of them.'

'Not even Uncle Ernest?'

Irina crossed her legs, lingered in a smile, aware that she was still beautiful in the firelight. 'Your Uncle Ernest was infatuated with me. As your father was with your mother. And infatuation has no respect for nationality, isn't that so, Edith?'

There was refuge in Leopold's room. The bed was high and wide, and she imagined that the dip in the middle had been pressed out by his warm portly bulk. In the wardrobe, like his effigy, hung a large crestfallen dinner suit above a splayed pair of brogues. Edith pressed her nose into the suit, but could not smell the sweaty, faintly sweet smell of him. Only mothballs, the smell of his mother's meticulous housekeeping. There were no school photographs or trophies or Boys' Annuals, no traces of Fat Leopold. On the desk was a blotter and pen-holder and a globe of the world. Otherwise all the surfaces of the room were bare.

'You know how untidy Leopold is,' Irina said. 'But before he left he burned all his papers and packed away his books.' She stood looking round the room shaking her head. 'He wouldn't even tell me, his mother, where he was going.'

Take your life in your hands. He would have written that letter at this desk.

In his bed at night Edith pondered the puzzle of Leopold. The room with its bareness, its high bed, the vista of rooftops from its one long window, seemed to speak of him, show her something about him that she hadn't seen before. Something detached, airy, austere. It comforted her. Something was finished in this room, in eternal readiness for departure.

The more she thought of Leopold, the less she could recall Aram, or, rather, Aram and Leopold were blending into one person. In this bed she was peaceful, as if she lay in Leopold's arms. It made her gentler with Jim.

Each afternoon, Edith watched Irina's speared hat and pouter chest and hurrying pointed shoes disappear down the street. She went downstairs into the tiny paved backyard and brought in Jim's nappies, damp, stained, threadbare squares. She hung them to dry in front of the fire, a sight Irina abhorred. She fed Jim a generous lunch in the kitchen and put him to bed. Then she went into Irina's room and looked in her cupboards and drawers. She found what she wanted in her writing-case: the secret address to which Irina sent her letters to Leopold. Was it so secret, or had Irina not offered it because she wanted to keep Leopold to herself? It was a post-office box number in London. She also took an envelope and stamp from the writing case and enclosed the letter she had written, asking Leopold if he had news of Aram. She told him she was going to Armenia and would send him her address from there. Shyly, she added that she was travelling with her little boy, and that she hoped Leopold would have a chance to meet him. She slipped out of the house and posted the letter into the red pillar-box on the corner. She returned to stand by the bay window and smoke one of Irina's exotic black cigarettes.

Was she up to her old tricks? she asked herself. Once a thief always a thief? There were some coins, threepences and pennies lying in a white china bowl on the dressing table, but she refused even to look at them. Irina had been so kind. She was having an old coat of hers altered by her dressmaker to fit Edith. She kissed Jim on the cheek morning and night, like a proper great-aunt. Their evenings together by the fire were very cosy. Irina said how glad she was to have Edith there, now that she was a lonely old woman whose son had left her.

But her attacks on Edith's plans were relentless. Every evening she asked Edith the same question: Have you given up your silly ideas yet? Edith shook her head. Then Irina said Edith didn't know how cold a northern winter could be. How the Caucasus was filled with brigands. How there were terrible spies and police in Russia. What life was like under the Communists. How this amounted to murder of her child. She fell into a bitter silence. Thwarted, her handsome face was sharp, almost vicious.

Some afternoons Edith took Jim into London, on errands for the journey. She was nervous as they queued for the bus, nervous of the crowds, but she told herself she must get used to this. A shoemaker resoled her shoes and on his shelves she caught sight of a little pair of leather boots, mended but unclaimed. She bought them though they were at least two sizes too big for Jim. But he was going to have to walk. She bought herself a square-folded map, of Europe and the Middle East. She went to Victoria Station and enquired about the price of a third-class ticket on the Orient Express. It cost as much as the boat trip from

Australia. She would be lucky to arrive in Istanbul with ten pounds.

As she grew tired the streets of London dispirited her. Behind the squares and parks, the regal rows of houses, the early spring beds of daffodils, were crowded lanes with overflowing gutters, ragged women and pale stunted children, sooty pavements, starving dogs. Jim was frightened and had to be carried. Once they passed three grubby brothers, the eldest held a baby boy who was laughing as the middle brother reached up to tickle him. Jim at least was clean and warmly dressed in Lavinia's stolen coat, and well-fed, thanks to Irina, but he had never known such adoration. They were strangers, and alone.

Everywhere the billboards shouted War. Germany had swallowed up Czechoslovakia. She shivered as she passed the steps leading down to the Tube, remembering the dream of her father disappearing into the underground. Beggars huddled on the steps beneath dirty blankets. She hurried on home to the fire, thinking of their blank, blinking faces. It was as if they waited at the gates of hell. Without family, this is what could happen to you.

She would have to leave soon before she lost her nerve.

'You are going for love,' Irina said. '*Love!* People die, not for love, but for hate where you are going. Do you know how many Jews are trying to get into England at the moment? You are leaving a sanctuary to go into the heart of a maelstrom. Love is a luxury. To die for love is a romantic luxury in the modern world.'

'I'm not going to die,' said Edith, 'and neither is Jim.'

'You know, Edith,' said Irina softly, deadly, 'no good ever came of chasing a man.'

'Aram didn't run away. He doesn't *know* about Jim.'

Irina cocked an eyebrow at her. 'Well, he *should* have, Edith.'

A hot wave ran over Edith.

'You'll end up in the brothels of Europe.' Irina's face subsided into bitterness. She leaned back as if this was her final word.

The next afternoon while Jim was sleeping, Edith removed a soft white flannel sheet from the bottom of the pile in Irina's cupboard, and with the scissors from Irina's work basket cut the sheet into squares. She was grim and workmanlike about it. Irina had many sheets, she would not miss it. She swept up the threads and put Jim's new nappies into the bottom of the Globite suitcase. The scissors were inviting. She looked at her face in the mirror over the fireplace. She picked up her long thick plait and chopped it off at the nape of her neck. It felt like an execution. She stood holding up her plait, thick as her forearm. But the mirror told her she had not been instantly transformed into a woman of fashion. Her hair hung limp and jagged around her neck. She threw the plait into the fire where it coiled and sizzled like something alive. The room filled with acrid smoke. She ran into the bedroom clutching her head, and threw herself down beside Jim. Regret, and fear as Sampson must have felt, was so sharp she could hardly breathe. Jim woke and looked at her curiously, reached across to pat her rough head. Edith made herself look again in the mirror. There was no getting past it, she looked like a mad girl, or a fever patient. And this was no way for a woman to face the world.

One morning Edith ran a deep bath for the two of them. She folded their towels, smoothed the eiderdown over Leopold's bed and made them each a large bowl of porridge. They ate it slowly, looking out the window at a sparrow nesting in a tree. She packed a parcel of bread and margarine in brown paper and filled Jim's bottle. Then, determined not to steal away this time, she woke her aunt to say goodbye.

Edith's new coat, grey flannel with fitted waist and wide cape collar was the most beautiful coat she had ever seen. She didn't know that emerging from it, her black-stockinged legs and newly bare neck looked pathetically long and thin. Bits of her hair stuck out from beneath a pulled-down beret. She stood in the hall next to her old brown Globite, holding Jim by the hand. He was very pleased with his shoes, though the toes stuffed with paper made him trip when he ran. Pushkin sneaked across the floor, but Jim stayed by Edith. She had told him he was going on a train and must be good.

Irina had turned old. Her face fell into formlessness, her eyes were watery and blurred. Her dressing gown was shabby, and her white hair hung thin down her back.

'If only Leopold were here. He would never let you go.'

'You did your very best to stop us.' Edith put her hand gently on Irina's shoulder.

Irina's face crumpled up. 'I feel something terrible is going to happen to the world. I wish he would come home.' She clutched her neck. 'I have something for you. Wait.' She hurried back into her bedroom. A chair scraped, a key turned. She came out and placed an envelope in Edith's hands. On the outside in shaky black script was written *The gods love those who are brave.* (*Gorki*). Inside the envelope was fifty pounds.

'It would have come to you one day,' Irina said. 'It is your mother's gift.' She looked shy and pleased, in spite of herself.

Edith wished she had time to love Irina. Just for a moment, she contemplated the pleasures of being a devoted niece, a virtuous daughter, a loyal sister. Living out her days in the shelter of approval. She felt a pang now about cutting up Irina's sheet. She had broken her own resolution to be honest and it weakened her. She would have liked to tell Irina and ask for her pardon. But then perhaps she might never leave.

Too late! There was no putting the sheet back.

But there was something else, she thought, as she and Jim turned to wave to Irina from the front gate. Something that made setting off down the street to the bus stop feel like a relief. Her mother had always tried to please Irina. Edith had grown up knowing this, thousands of miles away. Irina was one of those women, like Frances and Madge and Matron Linley, who wanted you to do what they wanted you to do. Who made you feel you had to agree with them. Perhaps in the end her mother had made her journey to escape Irina. Perhaps Leopold had.

None of the passengers in Edith's compartment could afford to eat in the dining car. Three times a day when the restaurant man came rushing down the corridor ringing his bell and shouting *Premier Service!* they pulled out crumpled packages of bread and cheese and sausage, and munched glumly, looking out the window. The Bulgarian man at the other end of the seat offered Edith some olives and a piece of flat bread that looked like damper, but she refused. She did not like to think that he had noticed her meagre rations and pitied her.

In the station in Milan, Edith bargained English pennies for a bag of soft white rolls from a bread-seller on the platform. The magnificent train, with its shining blue and gold carriages marked *Paris–Athènes, Paris–Bucharest, Paris–Stamboul,* gave a burst of steam and Jim, terrified like her that it would leave without them, screamed and struggled to run towards the carriage steps.

Pazienza, pazienza, Signor, said the bread-seller softly to Jim. Edith paid sixpence for the rolls though she knew it was far too much. As she helped Jim mount the train, she had the strange sensation, as she had had in Victoria Station and the Gare de Lyon, of being watched.

She felt it again on the platform at Belgrade as she tried to buy some tea from a ragged, fast-handed vendor who refused her coins. She walked Jim off down the platform, trying to disappear among the drab officials and rush of local passengers in their headscarfs and felt hats as they clambered onto the day cars with their bundles and pots and chickens in a cage. *Pazienza, pazienza*, she muttered, to calm herself. Hadn't Ronnie Tehoe once said that travel was a game, a puzzle that piece by piece fell into place?

On the first morning, with fatherly resignation, the Bulgarian man had relinquished his window seat to Jim who was wailing and straining to put his face against the glass. He was a fleshy family man—four sons, he showed Edith on his fingers—with sad brown eyes and slow deliberate movements: he did not smile once during the journey but sat slumped in sombre thought, or slept, his stomach sadly gurgling, a handkerchief over his face.

Nobody spoke. The couple on the opposite seat sat smiling as they watched everything Jim did. When he was fresh from sleep he jigged and crowed for them and they laughed and looked at one another. They each wore a shining gold wedding band and they longed to have a child. Edith knew this, as she knew that she in turn longed for the intimacy they shared. They had boarded in Paris but the language that they whispered together did not sound like French. The bride had grey streaks in the long curls of her hair and her shy dark eyes easily filled with tears. When she slept her husband kept his arm around her soft sloping shoulder. His face was worn, faintly pitted and a pulse seemed to beat above his jaw. As they approached a border he woke her and they held hands. But the *conducteur* of each carriage kept the passengers' passports and the Orient Express crossed all frontiers without hindrance from border guards.

As night fell they all studied their reflections in the black mirror of the windows. Edith saw that none of them was happy, each of them was worried and afraid. Stark haunted faces stared back at them until the *conducteur* came in and pulled down their beds. The men took the top bunks. Edith could hear the Bulgarian man making discreet adjustments to his clothing above her. The couple, like her, slept fully dressed. Jim lay wedged next to the window, sucking on his bottle, keeping his eyes on Edith, who was still sitting up. After he fell asleep she would let herself out into the corridor and have a cigarette by herself.

He had just closed his eyes when the compartment door discreetly rumbled open and the *conducteur* in his blue and gold uniform bowed from the corridor towards Edith. He beckoned her with his white gloved finger. 'Madame,' he whispered, 'if you please.'

Edith eased herself from her bunk and tiptoed out, closing the door. The *conducteur* did not speak but set off quickly down the length of the train. Her hands spurted perspiration, her knees went weak. Afterwards she would ask herself why she had been so obedient, left her child like that, left the precious Globite, why she had been so afraid. It was guilt of course, night and day guilt lay in wait for her, made her expect a reckoning at every border.

At the very end of the train the *conducteur* tapped on a door which slid open at once and with a brisk, paternal pat, he pushed Edith inside. She was in a dim private car lit by shaded lamps. A manservant whose shaven head gleamed in the shadows, slid the door closed behind her and led her towards a large desk. An old man was seated there, writing. He looked up as Edith approached. He stood, flicked his hand to dismiss the manservant, bowed his head.

'Mademoiselle, thank you for coming. Please, take a seat.' His voice was soft, rather high-pitched.

The room was like a salon in a hotel, not a compartment in a train. It was as big as three compartments, with the desk in the middle of the room and at the far end a leather chaise longue. The windows were hung with heavy velvet drapes and Oriental rugs covered the floor. There were bronze lampstands with lights softly glowing behind parchment shades. Embroidered cloths looped across the walls and a parrot pretended to be asleep in a hanging cage.

'Mademoiselle, will you join me in a glass of sherry?'

He did not seem to expect an answer from Edith, but, smiling as he moved to a small cabinet, filled two crystal goblets and set them down on the desk. He sat again, facing her. 'Cigarette?' He pushed an open wooden box towards her. 'I do not smoke myself, but you I think, do like to partake.' He smiled again to himself. Edith shook her head.

The man was wearing a silk dressing-gown the colour of liver, with a yellow cravat around his neck and trouser cuffs showing beneath. This was how she supposed an English aristocrat to dress, but he wasn't English. She didn't know what he was, except that he was very rich. He was stocky and cleanshaven with a high domed bald head. Each eyebrow was like a tangled moustache glued above his sharp grey stare. Those eyes, ringed in old dark skin, seemed to her to be the room's real source of light. With his aquiline nose and thin firm mouth, he was like an old owl, who can see in the dark, who comes out to hunt at night.

'Mademoiselle, do not be afraid. I simply want a little company. It is a long tiring journey, is it not?'

Edith nodded.

'Mademoiselle, forgive my curiosity! I saw you embark at the very beginning of our journey in London. Please, tell me about yourself. Why are you travelling with your little brother?'

'He's not my brother, he's my son. We're on our way to join my husband.'

'And where may I ask is your destination?'

'Armenia.'

'Armenia! Your husband is Armenian?' He raised his great tufted eyebrows, delighted to be surprised. 'I too am a member of that ancient, ingenious but accursed race. Born in Constantinople. For many years my headquarters have been London and Paris, but I still do business in Turkey.'

'Isn't it dangerous for an Armenian to go to Turkey?'

'My situation is such,' he said, amused, 'that I am welcome everywhere.'

Edith took a sip of the sherry, which was sweet and delicious.

'Tell me, why has this Armenian husband of yours allowed you to make such a long dangerous journey with his son?'

'It was unavoidable,' Edith said firmly. 'He is waiting for us.'

'But you have had to come such a long way!' How much did this old man know about her? 'May I ask, what is your husband's name?'

'Aram Sinanien.' It felt dangerous to say it, as if she were betraying him.

'Turkish Armenian. Not an uncommon name.' For two or three minutes he sat back and tapped his right palm on the dome of his bald head.

'My dear, do you know the old Turkish proverb: *In the fight between a Woman and the World, Allah will always back the World*?'

'No.'

'A pity. Or another: *The Cage goes in search of the Bird*? Eh, Polly?'

'No.'

'My dear, you are ignorant, but brave. Your soul is Armenian! Eh? Will you have dinner with me?'

'No thank you,' Edith said, rising from her chair. 'I must go back to my son. He might be awake.'

'Someone can look after him. That can be arranged.'

'Oh no, he would be terribly frightened. He never stays with anyone but me. In fact I must go at once. He'll scream if he wakes.' She stood and, out of politeness, drained her glass of sherry.

'I understand,' said the old man, rising and coming around his desk to pull back her chair. 'You need time to consider.'

'I'm very tired.' She heard her voice, high, flat-vowelled, Australian, as she edged towards the door.

'You could always sleep here.' He gestured at the chaise longue, his eyes suddenly gone black with calculation. '*Comme tu es charmante*,' he murmured, '*comme tu es gamine*.'

'I don't speak French,' Edith said, stepping around him towards the door.

He turned away abruptly. 'Madame, if you please.' He tapped at a map on the wall. Closer she saw it was of Europe and Russia and Asia Minor. With a practised eye she made out the tiny island of Armenia in the ocean of Russian green. All over the map, across Turkey and Persia and the deserts of Mesopotamia, were scattered coloured toothpick flags.

'Oil interests,' said the old Armenian, with a wave of his hand. '*Nous sommes ici*,' he said, stabbing at a point north of Greece. 'Tomorrow afternoon we will reach Istanbul. Tell me, what are you intending to do then?'

'I'm not sure yet.'

'Do you have a visa for the Soviet Union? No? And you think they will let you in! They will think you are a spy! Do you know what they do to spies?' Close up she could see the ring of his teeth, worn concave like an old dog's. His eyes peered at her, cold as stones. Perhaps *he* thought she was a spy. He took a card from a little pack in his pocket, held together with a rubber band. 'Here is the address of a hotel in Istanbul. The Hotel Pariz. Very comfortable, very clean. The courtyard and its birds are quite famous. You would be well taken care of there, and so would your son.'

'I'm afraid I could never afford it,' said Edith handing it back to him.

He steered her hand with the card back towards her. 'Foolish girl!' Fine specks of saliva flew from his mouth. 'You would not even have to pay for the taxi that took you there.' His eyes fixed hers. 'Listen to me. You do not know where it is you are going. You do not know the nature of those parts of the world. They do not have enough to eat there. Do you know how that feels, Australian girl?'

'Yes. I do.' So he had seen her passport, the *conducteur* must have shown it to him.

'A war is coming. All the men will go. You will be trapped. You will grow old there, if you survive. You will become a broken reed. Do you understand? A broken reed.' He opened the door for her. 'Keep this card. Believe me, you are going to need some help.'

'Thank you,' Edith gasped, stumbling out. *Thank you*! The servant with the shaven head was waiting outside. He closed the door behind her. Down the long intestine of the train she ran, head bowed, shivering. *Jim! Jim!* Sherry-red thoughts rose and bloomed in her. She thought of Jim's round head, his ten white milk teeth, his throaty voice, his simple joys and displeasures. The well-meaningness of their life together. She was desperate for the feel of his arms around her neck. She was running to him as if towards all that was good in life.

She could hear him screaming as she entered Third Class.

The Bulgarian man, tousled and unbuttoned, was holding Jim against his shoulder, patting him, his melancholy eyes looking over his head. He handed him over to Edith with an air of a duty discharged. Jim screamed louder as if to let Edith know of his outrage. The newlyweds were sitting upright on their bunks, haggard-faced. *Hush, hush*, they murmured, frightened of the attention he might attract. They looked at Edith with reproach. Edith was aware of the sherry on her breath. Jim didn't quieten until she took him into the corridor and showed him the outline of trees and fields in the moonlight and the white gleam of a herd of goats.

He fell asleep against her, wet and hiccuping, heavy as lead.

Here and there was a light from a house or shepherd's fire in the mysterious shelf of distant mountains. Sometimes they passed through a tiny wayside station and she could see the yellow lantern in the stationmaster's hut as he rushed out to present his flag to the huge foreign express.

What was her story in the great swirling darkness of the world? The old man in the train could take her life and use it and throw it away. It didn't matter to him what she was, or what she thought. He could enslave her if he wished to and nobody would care. He had watched her, or had her watched, he was everywhere, he could always find her. She could sense the immensity of his power. There was nobody like him where she came from, not even the richest guests at the Sea House. Such power was everything that her father disapproved of, but what did his values matter in these parts? She had to think as they did here. The struggle now was not just to find Aram, but to stay alive.

In the early hours of the morning the train stopped briefly at a siding and the Bulgarian man, transformed into a portly businessman in hat and coat, let himself out of the compartment without a backward glance. The train was just sliding off again when the door rumbled open and a new passenger entered, a slight man, hatless, whose springing black hair gave the impression of youth. He saw that Edith was awake and he smiled at her. She glimpsed something black in his mouth.

In the grey light the newlyweds slept on, hunched into troubled, separate sleep. Jim slept with one hand lying lightly across Edith's knee, the small king who had exhausted his court.

The newcomer leant down to Edith. 'Cigarette?' He held out a packet, smiling and nodded his head towards the corridor. She eased herself out. She drew on the thick aromatic cigarette that he offered and her head spun and his face blurred. She looked out the window.

Men and women, working at dawn in the fields by the tracks, straightened up to watch as they passed. 'The Bulgarian proletariat,' he said. It was the sort of thing Leopold would say. How did he know she spoke English? He spoke it with ease. There was something familiar about his accent. It was a shock to glimpse his bad teeth, rotten and black like the seeds of a mildewed pumpkin. She drew again on the cigarette.

'There's an old man in a private car at the back of the train. I think he must be very rich.'

'Oh yes he is rich! Haven't you heard of him? They call him Mr Five Percent. He makes oil deals for the British and Americans and Russians—maybe the Germans—and he always keeps five per cent for himself.'

'He is Armenian.'

'Yes, the Armenians are very proud of him. They're always hoping for a patriotic donation. But the only loyalty Mr Five Percent has is the loyalty of the capitalist—to himself.'

'How do you know about him?'

'Because he loves the Orient Express! Each time I travel on it he is travelling too. He has his own special car kept for him. They say that during the Armenian massacres in 1896 he escaped from Istanbul on the Express, dressed as a Turkish peasant with his baby son wrapped up in a carpet!'

She felt comfortable with him. His eyes were wide apart, deepset, slightly inflamed. A small smile never left his lightly-closed lips. He wore a tight black suit and a knotted scarf of sky-blue Chinese silk. Dandruff sprinkled his narrow shoulders. His hair was parted in the middle and rose in two tufts like horns above his temples. He looked like an artist, a Bohemian.

'Why do you travel on this train?'

'I'm a cloth merchant. I travel around the Black Sea, from Batum to Odessa and Sevastopol.' He winked. 'Sometimes I slip across to the Balkans, or down to Istanbul.'

'Where are you going now?'

'I'm on my way home, to Armenia.'

'That's where I'm going! Are you Armenian?'

He was smiling at her. 'I was born in Yerevan.'

'How are you travelling there?'

'I take a boat across the Black Sea to Georgia. Train to Tiflis. Then the train over the mountains into Armenia.' Ronnie's route.

His name was Hagop Essayan. He suggested they travel together.

'You speak very good English.'

'I learnt it in my studies in Yerevan and on my travels. But Armenians are quick with languages.'

The sun rose to reveal soft green woods, rich brown furrows, an old maternal landscape. She and Jim watched Hagop buy some hot meat soup for them in the station at Sofia. He walked with a slight limp. Jim gulped down every last drop of the soup. He waved with Hagop from the window at the Turkish children waving by the railway line, and pointed as Hagop pointed at the gleam of the passing village minarets. From the day cars came the wailing sound of singing as the Turkish passengers glimpsed the glittering blue of the ocean.

'The Sea of Marmara,' Hagop said. He was a black-toothed angel. It was as if he had been sent.

But in Istanbul's Serketchi Station she lost him. He stood back for her to join the line that bumped its way off the train. On the platform all the passengers became instant strangers, making their own way into the crowd. She was surrounded by porters and moneychangers and beggars, jostling and shouting at her in an unintelligible language. Turkish people, the cruellest people on earth, Aram once said. When she looked around for Hagop, he had disappeared.

With Jim in one arm and the Globite in the other she pushed her way through the men, eyes blurred, shaking her head. She found them a little shelter next to a great barred archway leading to the sunlit road outside the station. She gripped Jim's hand and stood there, trying to think. She fought an impulse to crouch down, pillow her head on the Globite and sleep. A sleep from which she would never wake. Through the archway, on the street outside, she saw a line of beggars clustered around the long black nose of a limousine. The shaven-headed valet, arms folded, was leaning on the car, kicking at those who came too close. She pulled her head back behind the archway and tried to breathe.

When next she peeped around, the limousine was gliding past the archway and she glimpsed the old man's profile in the back window. A flash of blue appeared in the darkness of the archway. Hagop was coming out of the sunshine back into the station. She hardly had the strength to call him.

He'd been negotiating for a taxi, he said. He was cheerful, didn't seem to notice Edith's distress.

'Did you see old Mr Five Percent?' she asked.

'Indeed yes. Off to his local harem no doubt.' Limping, smiling, smoking, he instructed the porters in fluent Turkish as they lowered his large iron-banded trunk from the luggage van.

It was nearly dusk by the time their taxi set off on its mad hooting way from the station to the port. Hagop told the driver to hurry. A boat was sailing to Batum that night. 'Istanbul is a wonderful city,' he said, 'but no Armenian stays too long here.' It was only after they had passed them that Edith recognised the newlyweds holding hands at the dusty kerb, about to disappear forever into the teeming crowd.

At the rail of the deck, Hagop offered her a swig from a tarnished silver flask that he kept in the pocket of his jacket. Armenian brandy, the best in the world, he said. Everything Armenian was best, to the Armenians, Edith thought. The Black Sea was indeed black, and calm as a lake, the white wake curling primly beside them, but the very smell of the cabins and the overcrowded saloon of the sooty old ferry made her familiarly queasy. Hagop said the brandy would settle her stomach. She set up a nest on the deck, between two benches. Jim lay asleep there, beneath Hagop's blanket. All along the deck were huddled groups of sleeping passengers, children gathered under the shawls of their mothers. A sickle-shaped moon blew out from the dark coast.

Music started up in the saloon, with no instrument that Edith could recognise, and nothing of what her father used to call 'a bit of tune', the melody strange, Oriental, from the unknown countries towards which she was sailing. Hagop lifted his head to listen, his hand beating gently on the rail.

'The doudek. Listen. The long single note. To hold that note is very hard. There must be an Armenian aboard.'

'Do you play the doudek?'

'I used to. I played many instruments. I was a student of music once at the State Conservatorium in Yerevan.'

'What happened?'

'There was an explosion in the school. A bomb was thrown. By Armenian nationalists, it was said. I was injured. It affected my leg and my ... my nerves. The school was closed for more than a year.'

He offered Edith more brandy.

'It's not so bad. My family in Yerevan has always traded in cloth. And after the accident I saw life in a different way. I saw what was my fate. Now I am a cloth merchant who also collects music on his travels.'

'I don't suppose you would have met a man called Aram Sinanien in Yerevan? A man about your age?' Edith kept looking at the waves.

'Perhaps I have.' Hagop screwed up his eyes as if to remember. He didn't ask her who Aram was. She had told him she was going to Armenia to find her husband. He hadn't asked her any questions. It was important for him, she thought, as it had been for Aram, to appear detached and never at a loss.

'The man I am talking of is slim, but strongly built, with dark eyes and hair and a nose like—'

'In other words, an Armenian.'

'Yes, but he has only been living in Armenia for the last couple of years.'

'Perhaps he is the same. Who knows?'

'Do you know where to find him?'

'Perhaps.' He threw his cigarette into the water. 'Do you want to come and listen to the music?'

'I'll stay with Jim.' She must be careful, she thought, that out of need she didn't turn him into her protector. From a friendly, tatty stranger he was becoming someone else to her now. There was a density behind his lightness.

He went below and she curled up under the blanket next to Jim. Hagop made finding Aram seem possible.

I am coming to you. Wait for me.

In the morning they woke cold, wet with salt dew. The Black

Sea was grey and heaved in a temperamental swell. Her head ached, she felt nauseated. Jim's nappy was so sodden that she threw it over the railing. Jim crowed as he watched Irina's unravelling flannel sink beneath the waves.

It wasn't until the coastline of Georgia appeared that Edith told Hagop she had no visa. He said nothing but walked off up the deck, smoking. She wondered if he would disappear again. But he returned as the boat was drawing close to Batum and all the passengers were milling around on the deck. He pulled a black headscarf from his pocket and handed it to her.

'Perhaps if you wear this it would be better.'

'Why?'

'You will look less different.'

'Is it going to be difficult?'

'Who knows?' He shrugged and lit another cigarette.

The headscarf was ample, of soft black woven cotton. It swathed Edith's forehead and shoulders. In the salt-smeared window of the saloon she caught sight of herself and Jim. They looked dwarf-like and lost, like a snapshot of somebody's children.

The passengers passed straight from the ship into a huge vaulted waiting room without benches or chairs. At the back of the room at high desks sat three soldiers in olive-green uniforms, with red stars on the epaulettes. They were dark, with moustaches and square high-boned faces, as if they were all relatives of Mr Stalin. They worked calmly, unsmiling, turning pages of passports, slowly applying their rubber stamps. Before them, families with bundles and crates and screaming babies squatted in groups on the floor. How at ease they seemed sitting in a circle, as if wherever they went they made a home. Some were veiled women from Azerbaijan, with only their eyes showing, like black ghosts. Black-suited Levantine merchants, bearded Russian Jewish traders, Polish and Lithuanian commercial travellers sat smoking on their trunks and sample boxes. At the doorway guards stood smoking, with ammunition belts strung across their olive-green fronts.

It was late afternoon by the time Edith uncoiled her stiff legs from the floor and stumbled with Jim to a desk. Hagop stood behind her, to translate. The Customs official turned her thin black passport over and over and hailed a comrade. They spoke to her and she didn't understand.

The kangaroo and emu on her passport looked as innocent as a nursery frieze.

Hagop spoke rapidly to the soldiers. More of them crowded round. Telephone calls were made. The soldiers looked worried. Hagop was still talking. She was shown with Jim into a little room, and the door was locked. There was nothing in the room but a table and two chairs and on the wall an old-fashioned wind-up telephone. In the high barred window the night rolled down. Jim ran round and round the room and climbed on the desk. She had no energy to keep him entertained. Another official came in, older, heavy-lidded, harassed-looking, who spoke a little English. She tried to explain her case.

'So the reason for your visit is sentimental.' He shook his head. 'This is hard to believe.'

'I am not sentimental,' said Edith. 'I am looking for the father of my son.'

The man stared at her. 'But that is not important. Personal histories are not important,' he said. Jim started to scream. The official shook his head and left the room.

Nothing consoled Jim. There was no water or food. He was

soaking wet, but they had taken away the Globite. His little hoarse voice reverberated against the walls. He beat his hands on the door. He slumped, whimpering, and they both fell asleep on the floor. This was what happened to spies.

She was shaken awake by Hagop. 'Edith, come on.' There was a faint light in the room, it must be dawn. The older official was with him and he handed Edith her passport.

'Here is your visa,' he said. 'You are very lucky. Comrade Stalin loves little children.' He shook his head at her and left the room slamming the door.

'We can go,' Hagop said. His face was shadowed with stubble and weariness. He didn't smile. How long had he been speaking on her account? What had he said? She had no doubt that it was Hagop who had saved them. Why had he done this for them? He was indeed a friend.

'Hagop, how long is the visa for?'

'Do not worry. Once we are in Armenia, all can be arranged.'

There was a guard outside the door, smoking. He looked away as they left. The huge waiting hall was empty. The port was deserted. A solitary taxi slid over to them. Hagop's trunk was strapped to its roof.

'What did you say to them?' Edith whispered, but he shook his head. They all squeezed into the back next to the Globite, which had magically reappeared.

'I can't believe it. I'm going to Armenia!'

'Yes,' said Hagop, turning to look out the back window. 'And they are going to watch you all the way.'

They were driving down tree-lined avenues, past houses of faded stucco with vine-entwined balconies and shutters. It looked like a sleepy seaside town.

So this was the Caucasus. By some fluke or magic, she, Edith Clark, had slipped across the line, left the safety of the pink territory and crossed over into the vast unknown green.

'There's an Armenian proverb, do you know it?' Hagop was saying. '*He crossed the sea safely but was drowned in a brook.* You must understand about these parts. Someone will always be watching.'

In the train from Batum to Tiflis, two men in hats and overcoats came to take up occupation in their compartment. They each opened a newspaper, causing the other passengers to squeeze up. From time to time the men looked up and pretended to peer out the window, their eyes running across faces with exaggerated casualness. They were dark and moustachioed like all the men here, but less anxious, more solid, better dressed. When they coughed or crossed their legs the whole compartment stiffened. In the end they fell asleep like everybody else, their necks lurching, their thick hands open on their crumpled newspapers, their hats knocked askew over anonymous, unloveable faces.

'Are they not charming, Edith, the gentlemen of the NKVD? And so hardworking. But today we'll give them a little holiday.' They had been the first to leave the train in Tiflis and now they were rushing in a taxi through dark squares and cobbled roads in the old quarter of the city to a guesthouse run by Hagop's friend. Tiflis was a favourite city of his, he said. Edith glimpsed wooden balconied houses tumbling down a cliff and high above the predawn mist a white church with a pointed roof like a witch's hat. She heard a rooster crow as she and Jim fell asleep in a high bed with pillows like bolsters. It was sunset, and the rooster was crowing again when they woke. Up a dark stairway, in the kitchen, a buxom woman in high heels, with a dead white face, snub nose and shock of raven-black dyed hair, was laying food out energetically on the table. Plates of sliced fatty sausage, a pink vinegary salad, boiled eggs, saucers of jam and flat stale bread. A kettle boiled and there was tea, and milk for Jim. Her name was Dodie and she kept laughing and touching Hagop's arm as she served him pale red Georgian wine.

Across the table Hagop handed Edith a slip of paper written in Armenian. 'An address in Yerevan. An apartment of a friend, a wonderful old friend. She is almost blind. She needs somebody to help her. You can stay with her. I live in the apartment next door. I am married, did I tell you?'

'No.'

'It is a marriage of convenience.' He lit a cigarette. Dodie squeezed his shoulders as she passed.

'It is better now if we do not travel together,' he said in the taxi back to the station. 'In Yerevan it is better if we do not go together to the apartments. Let the NKVD wonder where you are living for a little while at least.' He put a few roubles into Edith's hand. 'For your taxi ride in Yerevan.' When she tried to hand them back, he closed her fingers over them. 'No no, you must take the taxi straight from the train. Do not try to change money. Give the driver the written address. There will be time later for you to pay me back.'

No sooner had she and Jim settled down into their seat than a man let himself into the compartment, tow-headed with high cheekbones and flattened Slavonic features. Once again the other passengers sank into sullen reverie. There was something counterfeit about his coughs, his absorption in his newspaper, as if he were only pretending to be human. As night came on he slept, and Edith gathered up Jim and the Globite and tiptoed out. She found a place in a compartment at the furthest end of the train, between slumped and snoring bodies. Jim sprawled on her lap, awake but silent, as if he too realised this was the last lap. She caught his eyes on her, studying her face. He looked thinner, she thought with a pang, and older, flushed from a rash on his cheeks, perhaps from all the tears he had shed on this journey. Perhaps, in a way that was too deep yet to trace, it was his tears that had saved them? But they were not saved yet. She sat up straight, stiff with tiredness, and Jim slept. As the train whistled and rocked across the dark mountains into Armenia, she fancied for a moment that it was she who powered it, her will, her energy, her luck, and, like the driver, she must stay awake.

Armenia

Everybody said that war was coming, it was only a matter of days.

Zakian Street was short and quiet, lined on one side by five-storey apartment blocks and on the other by a grove of slender yellowing poplars, the Twenty-Six Commissars Park. At night it was so still you could hear the clock strike a few blocks away in Lenin Square. At six when the early morning traffic started up it seemed to set the air moving. Curtains stirred at the balconies. Light flickered in the long windows. In Tati's room, Edith woke.

She had trained herself to rise at once. She dressed where she stood, in the clothes she had taken off the night before. With minute turns of the key she let herself out and left the tiny boy and the old woman in their separate worlds of sleep. She shut the door on the smell of the room, musty old books, cigarette smoke, brimming chamber pot. She was still half asleep herself, but nothing was more important than leaving that room on her own. This was the time when she bought the bread, when she moved free in the city.

Nevart's wheelchair was parked in the corridor. Nevart had lost the use of her legs in the same explosion at the music school that had injured Hagop. The stage on which she had been singing had collapsed. She was a wonderful singer, the most promising the school had ever produced, Hagop said. With scholarships she had studied in Moscow and spoke many foreign languages. Three students had been killed by the bomb. Afterwards she and Hagop had married. That way they could share an apartment. Nevart needed constant help.

Edith tiptoed past their door. Nevart had sharp hearing: she was no patient invalid and did not hesitate to call out. More and more, Hagop depended on Edith to help look after her.

Edith splashed her face in the sink in the communal kitchen, taking care not to turn the tap on too hard so the pipes did not shudder and wail. She used the privy at the bottom of the stairs.

A little girl came running as Edith crossed the courtyard. She stopped short when she saw that Edith was not carrying Jim.

Bari lous, Nora.

Lous bari, the little girl said gravely. She had black hair cut into a fringe, serious black brows. Her pigtails were tightly plaited, and she trailed a satchel, ready for school. *Dmitri*?

Edith mimed sleep, laying her cheek on her clasped hands. Even with Nora she was careful to avoid talking, to draw attention to her foreignness. Of course it was known she was *odar*, a stranger, but Hagop had set off a rumour in the block that she was Tati's goddaughter. This wasn't impossible, as Tati had lived abroad when she was young for many years. *Tati* meant grandmother, and everyone called her that. For some reason, although she never left her room, Tati was known to all, respected and beloved. Her neighbours were glad that Edith was here to look after her. Edith was sheltered by goodwill for Tati. All the same, she aimed to be noticed as little as possible, until people grew used to her and she had learned the language. But little Nora Gasparian had befriended Jim. She lived in the apartment beneath Tati's, with her parents who both worked in the Yerevan wine factory. Sometimes when Edith was hanging out washing in the courtyard, she would turn to see Nora staggering about with Jim clutched to her chest. Or in the Twenty-Six Commissars Park, she would gather her friends around him, little dark, lively, neatly-dressed girls, and they would try to teach 'Dmitri' how to count and say their names. And Jim, who hated to be constrained or crowded, suffered these attentions with a strangely pleased, almost sensual look on his face.

The façade of the apartment block on Zakian Street was genteel, built like most of the buildings in Yerevan from blocks of pink tufa, the local vocanic stone. Neatly spaced plane trees waved in front of the little porticoed balconies and their leaves gathered in the arched doorways. But behind the building the apartments fell into a jumble of tack-ons, shaky wooden steps, patchy windows with broken panes. The large courtyard was almost rural. There were vegetable plots in wire enclosures, vines growing over chicken runs. Washing was strung from trees to windows on a web of pulleys and lines.

The courtyard led through an archway onto Lenin Avenue, one of the city's busiest streets. Ancient tin buses wheezed past carrying workers to outlying factories. Trams and trolleybuses trundled up and down. Heavy black Russian tourers threaded their way through the traffic, the drivers' hands on the horn. Like all the avenues and parks and squares here, Lenin Avenue was generously planned. Beneath the plane trees, on the wide pavements, old women with shawls wound across their mouths sold carnations and sunflower seeds in newspaper cones. Shops like cupboards carved into the gracious tufa façades sold newspapers and cigarettes. The signs on street corners, above doorways, on bus fronts, Cyrillic or Armenian, were indecipherable to Edith. She was illiterate here. The street ran on beyond the haze of petrol fumes to the city's gaunt surrounding hills.

Dry leaves rattled along the gutters. It was autumn, early September, the wind was cold. She had been here three months now. The winters in the Ararat basin were freezing, she'd been told. She had no calendar and could not read the newspapers. She knew the date by asking Hagop or Nevart. When she first arrived here everything was so bewildering that for a while she had taken to marking off days by pencil strokes on the back of an old book, like a prisoner. She'd been terrified of being lost in time as well as space.

She had lost 'Armenia'. It had been swallowed up by Yerevan's dusty, bustling streets. 'Armenia' could no longer comfort her at night. It was like a phrase of music that had slipped her mind. She understood now that 'Armenia' belonged, if anywhere, back home. In the hazy, petrol-laden air of Lenin Avenue, she thought of the blue-gold air of autumn in Australia.

She walked fast to keep pace with the crowds hurrying to work. The Armenians were industrious people, they swept along the footpaths like the blowing leaves. There was something expectant about the autumn chill that had to do with the coming war. Their faces were serious, aquiline, dark-browed. She felt her face showed up in the street and wished it did not. She knew her pallor was different from theirs, it had an Anglo-Saxon fairness to it. The darkness of her hair and eyes was less intense, as if darkness was a state of mind. She wondered if in time she would come to look Armenian.

I am surrounded by Armenians. When she'd arrived in Yerevan this was her first thought. The streets were full of dark men in tight black suits. She thought she saw Aram ten times a day. A profile in a bus, the stance of a figure in conversation under a plane tree, a driver stepping out of a car and lighting a cigarette. Her heart beat almost before her eyes registered. In the next moment she would see it was not him. It never was. Every face was put together differently, and yet, looking for Aram, she saw how much a race was marked by the way they moved and talked to one another, by the way they thought.

Had Aram lost his 'Armenia' too?

Hagop said he was making enquiries. He had heard of a Sinanien who was teaching in Leninakan, whose mother lived in

Yerevan. Aram has no mother, cried Edith. Hagop punched his forehead. But he had another lead, he said. Don't give up hope yet. She had not. She was reminded of childish treasure hunts. Warm, warmer, getting hot ... She felt he was here. There must be a reason he refused to step out of the ranks of his countrymen, stand in front of her on the footpath and declare himself. Or come running across a park to scoop Jim up in his arms. There *was* a reason, which she would find out.

Meanwhile she kept on looking, ducking her head when men looked back at her. It was easier when she was alone, Jim took so much of her attention. On the other hand, when she was with Jim she was more anonymous on the streets. A mother and child. It was her camouflage. The NKVD must know she was here, must be keeping an eye on her, but for some reason had not made their presence felt.

The bread shop was a cellar fragrant with baking that opened onto Lenin Avenue by a sliding window, the round soft flat loaves steaming on the sill. *Hatz*, bread, bought fresh each day with Tati's roubles. Tati insisted on paying for it, though she ate so little, while Edith and Jim tore at it all day like animals at a carcase. Edith bought milk for Jim from the roubles Hagop changed for her.

The bread-seller down in the window had a long pale oval face like a saint and eyes so velvety and expressive they seemed to hold the secret of the world. 'Have you ever seen a really beautiful Armenian woman, Ee-dit?' Nevart had asked her. 'To Armenian men no woman is more beautiful than an Armenian woman.' Edith counted out her money into the bread-seller's slender fingers, and imagined Aram bending down low across the sill, buying his bread from the beautiful Armenian woman.

It was always a struggle not to tear a piece from the bread as she carried it home. It was good to hold its warmth against her, and think of the tea she would make. Before she crossed Lenin Avenue she looked down a side street, and up at the far left-hand horizon. The day was hazy, but there it was like a shadow, a snowy flank so enormous that it looked to be on the outskirts of the city, although it stood far away, over the Turkish border. Ararat, the Armenians' mountain. In this she was becoming a Yerevani: each day, like a ritual, she scanned the horizon, hoping that Ararat would show itself to her.

Nevart and Hagop were awake. Every morning they went to the markets where Hagop had a stall to sell his cloth. She could hear Nevart's voice from the end of the corridor. She must have heard Edith coming up the stairs. 'I smell bread,' she called out. 'Oh, Ee-dit, tea, pleez. I cannot *move* this morning.'

'*Ha*,' Edith called back. 'OK.' She put the black tin pot of water onto the little spirit stove in the kitchen alcove that they shared.

When she opened Tati's door, her eyes went first to Jim lying on the pallet in their corner. He lay quietly, his eyes open. With Tati he always stayed calm. Edith opened the curtains at the balcony window and a shaft of morning light fell across him. *Gadou*, he said, holding up Tati's black velvet pincushion in the shape of a cat. *Gadou*. Cat. His first word in Armenian. He took things to the pallet like a bower bird to its nest. Edith gave him a piece of warm bread.

The apartment consisted of one room, about the size of a bedroom at the Sea House, but cluttered with the remnants of a lifetime's possessions. In the centre of the room was a faded red and blue Armenian carpet beneath a round dining table with four heavy studded chairs. In one corner was a little iron stove on which was placed a tarnished samovar. In another was a wooden folding screen hiding the tin washjug and basin and the chamber pot. Crowded against the walls were armchairs filled with embroidered cushions, and sideboards piled with dusty books. Paintings hung one beneath another down the walls. Edith held Jim up to look at them, they were so strange, like dreams or children's drawings, some blue pears on a table, a black-haired woman with roses instead of breasts, two ducks joined bill to bill. They were painted by Tati's friends, in Paris, in a former life.

In the high brass bed next to the window lay Tati, no more than a hank of silver hair, the curve of a skull on the pillow.

'*Bari lous, Tati*,' Edith whispered, bending over the bed, but the old woman did not stir. Asleep, it was as if she was already transformed into another state, withered and speckled, becoming nature, like old leaves or bark or stone. It took Jim, scrambling up the bedspread, crouching beside her, his warm breath on her cheek, to make her open one milky eye.

'*Te*?' Edith asked. 'I will bring you tea.'

By mid-morning she would have Tati sitting in her chair by the balcony, washed and fed, her white hair brushed, her hands on her lap, her high cheekbones dusted with powder. This was Edith's task, and she had discovered she was good at it. To give Tati form, bring her back into the world for one more day.

But this day was different. A commotion started up, loudspeakers in Lenin Square bellowed voices across the city. They echoed down Zakian Street. Out in the corridor, Hagop was pulling his jacket on over his braces, shoving his feet into his shoes. He ran towards the stairs, laces flying. Edith snatched up Jim and followed him. Nevart was screaming for her but she pretended not to hear. *This is it, this is it.* What? The end to waiting.

In the vast square cars and buses had pulled up anywhere, and people were running to join the crowds clustered around the loudspeakers set up under the porticoes of the monumental concert hall. The announcer's voice spoke slowly, with dramatic official pauses. Ear-splitting rings and pops blared out in the transmission. Everyone was silent. Edith understood nothing. She had lost sight of Hagop. Military music signified the end of the broadcast and the crowd broke up into talk. Men were talking by the fountains, around the giant statue of Lenin, under the plane trees. A carnival hum filled the square. *I am surrounded by Armenians.* Was Aram here?

She started to walk back to Zakian Street and Hagop was suddenly beside her, swinging Jim up onto his shoulders. Germany had invaded Poland, Hagop told her in low tones amongst the crowds. England and France had declared war on Germany. Ten days ago Russia had signed a non-aggression pact with Germany. 'You and I, Edith, are officially at war.' Already the pink tufa buildings behind the waving plane trees looked faintly unreal, prewar.

It was almost a celebration. They all drank tea and brandy in Tati's room. They smoked cigarette after cigarette. There were gusts of rain in the autumn wind outside the balcony. For once Hagop and Nevart were united as they instructed Edith. Armenians would have to fight for Russia, but it was not a patriotic war. All Armenians knew that whatever side they were on, some invader, Germany, England, or, worst of all, Turkey, was bound to try to trample across the Caucasus to get to Baku on the Caspian, for its precious oil. 'We are a crossroads. Over and over we have been invaded, for thousands of years.'

Tati sat sombrely, her eyes distant, her hands trembling a little. Tati had survived the Turkish Massacres, the Great War, the Communist purges of the thirties. She had lost everyone. Her only son had disappeared to the NKVD in Yerevan three years ago.

Edith was quiet. If England was at war then she supposed that Australia was also. War for her country was her father's story. Young men in slouch hats and khaki marching to the ships, their faces eager and innocent. To be slaughtered and maimed on the other side of the world. At this very moment boys from her district would be enlisting. Dave Robertson, Bob Riley, the McIntyre boys. She remembered her father's stories of the mates, the songs. Her mother talking of the bells ringing in London for the Armistice. Because, of course, their side always won. Their side was on the side of right. And now she was on the wrong side! Among strangers, behind enemy lines! How could she ever go home now? She was trapped: for the first time she admitted to herself that without Aram she had no place here.

She thought of Frances at the kitchen table reading about the war in *The West Australian*. Ada wandering around, indifferent, though war had taken her brother and given her a husband and a new country and a life of despair.

She thought of Aram as a crop-haired recruit, even harder to find now. And Leopold, Fat Leopold, unimaginable in uniform. Did he ever get her letter? Did he know she was here? Was he still in the Middle East? Not very far away but across impenetrable borders. She wanted to tell him about this new dilemma. She was always writing to him in her head.

September 23rd, 1940

Dear Leopold,

It's the beginning of my second autumn here. I recognise the sound of the dry leaves rattling in the street. The poplars are yellow in the park. Soon they will be bare. I know now what winter is like here. Winter and war seem to go together. The chill never leaves your bones. There have been fuel cuts. We collect twigs and branches in the park and cook on the little iron stove in Tati's room. There is never enough food.

What else is there to talk of but war? And yet what use is talk? The focus of the day is the news. All the neighbours gather in the corridor below to listen to the wireless in one family's apartment. H. comes back upstairs with the report. Europe is falling over like a pack of cards. Now the Luftwaffe is bombing London. I hope Aunt Irina is safe. Does Australia still exist? There is never any mention of it here.

I have not found A. At least I know that he has always been a survivor. I still think he is around. One night I could have sworn I heard his voice out in the corridor. I ran out but there was no one, just the echo of footsteps on the stairs. N. says I'm crazy. 'All Romantics go crazy in the end,' she says.

I am always writing letters to you, Leopold. I don't know why. Is it because you always listened to what I said? The little crazy girl I was. Because you are my cousin, and blood is everything in times of war? Because you know A. really does exist? This letter I will send. At least there is no shortage of paper or pens in Tati's room. Do you know why? Because she is a poet, a famous Armenian poet. Her name is—no, I had better not write it. I asked her if this was why everybody loves her. Tati said no, she is loved because she has lost everything and thus she is a symbol of an Armenian. She said she is not very famous because she has not written many poems. I asked her why not. Because she has had too many lovers, she said.

Jim is two and a half now. Most of his words are Armenian. He is called Dmitri here, the name of your uncle. All day Tati speaks to him in Armenian. 'Hokeet seerem,' she tells him. That means: I love your soul. I can understand a lot more now.

I'm writing to you though I know this letter may never reach you and that there cannot be a reply. It's too dangerous to give my address. H. says letters to or from foreign destinations would be opened at the post office. He's going to post this for me on his travels. He would post a letter to Australia too, but that feels like a lifetime away. Please tell Aunt Irina we are well and living a respectable life. Send her my love.

Leopold, I hope you are alive. Your cousin, E.

Hagop was often away now. It was a good time to buy cloth, he said. People in wartime panicked, sold everything while they could. He went to Baku, crossed the Caspian Sea, travelled by camel train to the bazaars of Bokhara and Samarkand and Tashkent. He spread out wondrous reams of silk in royal colours across Nevart's bed.

'Who will buy this?' said Nevart, in English, so Edith could hear. 'You are crazy. In a war silk is for parachutes. You buy cheap, yes, but you don't sell at all.'

Hagop was thinner, more tattered, smoking cigarettes down to the butt in his small stained tapering fingers. Nevart's criticisms affected him not at all. He was endlessly good-natured, though distracted, like a traveller who has not really come home. He rolled the cloth up expertly and stacked it with the other bolts and bales against the wall by the door. Half their room was used as a storehouse for cloth, the Essayan family inheritance, Hagop called it. After a week or two he set off again, this time on his old route, to Tiflis, and the ports of the Black Sea, and a day in Istanbul. Turkey was prevaricating, he reported, waiting to see which side was winning before entering the war.

When Hagop was away, Edith's duties increased three-fold. Every morning she ran between the two rooms, Jim following, helping Tati dress and then Nevart. Nevart's voice rang out every few minutes. *Ee-dit, pleez!* Edith helped her with the long print dresses that she wore, flowery prints from the Essayan inheritance, pulling them down over her startlingly voluptous breasts, her muscular torso, her poor withered legs. She brushed Nevart's long thin hair that ran in ripples over her shoulders. It was dyed dead black. The accident had turned her prematurely grey. While Edith ran back to Tati, Nevart wheeled herself to the window and peering in a hand mirror, outlined her eyes with kohl. Her eyes frightened Jim. He screamed whenever Nevart looked at him. Nevart raised her arm and jangled her gold bracelets at him. He beat on the door for Edith to come and save him.

'Nevart, please, he is easily upset in the morning.'

Nevart did not tolerate even mild criticism. 'Don't fool yourself, Ee-dit. He is upset *all the time*. He is always afraid. You must know, Ee-dit, he is a very strange child.

'You know what we do in Armenia with children like Jim when they grow a little older?' Nevart mused, as Edith carried her down the stairs. 'We send them to Industrial School.' Edith set her down in her wheelchair with a thump and ran back up the stairs for Jim. Once she forgot to put on the brake of the wheelchair and came down to find Nevart being picked up from the front steps by concerned passers-by. Tears ran black down her cheeks, she was a poor broken doll in her flowery dress, half old woman, half child. Nobody understood they were tears of rage. 'There are no *accidents*,' she hissed, as Edith, apologising at every step, wheeled her off down the street. 'Only jealous hearts.' She spoke loudly in English though Hagop had warned her to speak only in Armenian in the streets.

But when they reached the markets Nevart made an entrance like a queen, waving gaily as Edith, trailing Jim, pushed her wheelchair down the aisles. In the markets, the *shouka*, a great dark basement hall, farmers came down from the hills to sell apples, pears and cherries, walnuts, tomatoes, eggplants, brandy, home-cured tobacco and stacks of lavash bread. Here knives and scissors were sharpened, medicinal herbs dispensed, fortunes told. It was warm and communal in the *shouka*, a refuge from Yerevan's dour, business-like streets.

The cloth stall was set up in a dark corner, displaying only a fraction of the Essayan inheritance. A day's sale: a square of muslin for a cheesemaking. A length of navy blue serge for a schoolgirl's uniform. Occasionally a bride fingered the silk or lace, but weddings were frugal now. How did Nevart and Hagop survive? Nevart bartered Turkish braid for kasha, and the cheapest flannelette for turnip greens. The market folk looked after her. They brought her tea and *tahn*, a drink made from yoghurt, and, if she sang for them, a sweet made from walnuts preserved in grape juice. She sang rarely, only once did Edith hear her. Her voice filled the *shouka*. Even the sparrows stopped twittering among the roofbeams. She sang a folk song, centuries old. She sat in her chair, her hands folded over the drum of her chest, her eyes looking upward, her head rolling from side to side. It was impossible not to relent towards her, to forgive her when she sang.

If people gave her money she put it at once down the front of her dress, never to be seen again. After singing she was tired and liked to be wheeled home. All the way over the bumpy pavements of Yerevan she complained. 'Ouch! Ee-dit, pleez! I wish you knew how it is to be in a wheelchair. I hope you do some day.'

Nevart sulked when Edith left her at the market stall while she went back to Zakian Street to give Tati her lunch. Edith did not like to think of Tati too much alone. As she hurried home she sometimes thought of Frances running back to Ada.

All day Tati sat in her chair by the balcony, and let the movement of light and dark chase across her eyes. Her only connection with the world outside was the light in the window and the strip of light under the door. She could hear the footsteps in the corridor, the apartment doors opening and closing, the ring of the metal banisters on the stairs. She knew the time of day by the shades of light, the ebb and flow of traffic, the chiming of the Post Office clock in the square.

The first thing she asked Edith every morning was if Ararat was visible that day.

She liked her books and her notepads to be placed on a little table by her chair. She could not see to read them. But she knew so many poems by heart, that she would suddenly break into words, reciting them to herself.

One day when Edith came home from the markets, she found Tati had put herself back to bed. Someone had come to visit, Tati had seen the shadow of the feet beneath the door. He—the tread was masculine—had not knocked, but stood for a long time at the door. Tati had edged her way out of her chair towards the door, calling out hello, asking who was there, but the footsteps moved away. Now she lay on the bed exhausted, shivering in her shawl. Edith made her tea.

'Who do you think it was, Tati?'

'He walked like my son. Carefully, like someone who is always being followed. Like someone who doesn't want to bring you trouble.' She shook her head to herself, her eyes cloudy and inward.

'Could it have been the NKVD?'

'No. The steps were too—sensitive. Listen, I know those footsteps. I have heard them in the corridor before.'

'Tati ... could it have been Aram?'

'Perhaps. Perhaps it was my son. That is how it is with sons. They are beautiful strangers. They are angels that sometimes fly down to visit their old mothers.'

Perhaps Tati had agreed to take in Edith and Jim out of kindness. Or for Hagop's sake. She was very fond of Hagop. Her face brightened when she heard his quick, uneven step. But now she said that God had sent Edith to her, and that Jim was her own soul. Nevart rolled her eyes at this but said nothing. She was always civil around Tati. Tati was smoking a long-stemmed ivory pipe and drinking her evening tot of brandy. Nevart and Edith were smoking too, fierce little Armenian cigarettes, so that a blue cloud of smoke swirled around the ceiling of the room. Jim lay on his pallet, watching the smoke clouds and the three women's shadows on the wall. For Jim this was home, Edith thought. Three women. She had re-created what she had left.

Edith yawned. All day she had run up and down the stairs, washed, shopped and cooked, tended bodies, emptied slops.

'You are very strong,' Tati told her.

'I'm a farm girl,' Edith said. She thought of Frances again, running through the bush back to Ada. Ada's eyes were clear and empty, her body capering and agile, like a dried-up child's. Thought of Ada, even of Frances, sent a pain through her so sharp she held her breath. She couldn't afford to think about them. But sometimes she thought that as much as God had sent her to Tati, Tati had been sent to her. That somehow in looking after Tati she was making amends to Ada.

'But you of course always had enough to eat,' Nevart said. 'Did you ever eat rats or dogs like the peasants did here during the collectivisation? The stuffing from an armchair? Grass soup?

'But you're thin like a skeleton now, Ee-dit,' she said. 'Of course, you are *odar*. Look at the King of England's woman, Mrs Simpson. It is not the Armenian idea of beauty, I must say.'

In Tati's room they knew when Hagop was back because Nevart started screaming again. '*Eshon kulukh!*' Edith heard her screech ten times a day. Donkey head. If he stumbled as he carried her down the stairs, she smacked him across the head. At the bottom, she always remembered she had left her comb or shawl and sent him back for it. Some nights Hagop escaped. There was a bar where he liked to go late to listen to music. He went to wash at the sink in the kitchen. Nevart followed him across the corridor, pulling on the wheels of her chair. 'That's right, my little humming bird,' she called out, in English, so Edith would be sure to understand. 'Make yourself beautiful. So the whores will buy you vodka. Because there is no money for vodka, Hagop-djan, you know that, don't you? The money I make from singing is blood-money, you know that.' Hagop calmly dried his face, pulled on his jacket, saluted Edith, kissed his wife on the cheek and departed down the stairs. 'Where do you get your money for drink, Hagop-djan?' Nevart screamed down the stairwell. 'I'm curious, I really am. Or do the whores buy you drinks because they know they are safe with you?'

She rolled her way back to her room. 'Saint Hagop,' she sneered at Edith. Tears poured down her cheeks. She went inside and slammed the door.

'Why doesn't Hagop ever get angry with Nevart?' Edith asked Tati.

'Because,' said Tati, 'he owes her something. Or thinks he does.' She tapped her brow and shook her head.

One spring day when Edith had taken Jim to the Twenty-Six Commissars Park, Hagop suddenly appeared. Jim ran towards him. 'Where is Nevart?' Edith asked.

'At the markets.' He gave his black-toothed grin. 'I can run faster than her.' He picked up Jim. 'Come, I am inviting you to drink coffee with me.'

The café was several long streets away, at the base of the hills, where the city blocks gave way to roughly-built, flat-roofed houses, thorny bushes, old cars half repaired. The start of the countryside. The café was crowded with men, many in uniform, drinking brandy, playing chess or cards, smoking and talking. Everyone turned to look at Edith and Jim. A wireless above the bar blared out Armenian music. The central room was surrounded by a warren of cubby holes concealed by shabby velvet curtains. Hagop found them a table by the doorway and sat Edith and Jim facing the room. He seemed distracted. He drank vodka with his coffee and ordered *paklava*, oozing honey-coloured syrup. He fed the pastries to Jim, laughing, rather theatrically Edith thought, as the syrup formed a beard on Jim's chin. She wiped it away, told Jim to sit straight in his chair. The coffee was thick like mud, you could almost chew it. Something about the atmosphere made Edith uneasy, too self-conscious to light a cigarette. She felt watched.

'You know, Edith,' Hagop said, quietly, looking outside, 'it is only a matter of time before Germany attacks Russia.'

'What will happen then?'

'The Germans will almost certainly try to reach Baku. And if they look as if they are winning, the Turks will attack from the west. And then, my dear Edith, you would be caught in a bloodbath.'

'Why are you telling me this?'

'It may be better for you to leave, sooner rather than later.'

'Now? Where would I go? Europe is closed off.'

'There are other ways. It's a risk, but there is Persia.'

'Persia! Who do I know there? Where would I go? This is my life here now, Hagop. After all, Jim is half Armenian.'

'He is also half Australian.'

'Have you had news of Aram? Is that why you're saying this?'

Hagop shook his head. He turned away to order more coffee.

'I suppose you think I'm a crazy romantic, as Nevart tells me I am. Every single day. If you must know, I'm fed up with Nevart.' The coffee was making her hands shake. She looked down at them. She felt a savage dizziness.

When she looked up again Hagop was smiling at her. 'Oh, Edith, if you only knew Nevart before. How brilliant she was. We call it *jarbig*, you know, life, wit.'

'Wit at other people's expense.'

'You understand, all that power she once had, it has to go somewhere. The gift she had, that force has gone dark and crooked.'

'She beats you over the head, Hagop.'

'Ah, but you don't know what it is she gives to me. Each time I have to find my balance again. Each time I struggle and each time I come through.'

By the door two men, departing, embraced, kissed each other on the cheek. In Australia not even fathers and sons did that. What did she know of their ways, the dark men of this country? Was it her imagination, or did she hear among the conversations the name *Gilgamesh*?

A waiter wiped their table. It was time to go. As they stood up she felt so strongly that she was being watched that she looked behind her. Had that curtain just swung closed? Or was it nothing but a vibration in the smoky air?

⁂

Hagop organised an expedition to the country, to a house of a friend of his, a member of the Party. He borrowed an ancient car and strapped Nevart's wheelchair to the roof. They all went except Tati, who said she was impossible to move, now that she was a national monument. Besides, everything she saw now was in her head. 'But tell me how it is, *hokees*,' she said to Jim. 'Tell me about our mountains.'

The car wheezed up the Yerevan hills onto a plateau, surrounded in every direction by giant snow-capped mountains. The poplar-lined road passed settlements of wooden houses, State farms, with ragged sheep grazing beneath cables and pylons, and, in the valleys, the smoking chimneys of factories.

Nevart pointed out the looming peak of Mt Ara, named for Ara the Beautiful, an ancient Armenian king. An Assyrian queen fell in love with him but when he wouldn't marry her she went to war with him. He died, and she had his body carried to the top of this mountain, where she believed he would come to life again. But he didn't. His was an eternal sleep.

'You have to understand the stubbornness of Armenian men,' said Nevart, with a smirk at Edith.

The house of Hagop's friend, Bedros, was on the outskirts of a tiny village, no more than half a dozen rough stone houses with smoke rising thinly out of tin chimneys, and chicken and sheep wandering among sparse orchards. A country silence settled as they made their way along the dusty track, the noontime hum of insects, the rustle and chewing of goats hidden among thorny bushes.

Bedros had arranged everything. A woman from the village served them yoghurt and dolmas and lavash bread made fresh in a pit down the street. They drank tea on the porch sitting in a line-up of old chairs. Here in the clear cold air they could see beyond the orchard to a valley folded between great bare rocky hills. Far away you could just make out the cone-shaped roof of a little stone church. Behind it were mountain peaks lost in drifting cloud.

The Armenians gazed out, silent and dreamy.

'This is very beautiful,' said Edith. She remembered her touchy, proprietary attitude to Nunderup. The Armenians too liked their country to be praised.

Bedros had been a student with Hagop and Nevart at the music school. Now he was a Party official. Although he did not have any outward signs of injury, he was thin and stooped like an old man, his forehead creased into a knot of lines. He and Nevart fell into intense conversation. Bedros was giving Nevart figures, holding up his fingers. He was pointing to the factories further down the valley.

'You're a good little Party member now, Bedros,' Nevart said, in sugary tones. 'Better than playing third horn, eh?'

He and Hagop went for a walk down the lane. As they turned a corner, Edith saw Hagop take a swig from his brandy flask and hand it to Bedros.

'Why did you speak like that to Bedros?' she asked Nevart.

Nevart shrugged. 'After the bombing all the students were under suspicion. We all hated Moscow. Bedros was cleared and immediately joined the Party. Some of the students were arrested, never to be seen again. Hagop, of course, Saint Hagop, was spared.'

Nevart fell asleep, slumped down in her wheelchair. Suddenly Edith took Jim's hand and ran with him through the orchard to a sloping meadow, faster and faster, Jim laughing, through the stones and yellow grass. They came to a stream about to dive into the valley, far away from everybody, and they threw themselves down. They lay panting, listening to the water and the wind in the poplars and the call of the ravens soaring far above them. Space at last.

The wind in the trees reminded her of the sound of the surf. She remembered that they were landlocked, that this was a country with no sea.

August 12th, 1942

Dear Leopold,

Do you remember the hot day that was like summer when we went swimming, and the sea was smooth as a lake, as far as the eye could see?

In summer here the sun is a little high white fire-ball. There's a haze of heat over Yerevan which covers the hills. Ararat rises above it like a giant cone with an icecream tip. There's an icecream seller in Lenin Square, ringing his bell. But Yerevanis aren't in an icecream mood these days. In the evenings all that people do in the parks and squares is talk of the invasion. The Germans panzers have nearly reached Rostov. That's about five hundred miles north of Yerevan as the crow flies.

All that I would like to do is to go swimming and forget everything.

There's Lake Sevan in the north, it's a famous summer resort for families, but who would go north now? And only Party members could afford it. Besides, most families are only half families now. All the men, apart from the old or the lame, have gone to fight the Germans. Three hundred thousand Armenians are fighting in Russia's great patriotic war. Stalin says that there is to be no retreat. Anyone running back will be shot.

The avenues and the cafés are empty of men. Women queue for buses to the factories. Women drive the buses. Women distribute the ration cards and serve behind the counters in the government stores. It was a woman who came to show our apartment block how to tape our windows against explosions, and to explain the importance of the blackout. Women rush along the dusty streets in overalls and headscarfs. There's no one to look at them any more. Anyway they're too tired and worried to think about being looked at.

In the evenings it's so hot in the apartments that the women gather in the courtyard. They turn kebabs over little outdoor fires. There's the smell of charred peppers and eggplant. There's no meat any more. Children play evening games and the sparrows go mad in the trees. It's so light that women hang out washing, or water the vegetables. All along the back steps, women sit calling out to one another as they soak their feet or dry their hair.

Then at nine o'clock they all rush inside to the corridor outside the apartment with the wireless, to listen to the news.

I can't understand much of the broadcasts. I let Jim go out to play and I sit with Tati and N. looking out from our balcony. Of course Jim and I cannot have a ration card. We share Tati's coupons, and the food that N. and H. barter for at the markets. We survive because of the markets. H. (who is not fit enough for the army) also works for the State now, in some sort of war-effort job. He is usually away and N. is usually in a bad mood. It's only safe to be with her if Tati is around.

Jim is big and strong. He does not speak as much as most four-year-olds, perhaps he is confused between languages. He loves Tati and his friend who is ten. She teaches him everything, even how to read. Soon he will have to go to school.

The brightness of summer seems put on to tease us. Funny to walk beneath green leaves and feel so on edge. Not that life is so bad—not when you think of Leningrad. But will Yerevan go the same way?

I haven't found A. and I know he's not around. I can't feel *him any more. Does this mean he's at the front? Does this mean he's dead? I'm cut off from him, as from everything else in my life before the war. Except from you, I don't know why. I know you're there. Leopold, stay safe and well please, please survive. Your loving cousin, E.*

In autumn when the Eastern Front reached down as far as Grozny and Ordzhonikidze in the north of Georgia, Nevart was summoned to play the piano for the Russian officials in the grand hotel in the main square. It seemed there was a shortage of pianists in Yerevan, as well as of everything else. A car was to be sent for her at six o'clock. Nevart ruthlessly cut a strip of gold-threaded turquoise silk from a bolt of the Essayan family inheritance, and sewed it to the bottom of her black woollen shawl. She enlisted Edith to dye and curl her hair. By evening she was very nervous. She looked at herself in the long mirror in Tati's room and her face crumpled in rage. Edith had placed the shawl on her shoulders around the wrong way. 'You are very Antipodean, aren't you, Ee-dit?' she said, rearranging it with her little beringed hands. 'Everything upside down.'

'Why do you worry, Nevart?' Tati asked her. 'The Russians will be so drunk they will hardly listen to you. Just play Tchaikovsky for them, and let them cry into their vodka.' The Russians. Ada's fabled exotic people were boorish oppressors here.

Nevart's breath came in short gasps as Edith carried her down the stairs. She rubbed her hands to warm them. 'Oh, Ee-dit, I have not touched a piano for years.' A large black Russian limousine was waiting for her in Sakian Street. A uniformed driver took Nevart from Edith's arms and placed her in the back seat. Nevart swept off, her head just visible behind the limousine curtains, held high like a filmstar's.

Edith waited up for the limousine's return. The evening had been a great success. The Russians had complimented Nevart on her biting wit, her excellent Russian, the amazing span of her tiny hands. They offered her a job playing for them three times a week. 'So now at last I earn my living as an artist,' she said, as Edith carried her back up the stairs. 'I have become a circus freak. Well, somebody has to make some money around here.' Her eyes were bright, her cheeks flushed. Edith placed her on her bed and she fell straight asleep.

Nevart began to live only for her performances. She rose late and attended to her clothes, her nails and hair. She had Edith wheel her to visit her old piano teacher in an apartment on Lenin Avenue so that she could practise and learn new pieces. She was beginning to sing a little, a few comic songs. Bah, she said, it was no great thing to perform for barbarians. 'Though I must say, Ee-dit, one or two of the comrades are quite civilised men.'

Edith kept the cloth stall at the markets open for an hour or so each day, though usually she sold nothing. She stood in queues for bread and kasha and milk. Nevart sent her on errands, for honey to soothe her throat, black-market stockings, hairpins. At night she was Nevart's dresser. She was too tired now to find a response to Nevart's sharp tongue. Besides, she depended on the few roubles Nevart threw her way. She told herself that putting up with Nevart was how she earned her living.

Late one night as Edith tiptoed out from putting Nevart to bed, Hagop came softly up the corridor. He put his head to one side. 'Edith, *mairig*,' he whispered. 'You are tired.' His hair was cut ragged and short as a soldier's now and he carried a briefcase. Edith had not seen him for days. He was even thinner, haggard, unshaved. A single bulb swung above them in the draughts of the corridor. A point of soft light shone in each of his eyes. For the first time she thought of him as sad. 'Get your coat. It is time we make a party. Look.' He took the blue silk scarf out of his briefcase. 'Remember this?' He went into the kitchen alcove and stowed his briefcase in a cupboard. He splashed his face in the sink and wrapped the scarf around his neck. 'Come, Edith.'

'I'd better not. Somebody might wake . . .'

'You have become so dutiful, Edith. God smiles on you, I am sure.'

'God has more important things to do these days.'

'True. He doesn't seem to be paying much attention to us any more. That leaves us free to enjoy ourselves.' He smiled at her. 'Ah, Edith, you need music, you need vodka. You need kisses. I can tell.'

Edith fetched her coat from Tati's pitch-black room, blinking away a sudden spurt of self-pitying tears.

Their way was lit by the moon, for there was not a chink of light showing along the empty streets. Even the great hotel, where just an hour before Nevart had performed, was nothing but a dark outline as they crossed the deserted square. Hagop's club was not far away, in a basement entered from an insignificant side door. It was a small room crowded with tables, lit by candles. They were greeted by the owner, who hugged Hagop in the Armenian way. He introduced himself as Manouk to Edith, as if he knew her already, and in English invited her to sit at his table. All the candle-licked faces at the tables were male. Some were in uniform and some perhaps were on leave, but some, like Manouk, were not imaginable as soldiers. His hands, as he lit Edith's cigarette with a gold lighter, were plump and white and there was a ruby in his heavy gold ring. Hands that had never done a day's work, her father would have said.

Manouk snapped his fingers and brandy and vodka appeared. He excused himself, moving as smoothly as water between the tables, a word here, a handshake there, not smiling, but pleased and imperturbable. There were others like him there, in smart cut suits, their hair sleeked back from sharp carefully-shaved faces, smelling of pomade, men like boys, pulling wads of roubles from their pockets, men you never saw on the streets.

'Hagop,' Edith whispered, her mind looping and darting from the brandy, 'is this the *underworld*?'

'No, Edith. You are in heaven.' Hagop's eyes glittered, he seemed at ease, elated, as if he had come home. He clapped loudly as the music began. The sound curled up like smoke, Armenian music, familiar to her now, as were the instruments that looked like weird root vegetables, the *doudek*, the *kamanchar*, the *saz*. Soon the men were dancing, whirling and clapping. Back at the tables they raised their glasses again and again, making toasts, swallowing their vodka like medicine. A woman came out and sang, a beautiful woman with a slender-boned face and long curling black hair like a gypsy, in a dress made from red and purple gauzy scarfs, so you could see her plump body moving free within it, her breasts loose. The audience went wild with clapping and toasts and fondness for each other.

It was good, Edith thought, to be among happy people. It was good to feel so warm she could take her coat off. She realised she no longer had any expectation of seeing Aram. She put her head down on the table and slept.

She was sitting on the steps of the verandah, warm in sunlight. Her father was coming across the clearing. Oh, she thought, I have been here all the time. I must have dreamt Armenia and the war . . .

Manouk was helping her up from her chair, kindly as a father. There was no music, no guests, as if they too were a dream.

'Where is Hagop?'

'Hush. He is going to rest. He will be a little while.'

Sure enough, as Manouk led her through the empty tables, she saw Hagop's feet disappearing up a staircase.

'I must go home.'

'Hagop says that you are to wait for him. He will take you home, do not fear.' They too were climbing the staircase. Manouk had his arm around her. Her legs were spongy. 'You can rest here while you wait.'

They were in a store room crowded with boxes and furniture. There was a tattered lace curtain across the window but no blackout. Manouk helped her lie down on a narrow couch beneath the window. He covered her with a blanket. He pulled up an armchair and sat beside her. From the light through the curtain she could see the powdery smoothness of his skin, his trimmed moustache. He lit a cigarette, which was comforting. He was so calm. She felt high above the city. The ceiling whirled down close to her. Manouk stroked her arm. 'Rest,' he murmured. He stroked her forehead. He stroked her calf beneath the blanket, her thigh. He did not once leave his armchair. 'Rest.' He wheezed slightly, like an asthmatic. His wheezes grew rhythmic. 'Rest,' and she obeyed. Whoever would have thought those hands-which-hadn't-done-a-day's work could be so firm, so dedicated? This was their work. They made her skin into silk. They made her move like silk.

Pale light filled the window. The city was quiet. The roosters crowed in the courtyards of Yerevan. Another night had passed and still the Germans had not invaded.

Jim was sitting up in Tati's bed when Edith let herself in. Who had opened the curtains and untaped the blackout? It could only have been Jim. Tati was sitting up against her pillows, muttering to herself, writing in her notebook while Jim watched her. They were peaceful. The room was cold. 'We'll have to go to the park for some kindling,' Edith whispered to Jim. Everything was different, as if they had all become separate. She ran her hand through Jim's hair. She was grateful for his silence, that he didn't ask questions.

Tati lay back and closed her eyes.

'What are you writing, Tati?' She had never seen the old woman so alert in the morning.

'Memories. A poem.' The words were large and sprawling across the page. Tati couldn't read them back. Later Nevart or Hagop or Nora's mother, Nelly Gasparian, would read them to her, and she would dictate changes, line by line. Then she would know it by heart.

Through the wall they heard a crash, a tinkling, and words choked out between sobs. Hagop must have woken Nevart and now she was throwing china.

Winter deepened, and the whole city held its breath for the Soviet counter-attack. Nevart spent most of her day in Tati's room to save on fuel. Even when she was talking she watched herself in Tati's mirror, curling her hair around her fingers. Edith took Jim with her on her errands although the streets were so cold. She could not leave him with Nevart who only had to turn her eyes on him to torture him. Once Edith turned to see that Jim had squeezed his eyes shut and was spinning round and round.

'Jim, what are you doing?'

'He is trying to make me small,' Nevart said. 'So I will disappear. I know his tricks. He is not a normal child.'

She leant back in her chair with her hands behind her head and her cigarette burning beside her. There were dark half-moons beneath her eyes. 'Have you heard Tati's poem?' she said. 'Do you know what it is called? "Footsteps At Dawn". She says that is the time that invaders arrive, and babies, and lovers tiptoe home.' She threw her cigarette into the stove and spoke softly. 'Why did you come here, Ee-dit? Did you want to kill your child? Because you want to be free, don't you? If you found a man to love you, even a weak drunk with rotten teeth, you'd run away with him, wouldn't you.'

The water froze and the plumbing did not work. Edith fetched water from a tap in the courtyard. She put newspapers under Jim's coat and took him with her to collect twigs from the frozen park. Jim rustled like a parcel as he walked. She found herself singing old songs that she had learnt at school, 'The Skye Boat Song', and 'The Ashgrove' and 'Botany Bay'. English was beginning to sound exotic to her.

Only her childhood solitude had allowed her to survive.

She thought of the skin of cream on the top of a mug of Bourneville cocoa and of sucking hot marrow from bones boiled on the woodstove. She thought of food all the time now, she was too cold to think of anything else.

They heard Nevart's wails as they came up the stairs. Her door was open. Hagop was standing in the middle of the room with his hands in his pockets and his sad uneasy smile. His battered bag was at his feet. Nevart sat in her wheelchair by the window. She was clutching a small bolt of red silk. She lifted her head to him, pleading. Tears poured black down her cheeks.

'I beg you, Hagop.'

Hagop's smile stayed fixed as he shook his head.

There was a creaking and a shuffling. Tati crept into the room, one hand holding her stick, the other grasping the door frame.

Edith ran for a chair for her. Nevart bowled across the room and threw her head on Tati's lap. She closed her eyes and wailed shamelessly, like a child.

Hagop turned to Edith. 'I have to tell you, I am leaving. It is necessary. I must make a trip and I do not know when I will return. Nevart does not need me now, Edith. She has money and friends. She has you. And, as you may have noticed, I do not make her happy.' He smelt of vodka.

Nevart sat up. 'I won't let you have it, Hagop.' Her tears dripped onto the red silk.

'I am leaving her all the rest,' Hagop said to Edith. He waved his hand at the bolts of cloth piled up against the wall. 'But this silk my father gave to my mother when they married. And before that my grandfather to his wife. They say that when it came into the hands of my great-great-grandfather it had cost a human life. It is our luck. It must always stay in the family.'

'I am your wife,' Nevart sobbed. 'Have you forgotten?'

But Hagop leaned down and took the slender bolt from her. She screamed as if he were tearing away a limb. Why this silk? Edith thought, for there were other more opulent silks in the Essayan family inheritance. And why was Hagop so stubborn, he who never seemed to care for anything? But as he tucked the silk into his bag she glimpsed its sheen, raw, rippling, blood-coloured, like a beating heart.

He picked up his bag, saluted them all, and left.

It was only afterwards, after she and Tati had persuaded Nevart to drink some brandy, and to sleep, that Edith realised that Hagop, her friend and protector, had left her with no clue as to Aram's fate, and no advice for the future.

'Oh my God, Ee-dit, look how late it is! And I look like an old woman.' Nevart's cheeks were red from crying, her voice hoarse, but she was business-like as if she had decided to recover from sorrow. 'Of course my husband would decide to leave me on a day when I must perform. Oh yes, himself to the very end! Ee-dit, tea, pleez, and my curl papers. Let me tell you, this will make a good story for the comrades this evening.'

Nevart spent more and more time at the hotel. She had been given a room there for herself so she did not have to come back to the apartment at night. Then she stayed there even on the days when she was not performing. The hotel room was heated, there was also hot water, and a concierge gave her some help. She came back one day in a long black suit like a riding habit, a black beret stuck impossibly low on the side of her head. Her driver loaded up the limousine with bolts of silk. 'I have a friendly seamstress at the hotel,' she said with a wink to Edith. At least she did not speak in English when the driver was in the room. She seemed in very good spirits. Her hair was luxuriously curly, her cheeks were powdered white. 'I am quite the belle chanteuse these days,' she said, looking round for possessions to shove into her bag. 'A frrree woman. With a piano. I can practise all day if I want.' She had Edith carry her in to Tati, to kiss her on the cheek. She made a last face at Jim. 'You'll have to find someone else to hate now, little one,' she said.

'Look after my things for me, Ee-dit,' she murmured as the driver came up the corridor. 'You never know when I'll be back.'

It seemed that Nevart's comic turns, when she sat on a table and sang and told humorous stories of her life, of her student days, of her marriage, of life in a wheelchair and the deprivations of war, had become quite famous. Edith heard this from Nelly Gasparian, who came to visit Tati. Nelly's friend worked at the hotel. Nevart had admirers. There were parties till dawn. There were many jokes about her. Nelly shook her head. Nevart sent no word (and no roubles) and she did not come back.

By the end of January a hundred thousand German soldiers were captured at Stalingrad. The German forces were withdrawing from the Caucasus. But in February there was a massive German counterblow in the Ukraine. Nobody knew what the spring thaws would bring.

In the evenings it was so cold that Edith and Tati went to bed when Jim did. The room was pitch black, the city so quiet you could hear the wind whistling down Sakian Street. It was as if all Yerevan had gone into hibernation.

One night Tati whispered 'Edith.' Edith tip-toed over to her. She could just make out Tati's finger raised, pointing at the door. She could see nothing but the faintest shadow moving in the dark grey strip beneath it, perhaps no more than the movement of dust in the draughts of the corridor.

'A betrayer,' Tati whispered.

Edith ran to the door, her hands shaking as she unlocked it. By the time she opened it the corridor was empty.

'Who was it, Tati?'

'Hagop.'

'Hagop?'

The old woman nodded.

'Were you dreaming?'

'Perhaps.' Tati lay back on the pillow. 'I saw him waiting at our door. Poor tortured soul.'

Without Nevart, Edith had more time for Jim. She discovered that in all the time she had been attending to Nevart, Jim had learnt to look out for himself. Now that he'd turned five, he had his own way of doing things, his own strict routines. As summer came he woke before her, dressed himself and let himself out of the apartment. She followed him one day. She saw him take a drink from the tap in the courtyard, holding his legs apart so the water did not splash his shoes. He was very proud of his shoes, they had once belonged to Nora Gasparian. He chased a cat briefly and tried a roll over the stair railing as the older kids did, but he was a clumsy child and he fell. Nora came out and he ran to her. Edith saw that he had been waiting for Nora. How splendid she must look to him, her face rosy from cold water, her bright black eyes, her definitive black fringe. Jim's hair was bed-tossed, springing up in a cocky crown. Nora reached into her school bag, brought out a piece of bread smeared with red jam, held it from him until he said *Merci*. And then—oh, shameless Jim—he snatched it and gobbled it down. Nora wiped away the crumbs on his face. They clasped hands and set off across Sakian Street to the park, bright with green leaves now, where all the children met on their way to school.

Edith watched them from Tati's balcony. While Nora stood talking in a circle with her friends he waited, scuffling a little at a distance. When they all moved off together, Nora ran to him and said goodbye. Jim was left to the empty park and the long day's wait until she came home again. He sat looking into the bushes for a while as if someone else might appear. He crossed Sakian Street purposefully, a tiny solitary Armenian. He had a characteristic walk, for such a little boy, solid and rolling. What was he thinking? She was suddenly curious about what Jim thought of all the things that had happened to them.

Winter again and one cold day Nelly Gasparian, holding Nora's hand, knocked on the door with the news. Nevart was dead. She had fallen from the window of her room in the hotel. Nelly's face, normally clear and pretty, twisted up as she spoke. Nora and Jim shrank down on the pallet, listening to every word. Nelly spoke in a hoarse whisper. Her friend at the hotel said nobody knew how it happened. They did not know if she had jumped or was pushed. Somebody had heard her singing wildly at five in the morning. The Russians weren't saying anything. Nelly sighed. Her friend said Nevart drank too much and talked too much and took many risks. She thought she had more power than she really had. Already her clothes and jewellery had been pilfered. The funeral was tomorrow. She, Nelly would try to go. There was no time to gather her old friends from the conservatorium, if any were still alive. Poor Nevart had no family. And who knew where Hagop was?

On the afternoon of Nevart's funeral Edith took Jim for a long walk. Tati had advised her not to go the funeral, there would be Russians in attendance, there would be informers. Funerals were notorious for arrests, she said. The day was very cold, far too cold for Tati to go herself, although Nelly had offered to help her. She would write a poem instead. These days Tati spent most of her time in bed, writing down a word now and then in her book. In the quiet after Nevart's death, her mind seemed very clear. Edith brought tea for her before she left, and bread spread with a little of Nevart's honey. Every object once owned by Nevart, her cup, her curlers, her cluttered room, now seemed to speak of a doom which they should have foreseen.

'You have kept me alive, Edith,' Tati said. 'You and Jim. *Hokvov yev marmenov.* Body and soul.'

Edith and Jim, buttoned up, their scarves across their faces, paused at the door.

'But alive for what?' Tati went on, as if to herself. 'For death? For one more poem? *The* poem, at last?' She chuckled, wheezing, and waved her hand. 'Goodbye. *Hadjo!* Good luck.'

It was a place they often walked to, a wasteland high up over the river. It was just a few blocks away from Sakian Street and yet it was empty as a field, a stretch of rocky earth where no one went. There was a vista of the other side of the river gorge, barren and vast as a quarry, and, in the distance, a row of factory chimneys lined up along the horizon. In summer red poppies grew here and you could stretch out in the sun. She thought for a moment of Manouk's club, the only place she had been warm. Now the cold ate her hands, bit her cheeks, made her nose run. Far above, birds wheeled under a thick, blind sky. On the earth everything crouched, huddled, covered up. The whole world was filled with absence, seemed fearful, unconsoled.

Where was Jim? She turned to see him running towards a car, a battered black Russian tourer, which was bumping to a stop at the far end of the wasteland. Edith shouted, set off running after him, stride after stride, forcing her frozen legs. Jim reached the car and stood looking up at its blank curtained windows. The back door opened. Jim climbed inside. The door closed. The engine started up.

Edith reached the car and grabbed the handle of the door as it opened, knocking her back. There was Hagop, leaning over Jim. 'Get in quickly,' Hagop said. The car started moving. There was something familiar about the back of the driver's head.

'It is time for you to leave.'

'Why?'

'There is no longer anyone to protect you.'

'But I don't have my passport or my money or anything.'

'Here is your passport.' He took it out from inside his jacket and handed it to her.

'How did you get it?'

'I went to the apartment. After the funeral, but you had already left. Tati told me where you would be.'

'Who will look after Tati?'

'Edith, your first duty is to Jim.'

'Are we in danger?'

'Let's just say you are no longer useful.'

'Aram?'

'Edith, Aram is dead. You and Jim must live.'

'Where did he die? When?'

Hagop shook his head. 'In the Ukraine. At the front. I knew about his death on the night I took you to the club.'

Edith, staring ahead, saw there was a ruby in the gold ring on the driver's hand. 'Manouk!' she said.

The driver turned his head for a moment and smiled. He was thick necked, slick-haired like Manouk, but much younger.

'This is Ashot,' Hagop said. 'Manouk's cousin. He is making a business trip for Manouk. He has kindly agreed to take you to the border.'

'Are you coming?'

'No. I cannot.'

'How was the funeral?'

'As you would expect.' He looked the other way.

'Where are we going?'

'To a town called Djulfa. At the Persian border. You will be taken care of.'

It was nearly dark. They were on the outskirts of the city. Hagop called out to Ashot. The car slowed. Hagop ruffled Jim's hair and eased him off his knee. He picked up Edith's hand and kissed it, the only time he had ever touched her.

'*Hadjo*, Edith.' She saw his smile, his sad broken teeth. He had a ruined face. Why had she never thought of that? She clasped his hand and kissed it back.

They drove through the night. There was a rug on the back seat which Ashot said they should pull over themselves. They should keep low, he said. They slept. At some point Edith woke because they had stopped. She saw the red ends of cigarettes in the darkness. She stayed lying down. Ashot got back into the car, smelling of petrol. They were driving through a town of ghostly white buildings. 'Nakhchevan,' Ashot said. The stars were very bright. There was the outline of a ruined mosque by the side of the road. She saw the gleam of Ashot's ring as he lit a cigarette.

When next she woke, Ashot was shaking her by the shoulder. 'Djulfa.' It was dawn, they had stopped in the main street of a little town, lined with low white houses. Ashot handed her a piece of bread and offered a flask of vodka. Dreamily she and Jim tore at the bread, looking at the pink haze of the sky, and some chickens scratching at the roadside. Ashot stood smoking, leaning on the bonnet of the car. He looked at his watch, threw his cigarette away, and opened Edith's door. He bowed, beckoned them out. He pointed down the end of the road. There was a gatehouse, and beyond it a bridge. 'The river Araxes,' Ashot said. 'On the other side is Persia. You have your passport? It is time you went.'

Edith took Jim's hand. A cold wind was blowing off the river valley. She buttoned up Jim's coat. She looked at Ashot.

'Soon you will be warm,' Ashot said, nodding and smiling a little.

'*Merci*,' Edith said. She was too tired to do anything but trust him. Trust Hagop, trust Manouk. There was nothing else left.

They set off down the road. After a hundred yards or so Jim pulled away to piss, expertly, in the gutter. A ragged little brother and sister watched from a doorway. Edith looked back up the road. Ashot waved, encouraging them.

Two guards took her passport and conferred together. There was a page of stamps in her passport that Edith had never seen, and a cache of roubles. They put the roubles aside in a business-like way, stamped the passport, handed it back to her. They lifted a bar and nodded at her. Jim and Edith set out, high over the swiftly flowing river. Edith turned. Ashot and the car had disappeared. In the far distance was the black wall of the Caucasus. She turned back. Ahead were the light red mountains of Persia. Already the wind blowing in her face seemed warmer. 'I haven't even got a hairbrush,' she thought. Jim's head was down, he was muttering. He was counting his footsteps, in Armenian, the way Nora had taught him.

This was how Leopold saw them, coming across the bridge.

Orphanage

'Why did you come?'

'Because I was needed.'

Nobody ever engulfed her like this. He was a country she'd come home to. She would remember it all her life, the relief she felt when she saw the familiar bulk of his figure. She stepped back to take in what had changed. He was wearing desert khakis and an officer's peaked hat. The fine skin on his face and neck was stained warm brown as an onion. There was something taut around his eyes and mouth: he was wartime sombre. He spoke to the Persian guards and she saw he was used to authority. He was a thirty-year-old man.

Though even in uniform his trousers seemed about to fall down.

'This is Jim.'

'Hello, Jim. They want you to show them your passport, by the way.'

'Leopold, Aram—'

'I know. I know. Come on, there's a car waiting. Do you like jeeps, Jim?'

'He doesn't speak much English, I'm afraid.'

⁂

She stood at the window of the hotel, smoking a cigarette. The roofs of the houses along the street were flat-topped, their frondy gardens waving inside high mud walls. There was enough light left to make out distant pastel mountains. The muezzins of Tabriz had just called the faithful to prayer. The air was warm and clear.

They had all bathed, and eaten in the market, kebabs and rice, oranges and pears. The markets were bigger and as plentiful as a garden compared to the *shouka* in Yerevan. She had bought some clothes, a pair of loose black cotton trousers and an embroidered blouse which she tied at the waist. Also a hairbrush with which she'd brushed and rolled up her hair. It had taken five years for it to grow back to its old length.

Leopold had given her news of the war. The Blitz. The house in London had survived. Irina had refused to leave. The Italian campaign. The Burma campaign. The deportation of the Jews.

She crossed her arms and drew on her cigarette.

'You haven't said it yet.'

Leopold was showing Jim the journey they were about to make on a map spread across the bed. They were both sprawled on their stomachs. He spoke to Jim as if he understood everything he said. They would go through Persia, across Iraq, into Syria. He knew of a place, an orphanage in Aleppo where Jim and Edith could stay. And in Syria there were Australian troops. There would be a chance of repatriation. Jim nodded.

Leopold looked up at Edith. 'Said what?'

'You should have stayed in Australia.'

He looked more like his old self. He was wearing an army issue undershirt and baggy Arab pants. His uniform and hat were shoved into his kitbag. He was now officially on leave, he had two weeks and the loan of a jeep. Already he'd driven hundreds of miles from his post in Baghdad. Did he think she was a selfish little fool?

But his eyes were mild, benevolent. 'Haven't you always wanted to see the desert, Edith?' was all he said.

She threw her cigarette into the street.

They slept in the same bed, Jim between them. From now on, for the purposes of safety and Arab propriety, they would travel as a family, Leopold said. How soundly they slept to the soft rumble of his snores. Why did she wake thinking of Nunderup? He smelled as he did when he and Aram first arrived, the sweetish eastern smell. Jim, eyes open, lay very still so Leopold would stay sleeping beside him. Birds were calling in the walled gardens.

Across Iraq they followed the course of the mighty Euphrates. They rattled their way across the deserts of ancient Mesopotamia into Syria. The flaps were down on the side of the jeep but still the dust covered them. They wrapped their heads in squares of cloth they'd bought in a market. Jim stood behind the front seats with his head between them, a miniature sheik. He copied everything that Leopold did. Edith was proud of his stoicism. She turned to smile at him. At last, with Leopold, she could show her pride in Jim.

Leopold told them about the cities that lay buried beneath this landscape, Uruk, Larsa, Ur, Babylon. A dozen civilisations had been born and died here before Christ, each with its own gods and laws, stories and beliefs. All lost beneath the sands of the desert. He would have liked to take them to see his old dig, but there was no time for sightseeing. They were into their sixth day of his leave.

'Did you visit these sites with Aram?'

'Some of them, yes.'

'Did you drive along this road?'

'Yes. Aram took me to Aleppo. He showed me the orphanage where he grew up. That's where I'm taking you.'

He was always silent after he spoke of Aram. It was always she who brought his name up. And she was careful when she spoke of him, as if Leopold was the one bereaved. Not her. She didn't know why. It was as if she had thought and thought so much about Aram that there was nothing left to think. She had mourned him a long time before she heard of his death.

There was much that she and Leopold had not talked about yet. The jeep was noisy and they could only talk in short bursts. And at night they were too tired to do anything but sleep. Besides, she thought suddenly, Leopold didn't talk as much as he used to. He was often quiet.

'Do you still have the Gilgamesh book?'

'Yes, I always carry it. It's in my kitbag.'

'Would Gilgamesh have wandered in these parts?'

'He and Enkidu probably walked this very way to slay the giant Humbaba, or on another of their harrowing quests.'

'What were they looking for?'

'Action. Great deeds. You know, young men rushing off to fight, convincing themselves it's for the good of their civilisation. And they were arrogant, they thumbed their noses at the gods, they wanted to make the whole world lie down before them.'

'And after Enkidu dies?'

'Gilgamesh sets off like an outcast or a holy man. He grows his hair long, he wears animal skins. He walks hundred of miles, mourning, looking for the secret of eternal life.'

'He's afraid of dying, like his friend?'

'Aren't we all? He wants to become immortal, which is I suppose another form of arrogance, though common enough among us. So he sets off to find an ancient sage, the one immortal man, a Noah figure who survived a Great Flood. There's a school of thought that says he walked all the way to Mt Ararat, where the Ark was supposed to have been. Finally, after many trials, the great sage presents him with a magic plant that gives back one's youth. It's called "Old Man Grown Young". But on his way back home he falls asleep and a snake eats it and immediately sloughs its skin!'

'Does he give up then?'

'He accepts mortality and goes back home to Uruk to fulfil his responsibilities. He brings back all he has learnt to his people and writes it down on a tablet of stone. He becomes a wise and good king. His story, which is really a story about growing up, is told through the ages, as I am telling it to you. Paradoxically, of course, he does achieve immortality.'

'And Enkidu?'

'Enkidu? Enkidu stays in the Underworld. He never comes back.'

The desert seemed flatter and harsher as they drove into the oncoming dusk. There was no sign of army convoys, English or French, nor of the bands of nomads they sometimes glimpsed high on a rocky ridge. According to the map there would be a village soon where they could stay the night.

'I wonder why I heard his name in Armenia.'

'Whose?'

'Gilgamesh. I thought I overheard it once in a cafe in Yerevan.'

'He's a mythical figure. He belongs to everyone, everywhere. Take us, for instance. Aren't we on a heroic quest?' He reached across and patted Edith's knee. Ever since they crossed into Syria she'd noticed a change in Leopold's spirits. He'd become lighter, carefree, almost playful. This was the last lap of their journey. Was he relieved at the parting ahead? Or was this the light-headedness she'd heard of, soldiers on the eve of battle, their fate, like children's, taken out of their hands?

'Oh yes, very heroic.' It was easy to be ironic about themselves as travellers, the battered jeep's ragged canvas, the pathetic bundles that made up their luggage, the bag of pumpkin seeds Leopold snacked on from between his solid thighs. With their makeshift headdresses, red eyes and pale, unsuitable skin they were almost comical. And there was another unheroic feature of this journey. Little tantrums and sulks. Petty self-assertion: she had been far from a good sport. She accused Leopold of being bossy. He was so sure of himself. He was vain about his ability to find the best *khan*, to choose the sweetest fruit. You wouldn't think, she said, that for five years she had managed to keep Jim warm and fed. She hardly knew why she was saying these things. She even mimicked his English accent. She was like a child who has come home and can at last behave badly.

And he saw straight through her. Again and again he teased her with his patience and goodwill. Again and again she put him to the test.

Now she said: 'There are no women in this myth.'

'Yes there are. There's the temple girl who is sent to seduce Enkidu out of the wilds. There's Gilgamesh's mother, who prays for her son's *restless heart*.'

'But nothing happens to them. It's not their story. No woman goes off on quests like that. Women get stuck. They are left behind with the children.'

'What about you? All the way from Australia!'

'With a small child. I did it for Jim's sake. Well, all right, I did it for love.'

'Isn't that the same as eternal life?'

Edith blew out smoke. She was twenty-four and felt she could never be made young again. She drew on her cigarette and felt the lines on her dry face form some hard, predictive pattern. She was much too cross to tell him that she had found what she was looking for.

What happened next? Over the next rise, delicate plumes of smoke high and steady in the twilight. The cooking fires of a village. Thirty or so adobe houses that looked down on the Euphrates valley. Then there would be a cluster of little boys around the jeep, salaams with the elders, goats nudging them, messengers sent. Leopold speaking Arabic, bowing, enjoying the courtesies. Jim standing beside him. She with her scarf wrapped across her face.

It was always the same. They took off their shoes at the door of the *khan* where they would sleep. They sat on straw matting and were served by women moving in and out of the shadows from the oil lamp. Rice and grilled river fish and rough Arab bread. Goats' milk for Jim. They were so tired that time seemed to slow, almost stand still. This was how they lived in villages along the Euphrates five thousand years ago, Leopold said. People raised goats and ate fish while great civilisations came and went.

Then a mattress was rolled out for the three of them beneath a tiny star-crammed window. They huddled beneath woven blankets. At night beside him she saw their journey was unfolding at breakneck speed. Their hands touched over Jim's sleeping body and held a moment before they slept.

In Aleppo they stayed at the Baron Hotel. 'Everybody stays at the Baron,' Leopold said. 'The Lindberghs, Isadora Duncan, T.E. Lawrence. All the famous archaeologists. My dear, we simply couldn't stay anywhere else.' It had been built and owned by an Armenian family, the Mazloumians, since 1909. Edith recognised the arched windows and the Armenian designs carved into the stone walls. It seemed like the acme of luxury to her, the sweeping staircase, the parquet floors, the steam rising from the bath. In their room the provision of a cot bed for Jim, and the bowl of flowers beneath the window, almost made her weep. It had the same wood-panelled, slightly shabby gentility as the Sea House. Like any servant, she had always craved to be a guest.

They spent their last free day wandering in the Armenian quarter of Aleppo, down streets of Armenian gold shops, rug shops, spice shops, past Armenian schools and Orthodox churches. Thousands had fled here from Turkey during the 1915 massacres. This is where Aram had come as a tiny survivor. There was Armenian script over the shopfronts, the smell of Armenian food. They heard Armenian again in these streets. It intensified everything.

They wandered down the passageways of the famous Aleppo *souk*, the largest in the Levant, miles and miles of stalls along cobbled walks, under the domes of stone roofs. They watched the sun set over the Citadel.

After Jim fell asleep, avoiding the nuptial-looking bed, they went downstairs to the dark wood-panelled salon and drank Armenian brandy. The Free French and British soldiers drank here when they were in town. There was a poster hanging over the bar of a large ear with a swastika inside it. Beneath it was written: *Words can Kill.* Some Australian officers had been here not two weeks ago, the Armenian barman told Leopold. The Aleppo airfield had been bombed and there were rumours of mines in the desert. The salon was empty that night apart from an Armenian family in the far corner speaking together in French.

'Leopold, did Aram write to you?'

'Not after he went to Armenia.'

'How did you know he was dead?'

'Hagop. I was in touch with Hagop. Or rather, he got in touch with me. Through my address on your letters, actually.'

'So you got my letters?'

'Yes. Thank you. I enjoyed them immensely. They were very informative. I could start to find a way for you to leave.'

'How did you have the connections?'

'Ssh. Look at the poster. Let's just say it was in my line of duty.'

'Was Aram a friend of Hagop's?'

'Finding Aram was in Hagop's line of duty.'

'Who did Hagop work for?'

'He used to be in a nationalist group when he was a student before the war. Aram searched out and joined what was left of it. Do you know what his codename was, by the way? I believe it was Gilgamesh! In '42 they were all betrayed and sent off to Stalin's Penal Squadrons on the Russian front. They're marched in first to battle. About one per cent survive.'

'And Hagop?'

'The NKVD probably enlisted him after the bombing of a music school before the war. Nobody knows to this day whether it was caused by the nationalists or the NKVD.'

'It must have been the nationalists. Tati always said Hagop suffered from guilt.'

'Guilt from what? Was he in the NKVD before or after the bombing? You'd never know with Hagop. He serves many masters. You know, I met him before the war in Istanbul. He was a sort of part-time agent for an Armenian millionaire then, who wanted to do oil deals with the British.'

'You mean Mr Five Percent?'

'You've met?'

'On the Orient Express. He invited me to his compartment. I met Hagop on the same train.'

Leopold went silent for a while.

'Leopold, when Hagop sent Jim and me out of Armenia he said I was no longer useful.'

'As a lure to rope in Aram and his group. That's why you were left alone by the NKVD.'

'But Hagop said Aram died more than a year ago. Why did he keep on protecting us?'

'I don't think I'm being immodest in saying that I was the larger prize. He did some work for us. He wanted me to work for them. I think he wanted to do a deal with me, to help him to get out. He was always a bit of an Anglophile. He spoke excellent English.'

'Armenians are quick with languages,' said Edith, automatically.

'There was also the case of a modest but regular retainer from Mr Five Percent. Hagop would have been told to keep an eye on you.'

'What do you mean?'

'Your old Armenian gentleman is well known for this kind of thing. He has an eye for the ladies, a very specialised eye. He has agents in all the countries he travels to, to look out for him, his type. He has apartments in several countries and beautiful companions, specially trained in his tastes.'

'But I ran away from him.'

'Oh, he's renowned for his patience. He enjoys a challenge. And I suppose there was a chance, through you, of a link to the nationalists, or even to the British. He backs every horse in the region, old Mr Five Percent, any horse which might get him to Baku's oil. And of course, every government wants to do business with him.'

They were silent for a while.

'So Hagop was guarding me for that old man.'

Leopold thoughtfully shovelled up a fistful of pistachios.

'Is that why Jim and I survived? Even in Batum ... Is that why we got into Armenia in the first place?'

'Very likely.'

'Because of a lecherous old man.'

'Because of a beautiful face.'

Edith was warmed in spite of herself.

'You must remember that it was you and Jim who got out, not Hagop. He got you out, even though without you he has probably outlived *his* usefulness.'

'Why did he do that?'

'That was our deal. But you know, Edith, I think he was very fond of Jim. He always mentioned him in our communications.'

Because of Jim.

'What will happen to Hagop?'

'Didn't his wife die recently? I don't know how much he wants to live.'

They kept talking back in the room while Jim slept. She lay in Leopold's large arm, brown to the elbow and then soft and white.

'Do you feel funny?'

'Not with you, Edith. It would waste time. Besides I've given up hating myself. What's the point? In a war there's too much else to hate.'

He said that all the way back to Aden on the ship, he and Aram had talked about Nunderup. Nunderup always brought a smile to Aram's face.

'Did he ever talk about me?'

Leopold said that Aram never spoke of the personal. He'd once said that in the orphanage you had to hide what you wanted to keep for yourself.

So, no words of undying passion. Nothing to justify her journey.

'Leopold, Armenian men are very strict with their women. You know, wives, sisters.' It was painful to say this. It made her want a cigarette. 'Virgin brides, reputation . . .'

He understood it was a question.

'Aram was a survivor. What did he know of families, of mothers or sisters? He didn't feel he really belonged in the world. I don't believe he thought he would live.' He squeezed her close so she had to look up at him. 'If he'd heard about Jim, he would have tried to see him. I'm sure about that.'

'I think perhaps he did. Could that be why he died?'

'Oh, Edith, in wartime a group like his will never survive. It goes against popular feeling, the war effort. It will always be betrayed.'

'Who knows?' he said after a little while. 'Perhaps his last thought was of Jim.'

They held each other, their faces almost touching. Later Jim stirred and cried out. She lay and watched Leopold pad across the room in the moonlight, gather Jim up and carry him to their bed.

Who would have thought to put an orphanage out there, on the outskirts of the city, far from the hubbub of the *souk*, in the silence of the desert? What sort of place was this for children? Once it had been an inn for travellers from the west, from the port of Alexandretta, now ceded to the Turks. It sat beside the road in the lee of a hillside scattered with thorn trees, one-storeyed, flat roofed, behind a stone wall coloured red by the dust. The dormitories and school rooms were set around a large central court. The children were gathered in the shade of a roofed pavilion, eating their lunch. There was no fountain or garden. The only place to play was among a little grove of date palms outside the walls.

It was a Christian orphanage, the director, Miss Anoosh, a tiny Armenian woman, explained. They sat in her office, a little dark room with a high barred window and white-washed walls. There were Greek Orthodox and Maronite Catholic children here as well as Armenian Orthodox these days. Of course the original children from the Turkish Massacres had all grown up now. There were about forty children, some from the present war. Miss Anoosh said she would be glad of Edith's help if she stayed. There was an Armenian Orthodox cross on the wall behind her.

Edith's heart was pounding, her hands were cold. From the moment she woke up that morning, she had a conviction that someone had died.

Miss Anoosh spoke precise expressionless English. She remembered Aram as a child, and meeting Leopold with him before the war. When she heard of his death she crossed herself. There was so little of her, she was so plain and spare in her dress and manner, it was impossible to guess her age. She wore dark tinted glasses, her eyesight was very poor. No one was sure she wasn't blind, Leopold said. No one could remember a time when she had not been at the orphanage. She knew each stone of it as she knew the voice of each child. When she asked Jim his name and his age in Armenian, Jim answered her, unafraid.

Miss Anoosh led them to the pavilion where the children sat cross-legged at low benches smeared with grains of rice and drops of milk. She clapped her hands and the children raced each other across the courtyard and dropped their tin mugs and bowls into a keg by the kitchen door. Two or three helpers, older girls, ushered the children out into the palm grove and their voices blew into the courtyard in the desert wind.

They sat at one of the empty benches. A large girl brought them tea and a mug of milk for Jim. Leopold and Edith sat side by side, like an old couple who need say nothing more to each other. Edith watched the girl. She was about sixteen, with swinging hips and heavy breasts and a womanly headscarf. But the way she stood gazing at them, plucking at her mouth, was babylike. Edith could not take her eyes from her, her vast docility. She would be one of Edith's charges. Why did she feel this was her fate, coming to meet her? 'Sevan!' someone called—the name of the Armenian lake—and the girl turned and ambled back towards the kitchen. There was a wet patch at the back of her dress.

Leopold said that she must make contact with the Australian Seventh Division in Syria. That he would try to get in touch with them on her behalf.

'Can't we wait here for you?'

'Edith, you must take Jim home to Australia.'

'Will you come there again one day?'

'Oh yes. I want to see this chap grow up.'

He said she mustn't be afraid of going home.

At the jeep he dug into his kitbag and handed her the slim brown book she had last seen in the kitchen in Nunderup. 'This is for you. And Jim.'

In her memory, there was no trace of heaviness or clumsiness to him at the end. His touch was light on her face. His eyes were radiant. He seemed to vault into the jeep. He was lightness itself. He said that when he drove off he would not look back, but the jeep swerved a little as his hand emerged, waving. Perhaps he heard Jim's howls.

Jim always did her crying for her.

The jeep disappeared over the crest of the road.

A bell rang for siesta in the dormitory. Everything went quiet: the wind dropped. The sun fell in a solid shaft into the courtyard. Jim squeezed his eyes shut to make this place disappear.

There was an explosion in the desert. Not far away. A mine on the road.

Everyone came streaming out of the dormitory, following Edith as she ran up the hill. She left them all behind, even Jim.

Some nights, when the children were asleep, Edith sat with Miss Anoosh in her little white room. The carved stone cross, the worn Oriental carpet, the photographs on the wall reminded her of Yerevan. There was the snow-frosted cone of Mt Ararat, touched up with faded pastels. There was the fabled Lake Van in eastern Anatolia, once Turkish Armenia. Miss Anoosh had been born in the town of Van. There was the photograph of Miss Anoosh's family, taken in a studio in Van in 1912, her parents and three older brothers and her little sister, and young Anoosh in clear spectacles, a floppy bow at her neck. She always wanted to be a schoolteacher. She was the only survivor in her family. All the rest had died in the death marches of 1915.

The war went on. The Normandy landings, the race towards Berlin. The V-1 and then the V-2 rockets falling on London. Miss Anoosh served Edith brandy in ladylike thimble glasses and told her of the march along the Euphrates, the beautiful Euphrates bearing bloated Armenian bodies. Raped, murdered, or as with her mother and little sister, hands tied together in suicide. Hitler, the Jews, the Russian Front: for Miss Anoosh it was still the Turks murdering Armenians.

In this Miss Anoosh was like every Armenian Edith had ever met, starting with Aram. How you became aware of the place in their lives of loss, lost family, lost land. Of buried anger, for monstrous crimes unpunished, for the world's indifference. It was always there, as if the end of grieving would be the final loss.

The only place where Edith felt at ease now was Miss Anoosh's room.

Some nights Jim poked his bumpy forehead around the door. He had begun his lifelong career of never doing things when others did. He did not sleep when the children slept. He had been found wandering at night. No one was sure if he was walking in his sleep or out of contrariness. When Edith asked him he did not respond. Edith had seen him herself, walking in the moonlight along the top of the courtyard wall. Skimming through the date palm grove. She had not stopped him. He seemed happier in the night breeze, more of a child. He napped in short bursts in shaded corners of the courtyard at any hour of the day. Edith could not make him change. It wasn't just that she was too tired. There was a new authority about Jim. He was nearly seven, but seemed much older. He was grave, silent, and never joined in games. Sevan lumbered after him, as once he had followed Nora, and he was gracious to her.

For the first few weeks here Edith had lain on her bed in a dark corner of the dormitory. Miss Anoosh sent a message to a friend of hers asking for information about the mine. An English jeep, she was told, but no body could be identified. The wreckage had been blown far and wide and quickly disappeared beneath the sand. There were many English soldiers in the area, Miss Anoosh pointed out. But no letter from Baghdad ever arrived.

Edith lay without moving or speaking. Whenever she opened her eyes she saw Jim sitting beside her, as if on guard.

Many months later Edith wrote to Irina, asking for news of Leopold. She would find out if Irina had received official notification of his death, she thought, before she began to explain the exact set of circumstances that had led to that jeep being on that particular stretch of road in Syria that day. She dreaded the reply, dreaded Irina's grief.

Edith never knew if Irina had even received her letter, but she took Irina's silence as blame.

Edith and Jim joined an Australian transport bound for Palestine. It happened by chance. Some soldiers in khaki shorts and slouch hats came into the courtyard to ask for water for the radiator of their truck. Miss Anoosh could not understand the English of these large young men. She called Edith out of the schoolroom.

'I'm Australian,' Edith said and one of them said: 'Go on!' Twenty minutes later she and Jim were waving goodbye to Miss Anoosh and the orphans from the back of the truck as it drove off to join the transport.

It was April '45, the Red Army was fifty miles from Berlin.

All they could see was the shine of desert glare between the canvas curtains. Jim's face was smeared with chocolate. Family-hungry soldiers swung him high in the air as they lifted him in and out of the trucks. He was winked at, joked at, his bumpy forehead squashed down into somebody's hat. Edith was shown the wallet snaps, all those demurely smiling Australian faces. The eyes seemed innocent to her, touching. There were new pin-up girls in the cabs of the trucks, Betty Grable, Lana Turner. The shortwave wireless played songs she had never heard before. *You Must Remember This*, the men sang. Everybody knew the words. Everybody sang along.

Return

Edith told Jim that this was home but he didn't know what home meant. To him it was just another border, the queues on the wharf, the men in uniforms, the corrugated iron sheds. They were processed and stamped in a wave of Displaced Persons as the old troopship from Alexandria disgorged its cargo into Fremantle. Theirs was just one story among hundreds of sagas reaching an end here.

'Look, Jim.'

She was grey-faced from five weeks' seasickness, but her eyes were shining. He couldn't see what made her happy. They were standing on a railway platform looking at some old bush growing in gravel. Seagulls hung in air as clear as water. It was late winter, 1947.

The deeper they went into the country the closer they were to home. They descended from the bus into a great coolness and hush and the smell of forest. They walked down the driveway of a house as big as a palace and a tiny yellow-haired boy was rolling over and over on the lawn with a snarling woolly dog, and the boy, though very young, was laughing, completely unafraid.

Another dog was barking wildly at them as they crossed a clearing splashed with sunlight and Edith gasped, he knew she was afraid. She started running towards an angular figure in dungarees watching them from the verandah of a little house. She was calling out as she ran, the suitcase bumping against her legs.

Frances! Frances! Where's Mumma?

There was no grandmother to greet him, the Tati that Edith had promised him. Ada had caught pneumonia in the winter of '44, and couldn't seem to remember how to breathe. Dr Bly had stayed with her all one night, sent Frances off to sleep. At dawn he woke her to tell her that her mother had died. Madge Tehoe, a mother herself now, arranged the tiny funeral: the doctor and Reg and Madge with her arm clamped around Frances had watched as Ada was buried next to Frank. Afterwards Frances refused a glass of sherry at the Sea House, walked home alone to the empty house.

The Lord giveth and the Lord taketh away, Frances said, her eyes shining palely at them across the kitchen table. She bowed her head before she ate. *Oh Lord I give thanks for the safe return of my sister and the fruit of her womb, and for Thy divine forgiveness of them both. Amen.* Her voice was eerily loud and unabashed.

'I'd rather not be prayed for, if you don't mind,' Edith said.

Jim had never seen a face like his Aunt Frances's before. So pale and serious and exposed. Even Miss Anoosh had sheltered behind glasses and wispy tendrils of black hair. But something seemed to have rinsed out the blood from Frances's skin, chiselled her bones, bleached her eyes. Her hair was pulled back into a long stringy tail between her shoulder-blades. Her red-knuckled hands looked flayed. She didn't talk of everyday matters. She sounded as if she were reciting poetry all the time.

'I was lonely,' she said. 'I was lost. I thought about death day and night, nothing but death. Then Jesus came into my heart and I was saved. Now I know there is no death as Jesus showed us.'

Edith sat fiddling with her cup. Soon she went outside to smoke on the verandah.

'Jesus never promised that the Way would be easy,' Frances went on to Jim, as if she hadn't noticed he was a child. 'But what are the slings and arrows of unbelievers compared to the spear that pierced His side? I forgive them, I forgive my sister,

I was brought to forgiveness when I was saved. Praise the Lord!'

'Oh, for heaven's sake,' Jim heard Edith say.

The distant wireless roar of the ocean, the cries of the cockatoos released in the wind, came straight from childhood. Everything Edith saw moved her, the slow clouds, the olive-green headlands, the great bowl of the sea. She knew everything that met her eye in every direction. The space and light could make her dizzy with happiness. Whatever the terrors and mysteries of childhood, she thought, she must have known happiness here.

Once or twice in those first few weeks she swung her head around thinking she glimpsed a green hat bobbing across the clearing. She listened out for her mother's special call to the chooks. Sometimes at night she thought she heard slippers shuffling though the kitchen. She lay still until her heart stopped thumping. Her mother had fallen into silence here a long time ago. It was her silence Edith heard, in every moment.

She wanted to listen for her mother, but Frances's strange voice droned on and on. Her sister, once so familiar, too familiar, like a version of herself, had become alien. As if the real Frances had been abducted and replaced by some crazed enraptured saint. She lived, barely, on the eggs and vegetables she sold to the Sea House. She bought milk from the McKays once a week and Violet McKay slipped her a few chops if they were butchering. But she had few needs. She had no friends and wore threadbare clothes. All day she crouched and muttered to herself in the vegetable garden. At set hours she read her father's Bible or prayed in her room.

'How long have you been doing this?' Edith asked her.

'Doing what?'

'Praying all the time.'

Frances licked her lips in the old way. 'Ever since I was gathered to the bosom of the Lord.'

It horrified Edith to hear Frances, so reserved and prudish by nature, speak aloud of her yearnings, talk of wombs and hearts and bosoms. The way the floorboards creaked in her room as she carried out her devotions made Edith feel queasy. She didn't know how long she could bear it.

Worse, what she was conscious of every moment she was with her sister was the thought of the grief and loneliness, the desperation that had caused Frances to do this to herself. What anger did she hide, rolling her eyes with forgiveness at her and Jim, now that they were home, too late? She didn't seem interested in them. She never once asked about their travels.

This too was home. The feeling of closeness, with nowhere else to go.

Home was strange. Edith told him he had lived here as a baby but he could remember nothing. It was as if he had been asleep and was only now waking up. He stood just beyond the verandah and surveyed the great circle of the sky and clearing, the ragged horizon of the bush.

'Come on, Jim,' Edith said. He looked so foreign here, black-browed, with full serious lips. His shorts were too long. She led him down the shadowy tracks. The bush cracked and hummed all around them like something alive. Edith went into a special mood, alert but quiet. She had forgotten the great adventure of the bush, what it chose to show, what it withheld.

They walked along the beach, vast as a desert, paddled in the rock pools at low tide.

'Whose country is this?' There was not another person to be seen.

'Ours! Well, every Australian's. You belong here, Jim.'

Frances asked Edith if she was going to ask Madge for a job at the Sea House, but Edith said she was not. She avoided contact with the Sea House as much as possible.

Once she and Jim came across Madge chasing after her little son through the Honeymoon Gardens.

'Are all boys like this?' Madge called. She stopped to catch her breath. 'I'm counting the days till boarding school,' she confided. 'Let him loose amongst his own kind.' Her eyes flickered over Jim. Madge's skirt was creased over the mound of her stomach, her hair tumbled out of a hasty bun, her unpowdered face blossomed with broken veins. It was as if she'd never had time to recover from the shock of bearing a child. But she was friendlier to Edith, as if at last they walked on common ground. 'His father is no help at all, he's laid up with gout. He keeps his distance,' she said. 'Never marry an older man, that's what I tell my girls.'

Meanwhile Gareth Tehoe had run out of the depths of the garden to stand next to Jim. He turned his head up to him and stared, his eyes curious and impersonal, a wordless little animal.

'Come with Mother, Gareth. It's lunchtime, dear.'

Gareth did not seem to hear. He did indeed look too young and perfect for his old red-faced parents, light-boned, clear-featured, golden-haired. His mother could only ever lumber after him. He and Jim stared at one another. He was only a couple of years younger than Jim, but supremely at ease in the world.

'He's the image of his Uncle Ronnie,' Edith said.

'*Gareth*.' Madge leaned over and manacled his little wrist with her fingers. 'Come on, you naughty boy.' She rolled her eyes at Edith. Nobody was fooled, least of all Madge. She enjoyed being helpless with adoration. She dragged Gareth away from Jim without a backward glance. After all, a fatherless Clark was no playmate for her son. And such a *different*-looking boy, she told Reg.

But Gareth turned his head over his shoulder, his eyes meeting Jim's.

He wasn't a naughty boy, he was an angel, Jim saw that at once.

At the top of the stairs Madge stopped and turned. 'By the way, I had a letter from Ronnie the other day,' she called out to Edith. 'From California. He sends his regards. He was pleased to hear you made it back.'

Frances told Edith that her family in Christ was coming to take her preaching on a tour of the Great Southern. The Brothers and Sisters took the word all over the state, sleeping in tents, preaching at shows and race meetings, at roadsides, outside pubs. Often they were pelted with rotten fruit or empty bottles, Frances said proudly, jeered at, chased by dogs. During the War they had called on farmhouses, reaching out to the lonely souls of soldiers' wives and mothers and homesick internees. That was how they had saved Frances, braving the overgrown track to the clearing, the only visitors she had.

Not many souls stayed saved once the men came back. But Frances was a stayer. She believed in giving all of herself. She brought all of Frank Clark's Methodist integrity to this more flamboyant faith. Every word spoken between the Brothers and Sisters was in the Lord's breath, she said. At last she had found some people who saw the world as she did. Now that Edith was back to mind the farm, Frances was free to go with them. She believed she had a calling to preach.

They were going to set up their tents and sleep the night here. Frances made, with a handmaid's care, a pot of mutton bone soup and two loaves of bread. Jim was excited, he remembered the acre of soldiers' tents in the desert and the glimpses of Bedouin caravans. But the Brothers and Sisters arrived in one car, a battered utility that didn't seem to stop so much as conk out.

Three people, two in the cab and one in the back, climbed down. The dog barked and bared its teeth and Frances tied him up.

'Praise the Lord,' she called out shyly. 'Where is Brother Bob?'

'Heeding the call in Manjimup.' The driver, middle-aged, speckled pink, with a wispy beard and creased eyes high in his face, lifted his old straw hat and mopped his head with a piece of rag.

'He won't be touring no more,' called out the young man who had ridden in the back. Or perhaps not so young, he had bristles on his chin, and his stumpy arms and neck were thick as a man's, but he was short, as short as Edith, only a few inches taller than Jim. Like the older man he wore a dark suit and collarless shirt as crumpled and dirty as work clothes. 'He got a job in the baccy factory.' His voice was high as a boy's.

'Truth is,' said the woman, Frances's sister in Christ, 'Brother Bob's getting spliced.' Her voice was so flat, you couldn't tell if she was amused or disapproving. She was a tiny dried out woman, with sun-cracked lips and frizzy grey hair pressed down beneath her scarf.

'To an Eytalian girl!' shrieked the young man. 'A roaming cathlick.'

Compared to Frances they seemed a dust-blown, lukewarm lot. Not radiant with fervour, but ordinary, just a little grubbier and looser than people who stayed at home. Jim was disappointed. He had imagined the Brothers and Sisters to be more like the Orthodox priests he'd seen strolling through the Armenian quarter in Aleppo, like a breed of noble birds with their dead white aquiline faces. Brother Norris, Sister Leona and little Brother Fred, her son, used the lavatory one after the other, and drifted in to sit at the kitchen table without, Jim noted, bothering to wash their hands.

'Didn't know you had family, Sister,' Brother Norris said, with a quick bare-toothed smile at Edith. Edith kept her head down, slicing bread. Frances bit her lip nervously as she served the soup. Brother Norris stretched out his arms, and the Brothers and Sisters bowed their heads and held each other's hands.

'Come on, Jim,' Edith said, standing, gathering up her bowl. He'd never seen her be so rude. 'Jim!' she hissed from the doorway. He followed her into the front bedroom where Frances slept. They ate their soup sitting on the big bed.

'Trust Frances to fall for this,' Edith said savagely. They were hungry and she'd forgotten to bring in the bread.

It was strange to be eating in the melancholy twilight of the bedroom. For a moment Edith looked like a stranger, all deepened with seriousness, all clean and vivid with anger. For the first time he thought of the word 'beautiful' for his mother. So much more beautiful than the people in the kitchen. Frances too had looked more beautiful than those people. It grew dark and they hadn't brought a lamp in with them.

They lay back with their arms behind their heads. There was nothing else to do but listen to the conversation in the kitchen.

The voices were slightly raised, as if in opposition.

'But we belong to the poor and homeless, as Jesus taught us,' Frances was saying.

'All very well for you, Sister,' said Sister Leona. 'I'd just like a spell with a roof over my head.'

Perhaps Frances was too much for them too.

'It's like this,' said Brother Norris. 'Our number has dwindled. We are weary. Let the people come to us for a change. Let the lost souls come here and we will succour them. They can till the soil for their food and build shelter for their weary bodies. Learn to live in the love of God.' You could hear where Frances had learnt to talk the way she did.

'Here?' said Frances.'You mean this place?'

'You are the one with property, Sister. Where else could we find our pasture for the poor?'

'You should practise what you preach, Sister,' said Sister Leona.

Brother Fred giggled, his pitch out of control.

'But this is my sister's place too. It was our father's. He wouldn't want me to give it away.'

'Who's talking of giving it away, Sister? I'm talking of *sharing*, all our worldly possessions. I'm talking of holy matrimony, Sister. You and me.'

'Praise the Lord!' shrieked Little Brother.

'*Then* what could your sister say?' said Sister Leona.

'God sent you to me, Sister,' Brother Norris went on. 'I've always believed that. My eye fell upon you for God's work and you heard me straight away.'

'What about the tour?' Frances said in a small voice. 'Albany, Walpole, the Porongorups?'

'They threw us out of Manji,' Brother Fred called out. 'Brother Bob swore on the Bible no fornication did take place.'

'Think of it, Sister Frances,' said Brother Norris. 'Think of the orphans in their rows of little beds. *Let the little children come unto me.* Let your eyes be opened to the evil of selfishness. Let duty and pity enter your heart.'

Edith lay very still on the bed.

'Come to my arms, Sister.' Brother Norris's voice held a tenor's quaver. 'Let us hold each other in the Lord's embrace.'

Chairs scraped and bumped, footsteps ran outside, the dog started barking. 'Easy, Sister!' somebody called. Edith ran out. The Brothers and Sisters had stationed themselves around their utility, just beyond the ring of kitchen light. Edith stood in the doorway, her arms crossed, Jim peering around her.

'Sister Frances!' Brother Norris called out. 'This is your last chance. Do you wish us to leave?'

Frances was taking little steps up and down the edge of the verandah, her face very red.

'Get going!' Edith's voice cracked out. 'Or I'll call the police.'

'We go when Sister Frances tells us to,' said Brother Norris. But he had put his hat on.

'But if you do, don't think you're coming touring with us, Sister,' Sister Leona said.

'Sister Frances,' Brother Norris pleaded. 'Let us kneel and pray together.'

Frances stepped off the verandah and strode towards the bush.

Edith spoke loudly. 'Jim, run to the Sea House and ask them to telephone the police.'

'Bet I can run quicker'n him!' Little Brother yelled.

But Brother Norris and Sister Leona were already climbing back into their seats. The ignition turned, failed, turned again. The utility started to bump its way out of the clearing. It seemed they were used to making speedy departures. Little Brother scrambled up behind and stood holding the roof of the cab.

'You always was a crackpot!' he yelled towards the bush where Frances had disappeared. 'That's what we said.'

'I knew what they were up to the moment I laid eyes on them,' said Edith. Her hands shook as she lit a cigarette.

The frail beam of their single headlight soon dissolved into the darkness.

But the image of Little Brother, the man-boy still with his mother, stayed with Jim for many years.

Frances returned home hours later. She looked hollowed, tear-stained like a widow, the light in her all gone out. Edith sat waiting for her, smoking on the verandah. They faced each other.

'Did he ever say he loved you?'

'You don't understand. He loves God.'

'Does a man of God marry to get his hands on people's land?'

Frances swung off into her room.

For some time she was subdued. There was something crestfallen about her as she went about her tasks. She saw it as a weakness in her, that she had not been able to stand by her convictions, that she could not in the end give all of herself. That she loved the land more than God. She bowed her head over her plate, but if she prayed she kept it to herself.

Later she came to think that religion itself was her weakness, a dark attraction over which she had no control. In calm moments, weeding, tying up the beans, she knew this attraction was something inherited from her father. An appetite for moral judgement that she was always seeking to appease. She always felt watched. By whom? God or her father?

Bit by bit her eyes lost the glassy stare that didn't really seem to see other people. She started to see Jim only too well. Edith let him moon around too much. Frances mused about his education, how best to bring up a child. She taught him to use the axe, and told him he was now in charge of the stove. When she dug over the orchard she gave Jim the task of collecting stones. There did not seem to be time to pray any more. Thoughts of Jim, what he might be doing or not doing, disturbed her concentration.

She started to get angry like an ordinary human being. All her intensity became focused on Jim and he made her angry.

It started when he went to school.

From the first day he would not speak about it. How is school? Edith and Frances asked him and he just grunted, ashamed at his failure, for wasn't this an Australian school and wasn't he an Australian? He was more a foreigner here than he had ever been anywhere else. Scornful freckled faces loomed out of the glare of the gravel playground and called him names he couldn't understand.

'What's a bastard?' he asked Edith, out of earshot of Frances.

'Someone whose parents aren't married,' Edith said. She didn't offer any more information and he didn't ask for it because he knew it came from that area of her life which gave her pain. Ever since the orphanage he had protected her from pain.

How did these Australians know so much about him? Father, father, that seemed to be the question. *Where's ya father? What d'he do in the War?*

'He died,' Jim mumbled. Other kids had fathers who died in the War and that seemed to give them a sort of respect. But still they went on. *What side was he on? Go on, tell us.*

Just by standing there he seemed to send them into a frenzy. There were some older girls chatting on the schoolroom steps but they didn't come to save him. He knew he wasn't small and cute any more, but a blighted, big-nosed, gawky creature.

He brought home uneaten the sandwiches Frances had made him and she scolded him for waste. He did not say that he had no time to eat, he had to stay in the schoolroom and finish his work. This was because he was nearly ten years old and could hardly read or write. Nora had taught him to read Armenian and he'd learnt some Arabic in the orphanage, but the teacher, Sir, did not know that. *From what barbarous climes have you been delivered to us, Clark?*

Sir had been in the Airforce. He was very tall with bloodshot eyes and thin red-gold hair slicked back in a single strand to the nape of his neck. When he was angry, the strand fell over his face, like a signal. The swish of his cane nauseated Jim, it was like listening to an execution. Among his students there was a rumour, which Sir did nothing to dispel, that he had fought in the Battle of Britain. They admired his wit and bookish words in spite of their fear. They were proud he had come to Nunderup. What would make a man like that come to the bush? Whatever it was, he didn't go away. He stayed on, year after year.

He lived by himself in an old Settlement house near the school. Later it turned out that he had come to drink himself to death.

Blood drummed in Jim's ears, behind his eyes, his hands sweated, he knocked over his inkwell. There was ink everywhere, even in his mouth, it tasted like blood, metallic and salty. Six red stripes stung his blue palm, his hand bouncing like a spring, the room hushed, unreal. Sir's face was bland and suave.

Sometimes after school he went to the book called *Gilgamesh* which his mother kept beside her bed. Inside the book was a photograph of Leopold as a fat boy in shorts and cap, only a few years older than Jim was now. Jim spent long minutes studying the familiar face in its guise of schoolboy. Each time he saw something more. He saw Leopold's eyes with the knowledge in them deep in the flesh of the boy. The grin that stretched his cheeks he now saw as brave. He saw that this fat boy would also be a target in the Nunderup schoolyard.

He flicked through the yellowed rough-cut pages and breathed its musty smell. It filled him with a strange excitement, as if he'd caught a whiff of ancient, buried cities. Leopold had read these words, he loved the Gilgamesh myth, Edith said. That was why he'd wanted them to have this book. In bed at night Jim thought of Leopold the way he was in the evenings in Syria, all the dust washed from him, the calm he radiated. In this way he fell asleep.

He said he was sick. He would've run away into the bush every morning except that Sir said truancy was a crime, your parents could go to gaol. Most mornings he was sick anyway, sick with dread. Even alone with Edith he couldn't tell her how it was, how he'd entered a darkness and feared for his brain. He could never take a full week of it. Sore throat, stomach, ear, even leg ache. It annoyed Frances that Edith believed him. This was what motherhood had done to her, made her go soft in the head. By midmorning this so-called sick child would be up out of bed hanging around the verandah! The boy needed someone to stand up to him. *It's weak to tell lies*, she told Jim, *it's weak to run away from things. All children have to learn to read and write. That is their work.*

Edith had started work by then. He longed for her to stay home with him, put her hand on his forehead, spend all day by his bed as she had once in the camp in Alexandria when he was sick with measles. She'd sung a song about a kookaburra to him and he liked the young, free sound of her voice. Somehow she'd come by some ginger ale for him, and the taste would always remind him of her, her spicy smell, her cool fingers.

In the end he always went back. At least he could catch the bus with Edith to and from school. They could be together again away from Frances. Besides, he wanted to learn to read. He wanted to read his grandfather's books on the shelf in the kitchen. Also Leopold's book, which now belonged to him.

Edith had taken a job at the new nursing home in Busselton. A stone house on the inlet had been converted into a hospital with wheelchair ramps and handrails and a bathroom wing. Old farmers and farmers' wives, shopkeepers, fishermen, shire clerks, sun-blotched pioneers of the South West, would now be nursed here until they died. Edith was employed at first in the kitchen, but soon she was left to do what she was best at, the cleaning, feeding and dressing of old helpless bodies. Every morning now she caught the early bus from the Nunderup Hall in her bubblegum pink, double-breasted uniform, and her nurse's shoes which she whitened once a week with a special paste. She came home on the last bus, stepping down and fumbling for a cigarette.

The work was hard. It required all her concentration and precision, all her stamina. Sometimes she worked seven days a week, or stayed overnight if a patient of hers was dying or the hospital was understaffed. She gave her patients all the care that she had learnt to give Tati. That she would have given her own mother. She did not have time to chat with the other staff, though they respected her. Edith was always surrounded by her patients, yet always seemed alone.

Her feet and hands broadened, her back grew permanently round. At night she was silent with exhaustion. She wound her alarm clock and went to bed when Jim did. It was important to sleep enough, so that in the morning her heart didn't sink too much as she walked up the nursing home driveway and the thought came to her: *The House of the Dead.*

On her days off in the summer she went to the sea and let the swirling water engulf her, make her lighter. She taught Jim to swim and catch the waves. On the way back along the limestone track she listened to the ticking of the bush. Let me learn patience, she said to herself. She thought of the patience of Tati, who endured, who did not speak of her grief for the past. And of Hagop, caretaker of Nevart, paying for his sins.

She became aquainted with death. She peered down into it in order to learn about the deaths she had missed. She listened to the silence after the last breath and heard its echo far away in another country. The silence in the desert after the explosion, that even now vibrated through her. She bowed her head before the presence around that bed.

Yet her work was a battle for life. Day after day, to hold the end back a little longer. To serve life, which she had once too carelessly disregarded.

She moved calmly among the patients, knowing she could bring comfort. It was an instinct, sensing when a feeble body was lopsided, when an old back was cold, when a soul was about to disappear from loneliness. She learnt how to draw out of herself the exact words, the exact touch. Leopold had known how to do this, she thought.

She dreamt one night that Leopold came walking again into the clearing. This time he wore a coat of thick dark fur as if he were coming from a northern country. His light hair had turned to arctic silver, and his face was winter white. It was Leopold, walking and walking towards her *but he looked like someone else.*

She woke to hear herself gasping in the darkness. She put her head under the blanket so Jim wouldn't wake.

Jim loved to sit by Edith on the bus, to be travelling again. For a while he pretended to forget his true destination. He liked the morning smell of her fresh uniform, crisp with hospital starch. Her face was still dreamy from sleep. *Dmitri*, she sometimes called him, his old travelling name. He knew it was a gesture to another time, when they had been everything to each other. He understood that she knew he was suffering.

She watched him standing at the edge of the schoolyard, the first to arrive. The bus's exhaust blew the hair back from his forehead and as the morning light struck his face it seemed to her that his temples were bulging. As if his brain were overworking, or his emotions had crept up and filled his face. She felt a stab of disquiet. She raised her hand to him as the bus drove on.

He watched until the bus disappeared though she never turned back. He knew she would be glad to be alone. Ever since he was very young he had known this about his mother. Even if she was alone she set up a screen of cigarette smoke so she wouldn't be disturbed. She could never get enough solitude.

Edith sat near the front so she wouldn't have to talk to the locals. She knew they watched her and Jim, that their return would have been noted and talked about in the district. That here she would always be a woman with a past.

Sometimes she caught men watching her in a speculative way, even now, as she was, set-faced, tense-shouldered in her pink uniform. She looked straight ahead.

Sometimes, when she caught sight of the spire of the Anglican Church outside Torville, she remembered 'Armenia', that fabled mountain paradise where she had never been.

In the afternoons he didn't catch the crowded schoolbus, but walked all the way to the nursing home to wait for Edith. He sat on the verandah and watched the rows of sheets billow in the inlet breeze as peace settled over him. When Edith had a moment she brought him out a glass of milk and a piece of yellow fruit cake from the old people's afternoon tea, with instructions to stay outside. But he would never have willingly gone in.

Inside were corridors of cries and wails, glimpses of shrunken bodies so still they might be dead. He saw Edith wrestling with sheets and limbs like a sailor in high wind. The smell wafted out to the verandah, a sickly farmyard odour, so familiar it was almost comforting. Edith carried this smell home with her on the bus, it was the smell of the day's end, of release.

But the verandah was a place of respite. He sat in a cane chair swinging his legs, trying to make out the words in the magazines that were left by visitors, *Woman* and *Countryman* and *Pix*. Old survivors sat around him, bent over canes, parked in wheelchairs. They dozed and woke, watched the trees, muttered to themselves. They were indifferent to Jim, or asked him the same questions over and over as if he were one of theirs. Been a good boy? Done the milking yet? Eh? Eh? they screeched at him, enjoying the freedom of the breeze. Old yellow-nailed claws pushed their cake at him in offering. He took it but couldn't eat it, crumbled it down through a crack in the boards. Their watery eyes couldn't see him do that, he knew. After Tati, he felt at home with old people. Sometimes he glimpsed the little boy or girl in a face, peeping out through crumpled flesh, defiant. An old shearer swore like a boy behind a shed, winking at Jim. When I get better I'll get out of this place, he said. Jim saw that they were prisoners here, as he was at school. They were afraid of their weakness and helplessness, as he was afraid of his.

When Edith popped out for a smoko, the old people called to her, trembling in their chairs, fawning for a moment's attention. 'Sister! Oh, please, Sister!' Edith bent over them with kind hands, her white shoes flashing as she ran to them.

A huge black bird swooped into the clearing straight towards him so that he covered his head with his arms and heard its wings beat as it passed above him. It gave a hoarse cry as it circled and he fell down and lay on the earth. It hovered waiting, its cries grating and beating inside his head.

Jim, Jim, what are you lying there for? It's only an old crow, pull yourself together. You've got to get ready for school.

The long holidays were over and he could not face the classroom and yard again. Black hairs sprouted in his armpits and groin, there was even a line of silky black fur along his top lip. *No!* he croaked. He heard the wings beating in ever faster motion, so that the whole world veered, darkened, speeded up. *Leave me alone!* His voice had the harsh edge of the crow. He saw that his mother and aunt were startled and afraid.

He was surprised by his voice and the strength of his resolve. He stalked back into the house. Edith came after him, but he slammed the bedroom door. He heard their voices, rising and falling, attack and defence. But they couldn't make him go anywhere. He was as strong as they were now. Why hadn't this occurred to him before?

They didn't know what to do with him. Edith had to go to work. He roamed the bush and the beach, or lay in the bedroom with the door closed. This is what he had done in the holidays but there was no contentment for him in anything any more. After his rage a wretchedness took him over, which tightened his chest, weakened his legs, tainted the brightness of the summer. The faster his thoughts went round, the slower the day passed, from the ache of dawn to sunsets lurid with menace.

He heard Frances talking. 'He can't just run away from things. He isn't a child now. People won't put up with him.'

People. He saw a crowd gathered on the steps of a great civic building. He heard them murmuring, calling for his punishment.

'Jim.' Edith was leaning over him. 'Tell me. What's the matter?' But how could he tell her, when he knew this devastation joined up with hers, came from the same place. Loss had rained down on them like a sandstorm. In the orphanage dormitory his mother had lain all day on her bed. That was the day his childhood had ended.

Five weeks passed. His birthday came and went. A book, *Robinson Crusoe*, from Edith. A lopsided cake from Frances with thirteen childish candles. He couldn't thank her, couldn't bring himself to take a bite. Well *I'm* going to try it, said Frances, cutting herself a large slice. It nauseated him just to see her jaws move.

Day after day alone with her he felt her watching, thinking about everything he did. He felt trapped in her thoughts. Every morning she came into his room and told him to pull himself together. Once she tried to make him get up off the bed. She tugged and pulled at him, her face red. *Do you know your grandfather cleared this block with his bare hands? Do you know what he would think of you, a great big boy, lying around like this?* He kicked at her, she ducked, he split her lip. Blood poured down her chin as she stared at him, and her irises went large and dark for a moment as if at last she'd grasped a monstrous truth. She could not chew or smile or speak properly for more than a week. Edith wouldn't talk to him either. He was ashamed, but more, terrified by the pictures that came to him, those pale chiselled cheekbones squashed together, that obdurate skull with its thin plait crushed like an eggshell.

One day Sir came to look for him. Jim saw through the bedroom window the battered little Morris bump its way into the clearing and there Sir was, unfolding from his seat, spruced up in a tweed coat, tie and felt hat, disguised as a farmer going to the city. The voice too was in disguise, calling out from the verandah, reasonable and hearty, a wolf's voice sweetened for grownups. 'Miss Clark? I'm Howard Dowd, the boy's teacher.' It was Saturday, Edith was at work and here was Sir coming into the bedroom. Jim froze, lying there on his bed.

'There you are, Clark. Still *very sick?*'

Jim stared at him.

'Stand up when you speak to me, boy.'

Jim could not move.

'I've been hearing stories about you, Clark. About a boy who won't come to school. Do you know that's against the law, Clark? Do you know your mother could be in a lot of trouble because of you? You don't look very sick to me.'

Frances stood behind him, wiping her hands nervously on her overalls.

He shut the door and they sat down at the kitchen table. Jim heard the kettle whistle, and the growl of Sir's voice. Frances's voice was high, going on and on. *Run, run,* Jim whispered to himself, but he was too afraid to move. Frances and Sir talked for a long time. The shadows in the clearing grew longer, the bird calls lonelier, like a serenade for something ended. Jim thought of the empty schoolyard, and of all the other children playing freely and happily in the world.

They came into his room together. Frances was carrying his schoolbag, into which she started to stuff some of his clothes. 'You have to go to Perth, Jim. You have to do some tests. It's not for very long. Mr Dowd is driving you there himself. It's all for the best.' Her face, still a little puffy and bruised from his kick, was red. Sir was fitting some folded up papers into the inside pocket of his good tweed jacket. He spoke softly. In the classroom everyone shrank when Sir spoke softly. Soon someone would be crying. 'Find your shoes, Clark. Get in the car.'

There was a word for boys like him. Intractable. Sir said that was what Jim was and everything Frances told him in the kitchen had confirmed his opinion. Sir told Frances about Westlea, clean, large grounds, government-run, which straightened out intractables like Jim. He told her that it often didn't take very long, some discipline, a regime, nobody standing for any nonsense, sometimes after just a few weeks, half a term, a parent wouldn't know it was the same child. He advised her that action had to be taken. The boy was running amuck. It was obvious they needed help. A man's hand. Since he was going to Perth on private business that very day, he could take Jim now, and save a lot of trouble later, and the cost of two fares. Frances could sign the papers, she was the boy's legal guardian wasn't she, in his mother's absence? He gathered that Mother was often absent?

I thought it was for the best, Frances was to say to Edith. *I thought you would get into trouble.* She was biting her swollen lip when she handed Jim his bag. For a moment even Frances looked dear to him, his last link to the known world. He felt sorry for her. He understood how Sir made you do what he wanted you to do. Also that nothing and nobody could withstand the force of Sir's dislike of him. Except Edith. Yes, Edith could, he thought proudly as the car started up.

Sir and he said nothing for a long time in the car. Jim stared at the teacher's hands on the wheel, gingery fur on freckles, and his shoes on the pedals, the familiar punched-hole fountain pattern on the toes. Sir had polished the shoes for Perth. He knew every detail about Sir, having studied him in the classroom for three years, his papery earlobes, the comb-marks in his greasy hair, the glinting stubble like beer on his sharp jaw. In the sunlight streaming over the dashboard he gleamed pink and gold. Jim imagined him doing private manly things in his house, shaving, trimming his nosehairs, hunting for socks. He didn't have a wife or kids to soften him. Jim caught a whiff of his haircream, a small, hopeful smell. He knew Sir came from a terrible place, hard and cold, a man on his own.

'You have a dark colouring, Clark,' Sir said, his only effort at conversation. 'Your father was Albanian or something, wasn't he?'

'No.'

'No what?'

'No sir.'

Sir let the subject drop.

They were driving past the dense scrub along the Busselton shoreline. Jim glimpsed the driveway to the nursing home. *Howard Dowd*, said over and over in your head became *HowDow* and eventually *Dowdowdow*. He said it faster and faster to stop himself thinking of Edith going home and finding he wasn't there.

What if I am dying? he thought, watching the light fade over the road.

He was asleep when they arrived at Westlea. The journey took longer than usual because just before Mandurah the Morris had a puncture. Sir instructed Jim to hold a torch while he changed the tyre.

'I suppose you think the gods have answered your prayers, Clark. Let me assure you, I knew the tread was worn before I left.'

Jim had no such thoughts. He had abandoned all hope for his fate. He couldn't seem to direct the beam in the right places for

Sir, who spoke through clenched teeth. 'What have you done with the few brains you were born with, Clark? Haven't you any commonsense?'

The road was empty. The bush on either side was silent, a black mass. Sir relieved himself against a tree with an angry crackling sound. 'I take it, Clark, you'd avail yourself of the occasion if there was a need.'

There was a light in a doorway at the end of a broad verandah. A vast bright hallway, smelling of meals. The glare shocked him after the dark of the car.

A large woman loomed over him. Sir cupped the back of Jim's head. 'Answer when you're spoken to, son. Tell the Director your name.' His voice was pretend playful.

'Jim.'

'You can see what we're up against here,' said Sir. He let go of Jim's head with a little push.

The Director herself, her rear an immense flat shelf, her calves like clubs, led Jim up the wide staircase. All the other children were asleep, she said, panting a little, leading him past a corridor of open doors. He would have to sleep in the sickroom so as not to disturb them. She folded down the sheets of a high bed. He still hadn't looked at her face. 'It's like this at Westlea, Jim,' he heard her say, 'if you're fair to us, we're fair to you.' She saw he was too modest to undress in front of her. She snapped the light off as she left.

He climbed into the bed fully dressed. He was somewhere near a railway line. Trains rattled passed with a whooshing noise like breath. Further down the line they whistled into a station. Their lights chased across the pale curtains in the sickroom. He lay awake for a long time.

Something about it was familar, as if he'd died and found himself back in the past. Arrival at night, a strange bed, the collective sigh of rows of sleepers. The feeling that you were being punished for something. The steady glimpse, as you lay in bed, of the dark heart of the world. Except that in the past there had always been Edith, her body never far from his. Home was Edith, wherever they went. He was filled with childish longing for her. He couldn't remember spending a night apart from her before. And it was he, through his rages, who had sent her away! He groaned and ground his fists into his eyes.

Visions came to him. He was lying in another room, high-ceilinged like this one, thick with darkness, the only light a strip beneath the door. A shadow blocks the strip. A clock chimes across the city. The shadow disappears. Footsteps echo on the pavement beneath the window, pass away into the night.

He's in a park with golden shivery trees, a coppery tone to the light. There's a feeling of suspense, as if a storm is going to break. Standing a ball's throw away among rustling bushes is a man, watching him. A man's face, surrounded by leaves. Their eyes meet.

A haze of familiarity carried him through the day. He knew the routines. Breakfast, the morning energy of children, raw, seething, dangerous. A queue for porridge, a queue for washing dishes. A queue for inspection of nails and hair. Sunday School in the hall, *All Things Bright And Beautiful*, cutout Bible figures moved around on a felt board. Free Time Outside. Westlea had been a grand old mansion with a sweeping driveway and great dark Moreton Bay fig trees. Some of the boys were playing cricket. Girls paced the shade with their arms around each other. All around the grounds was a high wire fence. The world outside was out of bounds. He knew his first task was to make himself as inconspicuous as possible. He settled his back against a wide-girthed tree trunk, and closed his eyes. It was only a matter of time before assault.

He opened his eyes. Up the driveway, out of the sleepy white light of Sunday, a figure came walking, a small dark-haired woman in a beret, white blouse and white lace-up shoes. So familiar she was like a mirage sent to tease him. He wondered for a moment if all his longing had conjured her up. She was walking in the special way she had, very determined, so that her hair bobbed on her shoulders, and her feet seemed to rap on the ground. He stood up, the sun in his eyes.

'Come on, we're going,' Edith said, not even stopping to hug him, simply taking his hand. For the first time she noticed that he was taller than she was. As if misery had made him grow.

'We're not allowed to leave.'

Edith was leading him back down the driveway. 'And I say, leave while the going's good.'

'What about my bag?'

'Cut your losses.' She spoke like a spy on a mission. A bell was ringing as they reached the gate. He turned and saw that the boys had thrown down their bats and were running to queue at the front steps. Lunch.

'Don't look back,' hissed Edith. She reached up and unlatched the gate. They walked out onto the street. She shut the gate. There was a letterbox marked WESTLEA next to the driveway. Edith took an envelope out of her bag and posted it. 'That should keep them quiet for a while,' she said. 'I told them I'm going to write to the Premier. Now hurry, we've got a train to catch.' They tried to walk at a decorous pace until they passed the Westlea fence. Then they broke into an elbows-up walk and then a trot along the railway line. And then they ran.

It wasn't until the train was rocking comfortably past Pinjarra, and Edith had smoked a cigarette or two in the corridor and treated Jim to a plate of corned beef and pickle sandwiches in the dining car, and herself to a pot of tea, that she told him what had happened. As soon as Frances told her where he'd gone, her one thought had been that she must get him back at once. She knew her only chance was speed and surprise. Officialdom was slow and lumbering, too sure of itself.

She knew she'd missed the night train from Bunbury. The next train left early on Sunday morning. But on Sundays there was no early bus from Nunderup to Bunbury. So she walked up to the Sea House bar at closing time to see if she could find a lift.

'Frances was hysterical. I'd never seen her like that. But nothing could stop me, it was as if I heard you calling me.'

Old Reg Tehoe insisted on buying her a drink. She told him she had to get to Perth, that Jim was there and needed her. He drained his glass. Out came the old Rover, growling and rumbling from the garage, its leather seats all cracked now, but running sweetly as a bird, Reg said. He drove her to Bunbury: only fear of Madge prevented him from driving her straight on to Perth. Old Reg smelt of whisky and the Rover wandered all over the dark roads, but it was so late there were no other cars. He didn't like leaving her alone at the dark railway station, but he nodded when she said she had to go. He never once asked her why Jim was in Perth, or why he needed her.

She spent the night on a bench on the platform. When it was light the stationmaster came and she asked if she could buy a sheet of paper and an envelope—he gave it to her, with the West Australian Government Railways crest on the top—and she wrote her letter *To Whom It May Concern At Westlea School.* Then she caught the train to Perth.

'I've been doing some thinking, Jim,' she said. Although she hadn't slept for more than twenty-four hours, Edith seemed fresh and animated, like a younger self. She said she thought he could enrol in the Correspondence School, they lived far out enough for that, and do his lessons by the post. 'Then you are not a truant and nobody can lay a finger on us.' But if they tried, if they came after them, then the two of them would run away, go to live somewhere else, maybe Kalgoorlie, where her father had come from. Her father had always said Kalgoorlie was a law unto itself.

'Never let yourself fall into a stranger's hands,' Edith said. She looked out the dining car window at rolling yellow paddocks, long brown hills. Why had she thought they were safe here, that this was something that could never happen in Australia? She had forgotten. Australia was a place where they tried to take away your children.

'What did my father look like?'

Her eyes turned to him. He had eaten every last crumb of the sandwiches and now sat calmly with his arms folded. 'Like you,' she said.

All at once, like a gift, she remembered the exact look of Aram's face. His eyes looked out of Jim's eyes, withdrawn, sad, intense. Then he was gone and it was a boy's features she was looking at, with newly bushy eyebrows and a childish smear of pickle on the down of his upper lip. 'Go like this', she said, brushing her own lip.

He was not deterred. 'Why are there no photographs of him?'

'There was so little time.' She felt a warmth mount her neck and cheeks. She smiled. 'He was very good-looking, Jim.'

'How did he die?'

'He would have been at the front line. He was a prisoner, and the Russians sent the prisoners in first, as punishment. They didn't stand a chance.'

'Why was he in prison?'

And then, all the way past the scrubby coastlands, she told him everything she knew about Aram, from his birth to his death. What she didn't know she filled in with what she had imagined, all those years ago. 'What you have to understand, Jim,' she said, 'is that everything he did came from being that child marching through the desert.'

Why had she thought Jim wouldn't miss what he'd never known?

'He was a fighter, a man of action,' she said. 'A brave man.'

Was he? She was inventing a father for him.

They were passing through the forest near Bunbury when Jim asked her: 'Where did it happen between you and my father?' He felt curiously clear and empty after his ordeal. There seemed to be nothing left to fear.

'Where did what happen?'

'Where was I—'

'Conceived? In the Honeymoon Gardens. After a dance, on the last night he was here.' Edith spoke briskly, but her cheeks were pink.

'Did Leopold know?'

'Leopold always knew everything.'

'Why Aram? Why not Leopold?'

'In a funny way it was always as if the two of them were one person. Later in Syria it was as if Leopold was your father.'

'Do you think Leopold is dead?'

'Why on earth do you ask that?'

'He doesn't come back to me like my father does.'

She didn't tell him other thoughts she'd had, sitting up that night in the Bunbury station. Whenever she closed her eyes she saw Jim crouched by her bed day after day in the dormitory in Aleppo. Once she'd reached out to him and taken the thick black hair springing up from his forehead and pulled him towards her and looked into his little stubborn face, seen his loyalty and forbearance.

Hadn't he always done the crying for both of them? What if

all the raging in the past few months was a fight for life, hers as well as his?

She paced up and down the deserted platform. Even the moon had gone to bed. Her nerves were racing, the angry blood thumped through her heart. She was back in the heart of existence. It was clear to her now that for the last few years she had been living to one side, living in loss, she had been lost in death. For half of Jim's childhood.

So once again Edith brought Jim home but this time something had changed. Frances had lost her moral power over them. For as long as Edith could remember Frances had acted as if the fact of Jim's existence was something to be dealt with, forgiven or corrected, like a fault in Nature. Ever since they had returned from Armenia it was as if Frances expected something wrong to be made right.

He told me it was for tests, to see if Jim was, you know, normal, she said to Edith, looking at the autumn rain trickling down the window. She did not look at Jim.

Not since her mother's death had she felt as she did when she watched Jim disappear in the teacher's car. In that moment, as silence fell over the clearing, she realised that already she *missed* him, his mute, unyielding presence, so constant, so close, as close to her as anyone had ever been. She saw her raw ugly hands clutching each other and knew that her love was too large, it frightened her, she always drove those she loved away.

Why had she let him go? Out of fear, of a man, of the authority he seemed to represent. And from another sort of fear, even deeper, which was authority's fear too, that something might arise, something different, if the spirit wasn't tamed. This fear she had called 'care'. She had called it God.

God was the spirit. Where did that thought come from?

She felt dizzy, as if she were leaving a coastline. Her bruised face throbbed, the dog was whimpering. She let him off the chain.

A man called Len Corliss had bought the old McKay farm on the other side of the Sea House and was trying to make a go of dairying with his wife. One day he had a heart attack in the dairy and died. Frances started going over there to help the young widow with the milking. Lee Corliss turned out to be as keen on farming as Frances was. Together they put in a crop of lucerne, and passed long hours discussing how to improve the herd. Frances spent more and more time working at the Corliss place. She often stayed the night there. She seemed to lose all interest in Edith and Jim.

He started at Correspondence School with a teacher he never saw, a Miss Betts. He spent a lot of time thinking about Miss Betts, admiring her courteous instructions—*Something to keep you busy!*—and commendations—*Ably put!* He loved her delicate, joyful exclamation marks. He was sure that she was young, only a few years older than him. In his mind he saw her like Nora Gasparian, black-fringed, sisterly, judicious. Her girlish signature, *Letitia Betts*, seemed to put them on an equal footing. Was it or wasn't it an offer of friendship? He aimed at getting her to write just *Letitia*.

He spread the work books out on the kitchen table each morning. He felt a queer twinge of excitement at the clean page before him, a relish, an appetite, like wanting to run across an empty beach.

⁂

He took over Frances's chores, the chooks and vegetables. He delivered the eggs to the Sea House twice a week. It was the autumn holiday season. The world was suddenly full of beautiful women. Long-legged girls on the tennis courts, soft-faced newly-weds lying back on flowing green slopes. Wherever Jim looked he caught glimpses of women, their gleam and lightness, through shubbery, up stairways, disappearing into the leaf-mould tang of the gardens. They never seemed to see him.

In the great humming kitchen old Mrs Staines asked after Edith, and often a cup of tea was offered, or a slice of fresh cake or warm bread. It didn't matter that he was shy, he soon saw that in the hierarchy of the kitchen the Clark boy was too lowly to speak. It was enough that they let him sit there at a far corner of the table and observe them. He liked to watch them at their tasks, the cooks and waiters and the maids, and listen to the gossip tossed between them. One of the maids was always prettier than the rest.

Sometimes he left by the hall door, and stood looking up to where the light seemed to swirl at the top of the stairs. Upstairs, Edith had told him, they could feel the building sway in the storms. That was where Gareth Tehoe lived.

One day, he thought, he would go out into the world like other men. Meanwhile he read. He read Scott and Stevenson and Dickens, *Ex Libris Francis Clark*. He read the tattered magazines Edith found lying around the nursing home, read them from cover to cover, including the serials, beauty hints, Cake of the Week. He pored over Dorothy Dix.

A Lending Library had been set up by the Torville Road Board and each week he caught the bus to Torville and took out his allotted quota, two books. He read Kipling and Rider Haggard and *The Secret Agent* and more modern novels, *Shangri-la*, *Greenmantle*, *The Thirty-Nine Steps*. There was a set of books glued into uniform board covers, donated from the private library of Alfred F. Barker, an early settler in the area. Jim read all his collection, including Dumas' *Adventures in Czarist Russia*, *Sketches from a Hunter's Album* by Ivan Turgenev, Burton's *Personal Narrative of a Pilgimage to Al-Madinah and Meccah (1893)*. Where Mr Barker had trod, Jim went. Where would old Alfred take him next? He had collected histories of Persia and the Balkans, accounts of missions to Central Asia, of archaeological discoveries in the Near East. Jim read them all with a deep satisfaction that he couldn't explain.

Edith no longer kept *The Epic of Gilgamesh* at her bedside, but on the shelf with her father's books. At last Jim was ready for it, took it down, opened it at the prologue. *He who saw the Deep*, he read, *the country's foundation.*

He saw what was secret, discovered what was hidden
he brought back a tale of before the Deluge.

He came a far road, was weary, found peace,
and set all his labours on a tablet of stone.

He read it over many days, using Leopold's photo as a bookmark, skipping the repetitions, sounding out the strange names of the gods. Slowly the story took shape, emerging from the formal words and the strange ways of the past. Tiny figures began to strut, grew larger the more he read. Men wept and trembled, at the mercy of their gods and their terrifying dreams.

He began to understand that everything that happened to Gilgamesh was because he had a friend. *My friend Enkidu whom I loved so dear*, Gilgamesh cries after his death, *who with me went through every danger.*

When Jim looked at the photo now he saw that Leopold had a book stuffed in his pocket. In the background was a mother, a house, a grey grainy light. The focus point of the picture was the deep glint in his eyes. He knew that Leopold too lived in reading.

Why had he wanted Jim to have this book? Somehow he was becoming Gilgamesh in the myth. As Jim had last seen him, the light on his tanned face, his arm waving from the jeep, driving off into the desert. His face was Gilgamesh's face.

He wandered through the bush, carrying a stick. His head drummed with thoughts, complicated plots of heroism and rescue, Reds and Nazis. He wanted an accomplice, a lieutenant to be walking beside him. One day he came on Gareth Tehoe, barefoot like him, also trailing a stick, a slight boy, still childishly perfect, with long thin legs and big white teeth and the shine of privilege.

They stopped and looked at one another for a moment. Then wordless, they turned and walked together, like warriors too proud to explain themselves. At the lookout they clashed sticks for a while, soldiers on a rampart. They chucked stones from the top of the boulders, competing for the longest throw. All at once, from some shared impulse they raced each other down through the corridors of the dunes. Jim's longer legs reached the waves first, though Gareth was faster. At the water's edge they tried to throw each other in and fell down wrestling in the sand. Until Gareth, laughing, extricated himself and they ran home in separate directions.

For a long time Jim could recall the shock of the body against his, the life of it, its gritty resistance.

When he read about Gilgamesh and Enkidu, he saw that power came and went between them, one was always more or less than the other.

They said at the Sea House that Gareth ran wild when he was home for the holidays. Madge no longer chased after him.

From the day Gareth left for boarding school she had become a sort of invalid and rarely left the Tehoes' rooms. Sometimes in summer Jim spotted her on their balcony, sprawled out unabashed in a sagging bathing suit, bloated with indifference, white, immense.

There was a secret running joke in the kitchen and he came to understand that it was Madge.

Gareth got into trouble for practical jokes. Salt switched for sugar, frogs in beds. Once he'd turned the sprinklers on during a twilight garden party. He always ran away before anyone could catch him. In the kitchen the staff was outraged. Where was the boy's father? everybody asked. Drinking in the bar, of course.

But at the end of every holiday the Rover was backed out, and Gareth, in cap and blazer like a little English boy, was driven off to school.

Each time he came home he seemed older. Soon he brought friends to stay with him, and they played tennis and surfed and kicked a ball along the beach. Jim could hear Gareth and his friends shouting on the tennis courts. They wore white canvas shoes and called one another by surname.

A letter came from an English lawyer, acting on behalf of the late Mrs Irina Stubbs, who had perished in her house in July, 1944, in one of the V-1 raids on London. Two hundred pounds were to come to Mrs Ada Clark, née Stubbs, as her share of the estate. In the event of Mrs Clark's death, her daughters were the beneficiaries.

The delay in settlement was due to the demands on legal resources after the war, the lawyer said.

July '44. Edith remembered hearing about the V-1 raids sitting in Miss Anoosh's room in Syria. Did Irina ever read the letter she had written to her, asking for news of Leopold? She would never now know if Irina knew that Leopold had died. For a moment Edith saw Irina as she was when she said goodbye, standing in her dressing gown in the dim hall, her brown eyes brimming with foreboding. Saw the shaky writing on the envelope Irina thrust at her: *The gods love those who are brave.* Did old Vassily and Mr Osipov die with her in the house?

She hoped Irina did not have to live with Leopold's death.

'If this is just our share, I wonder where the rest went,' Frances said.

'You mean, Leopold's share?'

'Wouldn't a man make a will if he was going off to war? We could write to the lawyer. He might be able to give you the official story on what happened to Leopold.'

'We could,' Edith said vaguely, knowing this was a letter she could never write. It would be read as a relative's greedy, veiled enquiry. And for her it would be like querying Leopold himself.

Edith offered to give Frances half of the fifty pounds that Irina had given her in London, but Frances refused. She and Lee Corliss had decided to pool their resources. Lee sold the McKay place and they put in an offer on a dairy farm out of Albany. A *real* farm, Frances said. They had plans for crops and a piggery. She was going to fulfil her father's dream.

Then something happened. The deal was off. Frances came home and could not speak of it, the words made her choke. Her grief filled the house. She stumbled through the rooms, knocking furniture. She stood immoveable in the kitchen, staring into space. She set off across the clearing and collapsed, folded up as if she had been stabbed. Tears washed her face in torrents. Rain set in and the air in the house seemed sodden with misery. One night Edith woke. She felt she was suffocating in Frances's grief.

She stood at Frances's door and whispered: 'Can't you sleep?' Frances groaned. Edith went over to her bed.

'Is it Lee?' Frances had not gone to the Corliss place for over a week. Nor had Lee visited Frances.

'It's been very wet,' Edith said. But they both knew that a bit of rain wouldn't stop a woman like Lee.

Then Frances started talking in the darkness in a rapid desperate whisper, more personal than she had ever been. 'We fell out. It was over nothing really, a visitor she had. I thought she ignored me. I said some silly things. I was sort of possessive, which is silly with friends. I'm not good with people. I'm only fit to live by myself.'

Edith stoked up the stove in the kitchen and warmed some milk. She stood by the bedroom window and watched Frances as she drank it. She was surprised at how she felt, calm and wise, deadly sure. 'It's nearly dawn,' she said. 'When it's light, go to her.'

They left without ceremony, driving out of the clearing in Lee's truck, Frances so intent on talking she forgot to look back. Edith made sandwiches and she and Jim sat on the verandah steps, munching dreamily in the sun. Then Edith brought out the little work table from her mother's room and set it up on the verandah. From that night they ate every meal there, unless it was very cold or wet or the flies were bad. They read while they ate, or stared out across the clearing. They didn't speak of why they did this: they fell back into their old wordless companionship. They felt a great relief, an unfolding.

At last they each had their own room. Edith now slept in the big bed. Jim set up some planks as a table under the window in his room off the kitchen. He laid out his books. For his fourteenth birthday Edith had given him a globe of the world, the span of his hands, set on a curved brass axis. He spent hours studying it. The way he sat, his black bushy head bent over his books in the lamplight, reminded Edith of her father.

One day in early summer, when Edith was at work and Jim was sitting at his desk, he heard a faint creak on the back step and the dog's pattering feet.

On the verandah Gareth was bent over the dog, expertly massaging its ears.

Jim stood at the door. 'How come he didn't bark?' The dog's eyes were closed, in a trance.

'Dogs like me.' That was the most that Gareth had ever said to him.

Gareth straightened up, looking around him. He seemed to have no message or purpose for his visit. Was he curious about Jim's place, as Jim was about his? Jim made a gesture for Gareth to come inside and offered him water. He stood watching Gareth. The whole kitchen seemed alight. Gareth Tehoe was drinking from his cup! Gareth Tehoe, thirteen now, less sunny, more private, was drinking water in his kitchen, modestly looking at the floor. He was barefoot, in shorts, like Jim. He must have slipped away from his friends.

Jim took him to his desk, showed him his globe, his books, the pile of old Correspondence envelopes on which he drew maps and jotted down thoughts. Gareth reached out one finger and gently spun the globe. He wasn't a reader, Jim could see that at once, he didn't even pick up *Gilgamesh*.

'D'you want to go away?' Jim asked.

He nodded.

'Where to?'

Gareth traced his finger across two oceans and stopped on the west coast of North America.

'California? Why there?'

Gareth shrugged. 'S'where my uncle lives.'

In the greenish light flickering through the vines at the window the tan on his face and hands and limbs was almost luminous. His eyes shone, thoughtful. How did he see Jim's desk? As something poor and makeshift, or as Jim saw it, a whole terrain, as familiar as the hot, still land outside?

Each time they met was a sort of test, Jim thought.

But Gareth turned away, smiled at Jim from the doorway and left. He never stayed in one place for long. He slipped out of Jim's world as easily as he had come in, stopping only to pat the dog. Jim watched the dog creep after him, half-way across the yellow grass.

Edith was aware of a restlessness in her body, a nervous energy. She ran when she had no need to, she pushed wheelchairs at breakneck speed. She would break off suddenly and wheel some startled old patient up the driveway, for a breath of fresh air, she'd say. But it was Edith who was finding it difficult to breathe.

What had happened to her? Images came to her in unexpected moments, of caresses, blunt male hands, solid forearms, the rasp of a cheekbone. She pulled sheets smooth beneath skeletal forms and thought of bodies in their glory, in abandon. They were attached to no figure that she knew of, now or in the past. They seemed sent to taunt her.

⁂

A man called Lawrence Ford came to sit with his old aunt, who was dying. Emmeline Ford was Edith's patient, and she was fond of her. On what she knew was to be Emmeline's last day she gave up all her other tasks to nurse her. She told Jim it was likely she wouldn't be home that night.

She liked the way the man was with his aunt, neither falsely jolly nor po-faced, not afraid to hold her hand or sponge her lips. He didn't try to make nervous conversation as some relatives did, but attended fully to Emmeline's quiet labour. Hours passed. The rest of the hospital slept. 'She's tough,' he said. 'She and I used to fight. She belted the living daylights out of me once.' His eyes glittered at Edith. 'I deserved it.' A chumminess had grown between them over the past few days.

Edith knew he watched her as she went about her tasks. She found she was performing with an extra flourish, in spite of herself. She caught his eyes on her, warm with something like amusement. There was talk of him in the kitchen. He was a farmer on the other side of Busselton. The Fords had always been in the area. Emmeline was his last surviving relative. He'd served in New Guinea during the War, and his wife had cleared off to Perth to be a good-time girl. She ran away with a Yankee sailor. He was bitter, they said, and a drinker.

He was a large man, tall and heavy-set, with narrow brown eyes and floppy straight hair which looked as if he cut it himself. It fell like a friar's around his long full cheeks. He wore an out-sized duffle coat, and walked slightly pigeon-toed, which gave a shambling impression, like a bear. His broad brown hand, surprisingly long-nailed, wrapped his aunt's hand like a paw.

He wept as Edith closed Emmeline's eyes and she left him with her. He found her in the kitchen, boiling a kettle in the grey light before dawn.

'What are you going to do now?' he said.

'It's too late to sleep. I'll attend to your aunt, when you're ready. Then I'll catch the first bus home.'

'Go to her now. I'll drive you home, if you'll let me.'

Neither was sleepy. The sunrise seemed majestic to them, the gleaming trees rustling a benediction. They drove in Lawrence's truck along the pearly shoreline and cruised down empty back roads to the property which Emmeline had helped carve out of the bush as a young woman. He showed her over the house, a large stone cottage sprawling with wide verandahs, surrounded by Emmeline's garden. Flickering early morning sunshine fell into the dusty rooms. It was a peaceful, untidy place, its stillness made poignant through death. He was going to cook her breakfast, but then suddenly there was a cascade of birdcalls outside the windows and he put his arms around her. And then, because death had reduced them to very simple creatures, they fell into his bed.

On the day of Emmeline's funeral he was waiting for her in the nursing home carpark when she finished work. It was a shock to see him coming towards her, a dark shambling man again, his guise as a stranger.

'Will you come with me for a drink?' He smelt of whisky.

'I can't. I have to go home to my son.'

He nodded and turned away back to his truck, head down, hands shoved in his pockets.

A week later he telephoned her at work and asked her to come with him to a party the next night. She supposed this was what the Americans called a date. Her first date. She changed out of her uniform at the nursing home and splashed herself with a patient's lavender water. It was just a group of old friends getting together to play darts in a pub in Bunbury, he explained as, rather stiffly, they sat together in the truck.

They were a bright crowd, robust drinkers, with a teasing, romping manner together. Edith gathered that most of them were single, unmarried or divorced, in their thirties or early forties, farmers and teachers, stock agents, nurses, clerks. People who'd been young in the War. War victims, in their own way. Among them Lawrence looked slightly eccentric, with his duffle coat and long hair and friar cheeks.

The girls, as they were called, were more daring, sharper and noisier than married women. They joked and drank along with the men. There was something too familiar about the way Lawrence clapped them on the shoulders with his broad hand, Edith thought, something coarse about his laugh. And he had brought her to join them! She sat stony-faced, smoking in an armchair at the far end of the room. He came and perched his great bulk on the armrest.

'So, Edith,' he said, looking down at her, 'tell me about yourself. What do you do when you're not playing angel of mercy?'

'I look after my son.'

'But what do you do for yourself? Everyone has to have some pleasure.' He wouldn't ask her these questions if he hadn't been drinking, she knew. Sober, he was guarded and subtle.

'I read. I swim.' She spoke coldly. Her true pleasures, eating outside with Jim, a room of her own, the last cigarette alone on the verandah, seemed pitiful and thin in this brightness, indistinguishable from routine.

'What sort of life is that for a woman like you?'

She told him she would like to go home.

They were silent all the way back. 'I'll get down here,' she said as the Sea House came into view. All she wanted was to be walking alone again through the bush.

As she climbed out he leaned over the seat to her. 'Do you always keep yourself the stranger, Edith, everywhere you go?'

Thank goodness, she thought as she walked down through the Honeymoon Gardens. She had been rescued from the turmoil of the past few days, longing and exposure and defiance, and a strange guilt, as if she had betrayed someone.

He kept away for a few weeks. Then one spring evening the truck was waiting for her again in the carpark. He asked if he could drive her home. As soon as they were out of sight of the nursing home, he stopped the truck and put his arms around her. Purposeful but with the gleam of a smile, as if ironic even about this, his need for her, he kissed her neck and lap and ran his hands over her breasts. She was taken over by the smell of him, which had to do with the sweat of his hair and the soap of his cheeks, the warm splitting leather of the truck's seats, and, even deeper, the particular essence of his room in the stone farmhouse.

'You're different when you drink,' she whispered. They had crossed over again into that other realm where they could speak as directly as children.

He started up the truck again and drove with one hand on the wheel, the other holding onto her.

Jim grew used to Edith staying more often at the hospital. 'I'll be overnighting,' she'd tell him as she left in the morning, with instructions for his evening meal.

As darkness fell he paced the verandah, his arms folded, his heart racing a little. He was master of his own time, he could move at his own imperatives. The house itself seemed changed. The rooms held another aspect as if already they were angled to the future. He didn't light the lamp for a long time but let himself inhabit twilight spaces where he might live one day. On his desk beneath the window he could just make out the glow of an open page. He approached it and retreated, too restless to sit down. He tested himself outside, walking into the bush until he saw through darkness. He lay down on the earth and fell into the vast rushing space above him.

She liked to wake in the bedroom of the stone house. It was a treat that she rationed herself because she didn't like to leave Jim too much alone. She liked the solidity of the walls and the silence. It was milder land here, flatter and less romantic than the Clark block, without the relentless hollow roar of the sea. Cows grazed under silvery peppermint trees, pasture spread in every direction. Everything spoke, not of prosperity, but of self-sufficiency, of decades of patient management, of good sense and work. The light was dappled as a park. Birds dived into Emmeline's roses, left to themselves now, one, two seasons on, their long necks dipping and entwining beside the verandah, like gangly mating birds.

She felt different here, carefree and wilful. She liked to run the taps in the deep Ford bath and lie and listen to the sociable sounds of the kitchen, spitting fat and the trumpet call of the morning news. When she wasn't around, Lawrence listened all the time to the wireless. She knew a little about his life now. Most of his nights he spent alone here. He read journals and newspapers, articles on politics. He voted Labor. The Fords had always been left-wing. She was shocked and a little thrilled when he told her that a branch of the family was Communist.

He drank when she wasn't here. Whisky, or crude red wine he bought from Italian neighbours. He didn't try to hide the line of bottles in the kitchen. She'd telephoned him from the nursing home one night and heard his voice thickened and abrupt, holding himself in check from her. They didn't speak of this. Nor of his marriage. She didn't even know the name of his wife.

While she, right from the start, had felt the need to mention the name Leopold. One night, her elbow propped against his chest, she had yielded to the compulsion to tell him her whole story. She watched his eyes for irony but they were still and grave.

In daylight, once they detached themselves, they were resolutely unsentimental with each other. He cast a critical eye on everything, including Edith's life. As he drove her to work he told her that he thought she should leave the nursing home, she was overworked and underpaid. She was quick and smart, she should find another job, something where she could get ahead a bit. A business of her own perhaps. Nunderup was crying out for a post-office store for example.

'Who are you doing penance for? Your mother? This bloke, your cousin?'

'I caused his death.'

'Come on, it was wartime! Syria was crawling with English jeeps. How do you know it was him who was blown up? Why do you believe he's dead?'

'Because he never wrote!' It came out as a cry, for the letter that she'd never allowed herself to hope for.

'From what you've told me it sounds as if your cousin worked for the Secret Service. You said he spoke fluent Russian. By the end of the war Stalin had become enemy number one to the Brits. Who knows what he was asked to do?'

'He wouldn't just disappear.'

'Those were times when a lot of people took the chance to do just that.'

'You don't know Leopold. He wouldn't do that to us.'

'Have you ever thought of contacting the Red Cross or the British government or something?' He shook his head at her.

'You've done your time, Edith,' he said.

She could become angry with him. Then he knew she wouldn't see him for a few weeks. That was their pattern. She fell back into her solitary ways. Anger took her over, seemed to spread right back to the past. In spite of herself she had let Lawrence's words do their work and she now felt an obscure resentment towards Leopold. For what? In the end, for nothing but his desertion. The oldest grievance of the living for the dead.

Lawrence has infected me with his cynicism, she thought.

Then one morning she would wake up missing him and she knew the truck would be waiting for her in the carpark. Or sometimes he came for her at home, the truck bumping urgently into the clearing. As soon as he had shaken Jim's hand, he'd ask her to come for a drive with him, a defiant little grin on his face.

He always came back.

Jim and Lawrence, face to face, held themselves in neutral. Neither gave anything away. Nor did they speak of each other to Edith. Sometimes Lawrence invited Jim to come along with them to the outdoor picture show in Busselton. The three of them sank deep into their deckchairs, licking icecreams, a silent trio, Edith in the middle. They saw *From Here To Eternity*, the picture everybody was talking about, famous for its steamy romantic scenes.

I never knew I could be kissed like this, said Deborah Kerr.

Edith slapped at mosquitoes in a business-like way. She didn't want either of them to think she identified with this. *Only you.*

Forever. Did she believe that any more? She lit a cigarette. *Men Must Fight and Women Must Weep.* That was all in the past. In the Busselton Open-Air Cinema, 1954, she existed on a very different plane.

'Hysterical Yankee patriotism,' said Lawrence as they drove home.

Lawrence had no faith, Jim thought, wedged into the cab on the other side of Edith. Not in the War, or God or the Queen, or countries which were good or bad. He hadn't stood for the National Anthem at the pictures, the only person to stay seated. These were things that he, Jim, didn't yet know enough about to reject. He studied Lawrence carefully and listened to everything he said. He knew that Lawrence did not wish him or Edith harm—after Sir his senses were always on the alert for this. Lawrence was benign, but what did he believe in?

He'd felt uncomfortable with them, watching that couple on the screen. As if they were exposed. He knew his mother had a secret, not just her aloneness, which was still there, but a private sheen, a playfulness that she'd never had before.

It came to him as he watched Lawrence's competent hands on the wheel, that what Lawrence had put his faith in was Edith. It gave him a strange thrill of loneliness, but also of freedom ahead.

They were lovers in all seasons. Winter rain on the windows of the cab enclosed them. Afterwards they would wind down the windows and smell the soft air of the bush and the crushed eucalypts where the truck had pulled off from the track. In summer twilight if he picked her up from work, the hazy paddocks smelt of hot earth, and the trees' shadows falling rhythmically across the windscreen made them dreamily ecstatic.

One hot night at the farmhouse they left the bed and walked naked around the wide verandahs, splashing each other from the water bag hung to catch the breeze by the back door. The air dried them as they wandered around the yard, past the sheds, around the peppermint trees. He made her laugh, ambling ahead of her, his flat vulnerable buttocks very white in the darkness, his arms and shoulders brown. They were like strange creatures who didn't really belong here, like ghosts of the original settlers. Is this what they did, those Victorian couples, maddened by heat and isolation, rip off their high-necked clothing and wander naked, past caring whose eyes were watching them from the bush?

Had her parents ever wandered like this around the clearing while their little girls slept? Her father was too serious and her mother too afraid. Many nights Ada had crept into bed to sleep with her or Frances, from fear. What was it? The fear of death? Or pleasure?

Sometimes she remembered the room above the nightclub in Yerevan, the curl of Manouk's cigarette smoke, the princely ruby on his soft hand.

I shall miss our exchange, wrote Miss Betts on the last of Jim's Correspondence papers, in her girlish immaculate hand. *You're a gifted student, Jim, and I hope that, after discussion with your mother of course, you will consider going on to further study. There are bursaries available to help country students come to city schools to complete their matriculation. I recommend that, circumstances permitting, you apply for one of these.*

I myself have reached retirement age and am taking Mother on a sea cruise to the Eastern States. So it is time to say goodbye and good luck!

She never did sign just *Letitia.*

'You know, Jim,' Edith said that night on the verandah, 'your grandfather studied to become a teacher.'

'That's the last thing in the world I want to be.'

'Leopold studied. He went to university and became an archaeologist.'

Jim looked out into the bush and didn't say anything. Leopold's life was the stuff of myth, of books, and what use was that to him here?

'There is Irina's money,' Edith said. 'It's put away for you.'

It wasn't just that school, or university or any institution was a black hole that didn't bear thinking about. It was out of the question that he could ever leave Edith alone here, slaving to support him, sending him what little money she had. It was time for him to take his place in the world, but what was he to do? Hire himself out to farmers? He knew nothing about farming. Nor did he want to be a clerk filing cards at the Torville Road Board. He went and lay on his bed. He was nearly seventeen and ashamed as each day passed that he had no job.

He thought about his future so much it was as if he became detached from the present. It felt strange just to feed the chooks. Everything he did seemed provisional. He slunk into the Sea House kitchen with the eggs and out again without a word. At night the cicadas began to disturb him. He couldn't concentrate because the creaks of the house were so loud. The summer breeze played its endless game with the curtain above his desk. The curtain had no colour or pattern and like an ancient shroud disintegrated to the touch. It had not been changed since his grandfather built the place.

His desk was a wasteland, blasted, pathetic. He opened books but the words seemed dead to him. He picked up *The Epic of Gilgamesh* and studied the photograph of Leopold. He saw the fatherless boy this time, shadowed by mother, burdened by cap, badge, bike. He saw fear in Leopold's eyes, as if he knew the future would consume him. '*Oh Gilgamesh, where are you wandering?*' he read on the open page. '*The life that you seek you will never find . . .*'

'But you, Gilgamesh, let your belly be full
enjoy yourself always by day and by night!
Make merry each day,
dance and play each night!

'Let your clothes be clean,
let your head be washed, may you bathe in water!
Gaze on the child who holds your hand.
let your wife enjoy your repeated embrace!'

What use was that advice, for a young man? Jim could not eat. He felt sick, as if something terrible was going to happen. He roamed the bush at night and in the day he could see no point in getting up off his bed. His heart beat when a crow called overhead. The days ground on, week after week.

One day he dragged himself up to the Sea House, his springy hair damped down with water, his face nicked with shaving cuts. He asked to see Reg.

'What can I do for you, Jim?' Everything in Reg's office, the ceiling, the dusty fan, the diamond-paned windows, seemed stained a blurry yellow-brown, like Reg himself.

'I need a job.' Jim was surprised by his voice, thick and urgent. He had the odd impression that a stranger had taken him over, cruder but more decisive than him, a man of action, and he was curious to see what he'd do next.

'I see. What did you have in mind?'

'Anything. Groundsman. I can chop wood. Or kitchen hand. I know how to cook a bit.'

'Do you now?' Reg said mildly, his kind, tired eyes blinking at Jim.

Suddenly there was a series of loud, angry knocks on the ceiling above them. Someone was pounding the floor with a stick.

Reg jumped up as if he'd been recalled to his senses. 'Excuse me, Jim, I have to go. I suppose you've heard Mrs Tehoe's had a spot of bother with her health?'

Smiling, he came around his desk. He put his arm up around Jim's shoulders and steered him out into the lobby. Jim could see the sad, dandruffy strands draped like seaweed across Reg's sunburnt head.

'I'm afraid there's no jobs going at the moment, old man.' His breath was rough and sweet from his afternoon aperitif.

'Then what am I to do?' Jim said. He'd thought of this as his last hope.

'Go home,' said Reg, 'there's a good lad. Give my regards to your mother.' He added in a whisper beneath his stained moustache: 'I'll see what I can do.' Soothing, as to a mad boy. He hobbled urgently up the stairs.

The late afternoon sun streaming into the hall of the Sea House showed flaky paint, dusty panelling, motheaten carpet. The palace of Jim's childhood had grown tawdry, it could no longer offer protection. There was death in the air here, Jim could smell it. An era was drawing to an end.

The reckless stranger seemed to have deserted him as he made his way home through the Honeymoon Gardens. The kookaburras' evening chorus filled him with weariness. He heard the whip-whip-whip of the sprinklers like the hum of his self-dislike. Some college boys ran past on their way to the surf, towels flying from their bare shoulders.

He met Gareth on the track along the top of the headland. Gareth was coming back from the sea, barefoot, without shirt or towel, wind-dried, sand and salt stiffening his hair, streaked across his small, strong torso.

They stopped and faced each other in the old way.

'I've just seen your old man,' Jim said. Why did he say that? It broke their warrior pact of silence.

Gareth shrugged. A cool breeze seemed to blow from his salty body. It was restful standing here with him.

Words came to Jim, filed away over the years. Scraps of Tehoe gossip overheard in the Sea House kitchen. Reg had a brother who was here when war broke out. *She* fancied him. He'd had to do a runner, joined the Merchant Navy. A few months later, Gareth comes along. Poor old Reg. *Reg is laid up with gout, he keeps his distance. Ronnie sends his regards.*

Gareth wasn't a carefree schoolboy like his friends. He always seemed alone, adrift, unattached. His eyes watched Jim with the old, impersonal curiosity. He'd never seemed young to Jim.

Without a father, you had no youth.

What he really wanted to say to Gareth was: *When are you going to leave?*

But not yet. They nodded and passed on. It occurred to Jim for the first time that for Gareth he must be the dark man, the wild man from the plains.

But he was tired of old men's myths. He was oppressed by them.

Edith was smoking on the verandah, waiting for him. These days she started work an hour earlier so she could be home before nightfall. Her son was unwell, she said, some sort of night fever. She didn't do any more overnighting. She didn't go anywhere with Lawrence.

She watched Jim as he came across the clearing. He'd shaved and put on shoes, but was still sombre, his head lowered. Each evening when she saw him she hoped his mood had changed. These days the quietness between them wasn't companionable.

He was too much alone. It wasn't right for a boy to have nobody but his mother to talk to. It wasn't normal for a healthy young man to be so wretched. She had a fear for him that she found difficult to name.

She stayed up all night while he went roaming. She didn't know what else to do for him except to wait and keep the lamp burning on the kitchen table. Sometimes she thought of that other Dmitri, Irina's little brother who had walked off forever into the snow. When Jim came home at dawn and fell into his bed, she dressed and went to work.

Hour after hour she sat on the dark verandah and smoked and searched the past. What if despair was inherited? Was there a darkness to Jim's grief that went beyond the facts of his own childhood? His Armenian grandparents had been murdered. Aram had seen his mother die. Did Aram's actions in Armenia amount to suicide? Did he die in despair?

He didn't feel he really belonged in the world, Leopold had once said of Aram. She would have liked to discuss this now with Leopold. He was the only one she could have shared this vigil with. Once, in moments of need, he would have come back to her, she could conjure up his words, they were a part of her. But some time in the past few years, without knowing she did it, she had let him go, floating into the ether.

And what about her own parents, driven to despair in this clearing? Could melancholy be passed on? She might have escaped, but what use was that to her if Jim bore the burden?

She was too tired to bear such guilt.

How could she save him, this time? There was nobody she could talk to, or ask for advice. She didn't trust doctors or teachers, or even her own sister. She'd told Lawrence she could not see him for a while. She was alone in this, as always, with Jim.

'Let him be,' Lawrence said.

He'd arrived to sit with her on the verandah. 'Mohammed comes to the mountain,' he said, jumping out of his truck one night. 'What's all this about?' He was carrying a bottle of wine, and she saw he was already a little bright-eyed.

Jim was in his room. In a low voice Edith said that he was rather down in the dumps. 'I don't know what to do for him,' she said, trying to be casual, lighting another cigarette, refusing to show the relief she felt at seeing Lawrence. She waited for him to say: *What he needs is a good kick in the pants.*

'You should have told me sooner, Edith,' was all he said.

He insisted that a glass of wine would do her good. 'Got a corkscrew?' he asked. He lumbered into the kitchen, too big for this house, whistling, somehow happy. She heard him rummaging in the dresser and then knocking on Jim's door. He went in. After a little while he came out, winked at Edith and set about opening his bottle. Jim came out. Lawrence poured them all a drink and he and Jim sat down at the little table.

Then Lawrence, who usually couldn't be bothered with chat, started to talk. Of football—he had a cousin playing for Bunbury. Of the latest crazy thing the government had done. Of the unsettled summer weather. Calm and genial, he addressed himself to Jim, without asking for a response. Offered him news of the world.

It touched her, sitting on the steps, to see Lawrence there, his huge shadow hovering over the verandah, his movements curiously tactful. Because he was there she felt able to sit back and let her thoughts race a little with the wine. The night was hot with distant growls of thunder. Moths thumped against the lamp on the table. Jim's eyes were less sunken and his mouth made the movements of smiling. She studied the two of them together, the solidity of the man, the nervous slenderness of the boy. Lawrence raised his arm to tip the last dregs from the bottle and she saw a dark ring of sweat on his shirt. She could feel his energy, steamy and hidden, like a slow-moving summer river.

'You're good for me, Edith,' he'd said once, after one of their reunions. 'I'm lazy.' He was a successful farmer by habit and upbringing, he said, not out of ambition. One day he'd sell up and build a shack on the coast and go fishing. He liked to have no obligations. He found it suited him to be a bachelor.

All the same, he never let her go away too far or for too long.

Strange to be in something like this, with no future, no path leading elsewhere, no distant, ideal destination.

She remembered Lawrence telling her how strict his father was, even by standards of the time, how hard he'd worked him, from very young. She pictured Lawrence as he would have been when he was Jim's age: the quietness of a boy held too much in check, his secret wildness, his powers of observation.

He leaned his head down to her as she saw him off in the truck. 'Let him be, Edith,' he said.

Late that night the black sky above the cliffs cracked open with a gash of light. Thunder rumbled over Jim's head as he was walking and a fiery scribble lit up the sea's horizon. He turned back into the bush. Just as he reached the clearing there was a flash of lightning so close that he fell to his knees. The sky flicked on and off above him, and he saw as in a dream the blue dance of the bush, the frail crouching house with its pinpoint of light. And then the obliterating rain.

In autumn a letter came from Frances, inviting them to Albany. *I'm sure you're in need of a holiday*, Frances wrote, *and now that we've got the pigs we could do with a hand from Jim.* Edith's eyes pricked for a moment, in spite of herself. She was indeed tired. She took a week off from the nursing home, and they caught the bus south.

It was raining in the Great Southern. The hills of Albany rose up from the Sound and disappeared into mist, as if they were great mountains. Frances's world was *more* than theirs in every way. The farm stretched across acres of scrubby headland. The farmhouse was a large fibro bungalow with a nest of small dark rooms. Striped canvas blinds on the front porch flapped day and night against rope moorings. The wind here was fiercer, blowing straight in from the Antarctic. The Southern Ocean was a colder ocean than the Indian, the coastline more treacherous.

Frances and Lee collected things. You could hardly shut the doors of the little bedrooms, they were so full of what they called antiques, battered preserving pots and horse tackle and rocking chairs that they bought at sales of old houses in the area. Manuals and farming journals were piled up on every surface in the lounge room. The kitchen was so crowded with projects that they lined up their pots and pans along the hall.

It soon became clear that Jim was their latest project. At first light the next morning Frances knocked on his door. He went out with them into the freezing dawn to shovel out pigsties. We've been keeping these jobs for you, Jim, they said.

Jim discovered that he hated pigs, their brutal shrewdness, their shocking smell. But worse than that, he knew he was being tested. He sneaked away for long sessions reading in the lavatory. He disappeared for whole afternoons, walking along the headlands and miles of windswept beach. But he knew that sooner or later he must face it, the enormous mystery of work.

Every task must have its rules, he thought, a system, a secret knowledge. Like cricket and football, those endless games some boys seemed born knowing how to play. The shovelling of pig shit. Point one. The correct placement of hands on the handle of the shovel. Point two. The approach. Start at the back of the pen and move outwards?

Jim, Jim, how're you going? Haven't you even started yet! . . .

The work stretched out ahead of him like a series of impossible tasks in a fairytale. All that he could count on was that something would always go wrong, the shovel handle would snap, the pigs would bolt . . . *Jim, what on earth were you thinking about . . .*

He thought about work all day. There wasn't one job he didn't try to analyse, that didn't have its own mystery, its own sort of radiance. It was as if *that* was his work.

I'm not a farmer, I never wanted to be a bloody farmer, he fantasised saying to Frances. But what *did* he want? Time and space. For what? To think. To wait for the revelation. But how could he ask for that?

At night as the blinds slapped in the icy wind, he dreamt he saw his father standing in a barren field high above a river gorge. Jim knew the rocky earth, the metal-grey light was Armenia. His father, in a long black coat, was standing with his arms crossed, looking at him. How did he know it was his father? He had the same face as the man among the leaves. A sombre face, his eyes challenging. The message of the dream seemed clear when Jim woke, but a moment later he could not recall it.

They cooked up huge rich meals, stews, steak and kidney pie, liver and bacon. Apple turnover with cream. *We've got to fatten you up, Edith!* Frances was strong and solid now, and her cheeks were rosy. How the two farmers tucked in, how comfortable they seemed! They were beginning to resemble each other. Once they were opposites, Lee voluptuous, chunky, oily-skinned, Frances all dry and bony and ascetic. Their smiles were similar, loyal but slow to trust, and their eyes, deepset farmer's eyes, watched him in the same way. They insisted Edith should be spoiled and she sat all day with her feet in the oven. The sisters didn't seem angry with each other any more. In fact his mother had adopted a girlish persona that he'd never seen before, idle and airy, slightly wicked.

Jim retreated up the draughty pot-lined hall to his room.

He found himself wishing for his table at home, for paper and a pencil. He felt his old need to set down the commentary running through his head.

It was then as Jim lay on his bed and heard their voices in the kitchen, that he realised that these sisters, *the Clark girls*, beneath all their travails, their air of martyrdom, their touchy pride, *had never denied themselves anything that they really wanted.* They did what they wanted to do, and always had, and they had a good time, in their own way.

He thought of the generations of nameless dogs in their family, trained to stay home and guard the women.

He had to get away.

He stalked into the kitchen and told them that he was leaving that night, that minute, if they couldn't give him a lift he would walk. Edith could come or stay, it was up to her. They didn't try to argue with him, his anger was too pure. It was too late for the bus to Bunbury, but he said he'd catch the night train to Perth. Frances drove them to the station and he saw that she was nervous, she had trouble with the gears. He realised that she still thought he blamed her for Westlea, she didn't understand that he'd forgiven her from the very beginning. But he said nothing because he'd learnt a long time ago that anger protected him from her.

The night train was half empty and they managed to find a compartment on their own. It seemed like a good omen for the journey: at once their mood changed. As the whistle blew their eyes met and they couldn't help smiling for a moment at the old exhilaration of escape.

'Poor old Frances,' Edith said, as the train slid out of the station. Still, she had Lee to go home to now. Edith pictured them sitting in their cluttered little kitchen, deep in discussion of Frances's impossible relatives.

'Why do you say that?' Jim sat back, his man's legs stretched out between them, one half of his face lit from the lights of the passing town outside the window, the other half in shadow.

'Because she meant well. She wanted to help you. I've been thinking about her these last few days. How she was as a young girl. She didn't get enough affection. Our parents were always so preoccupied. And you know, Frances is a person who craves affection.'

He did know. He felt he was on the verge of knowing everything. He closed his eyes and for a moment he saw 'the world', as he called it, which for him was always a street at night in the old quarter of a city, the voices coming from the rooms, snatches of music, the smell of food, the soft, red, dangerous lights. One day he would go there and come to know it and write it all down.

'And there you are,' Edith was saying, 'she found it. She got what she really wanted.'

The night was cold and clear. Sometimes the dark bush opened for a moment to reveal a patch of moonlight across a clearing or the surface of a dam.

Why did she feel this way, a lightness, as if a shadow had lifted from them? As if a great wing had brushed over the carriage roof and flapped away into the darkness. She felt free. She had a conviction, without quite knowing why, that whatever Jim did now was out of her hands.

When this train reached Perth they would catch the early train to Bunbury. She would phone Lawrence from the station and he would pick them up in the truck. He'd told her to do this. Lawrence was feeding the dog and the chooks for them, and collecting their mail. He was working on a car for her, Emmeline's old Hillman that had been lying for years around the farm. She'd do him a favour to take it off the place, he said. He was going to teach her to drive. He'd take a bet, he said, wiping his hands on a rag, slowly, infuriatingly, that they wouldn't be speaking by the time she passed her test.

They creaked to a stop at every tiny siding. Some were lit by a single kerosene lamp. Sometimes Jim saw men come and go in the shadows, in coats for the cold inland night. Some exchange went on further down the track, the thump of a mail sack, quick voices in the sleeping dark. Sometimes there seemed to be no reason for stopping, nothing moved, there was nothing but the empty platform and silence.

He felt detached, as if this journey was a farewell to his past and also a prologue to all the journeys he was going to make. He didn't know how yet or where to. He'd tell Edith of his decision when they got home. He'd tell Gareth.

They'd gathered speed, the wheels were rushing them into the night. One day, he thought, he would be older than his father was when he died.

What they didn't know yet was that there was a letter waiting for them in the kitchen, a mute white rectangle lying on the table as the mice ran across the floor and the birds pecked in the vine over the window. Lawrence had collected it from their mailbox, turned it over, examined the stamp and the confident script, an educated hand, he thought. Someone who had forgotten their full address, yet knew this would be enough to find them. *Nunderup, Western Australia.* He fleetingly considered all it might have survived—theft (the stamp was unusual), fire, shipwreck, the carelessness of a clerk—before he propped it up against the teapot. He knew it was auspicious. He ran his eyes around the battered little kitchen for a moment, locked the door behind him, left.

Strange how one small object could seem to hold all the light in a room. Edith, still in her coat, with the dog winding itself around her legs, saw the letter before anything else.

Jim had gone straight to his room. Lawrence was bent over the stove, lighting the fire he had set.

She recognised the thick black script, had time to think that writing too grew older, sadder.

'Jim,' she called, and something in the quietness of her voice made him come at once. Lawrence went outside to fill the kettle. She pointed at the letter. 'You open it.' She sank into a chair. 'Read it out to me.'

Dearest Edith, Dearest Jim, he began, in his young, honest voice, frowning slightly, slightly embarrassed.

I am only now ready to write this letter. His head jerked up and his eyes met Edith's for a moment. He went on.

I know that long ago you will have learnt to live without me. As I never quite have, without you both. I wonder if you will ever be able to forgive me.

The real war began for me before the official war ended, soon after I left you in Syria. It was a time when 'one did what was requested of one', as they used to say. In this spirit I was recruited. But no cause redeems putting yourself above simple moral rules. I made a choice. I have had many years to live with the consequences.

All I can say is that I thought you would be in touch with my mother. I didn't know how soon she was to die. I was not informed of her death for a long time.

And Aunt Ada? I hardly dare ask. Please give my fondest regards to Frances, wherever she may be.

From the first day of my new life I began to count the cost. In a matter of weeks my hair turned white. I started to see that once in this game, you're never really out. I was taken over by a futility and desolation of which I will not speak. When finally I managed to resurface, I was in no shape to contact you for quite some years.

Do you still have the book of Gilgamesh? It's a consolation sometimes to think that thousands of years ago, men knew about all this. The return. Wasn't he told to go home, eat, drink and be merry? Take the hand of his child? Something like that.

If I trust my intuition—I've learnt to trust little else—I would say that you, Edith, have found your place by now. And Jim? At seventeen, at the start of it all? Perhaps in need of some new horizons.

I live quietly here in Baghdad. I have a small house in the Moslem quarter, a servant, a café where I read and drink my coffee. I continue my studies of Arabic, teach a little, visit sites in the desert. I plan to join an expedition to my old dig one day.

My dear ones, my one wish now is that this letter finds you, in happiness and good health.

'So,' said Lawrence from the doorway. 'He's come back?'

She heard the branch brushing across the roof, the distant crack of the surf. The sea breeze had started up as it always did, at the same time every day.

'Why don't you write to him?' she said to Jim.

Jim said he wanted to leave by himself. Lawrence offered to drive them all up to Fremantle, but Jim said he would rather go by train. He wanted to leave Edith as casually as possible, to stroll out of the clearing as if he were going to Torville, hurrying a little by the time he reached the track as he always did for the bus, because he was always a little late. He wanted it crystalline, the air clear, the break swift and clean.

But they woke to soft rain. A curtain seemed to have fallen over the clearing, the birds were silent, the world in shadow. 'Take the old oilskin,' Edith said. Her voice trailed. When would she give that up? Jim shook his head. He was wearing a black fisherman's cap from the Army Surplus store in Bunbury. It suited him. His eyes were dark with resolution. He spoke like an Australian, but he looked like a young foreign man.

I am exercising, Leopold wrote in his last letter, *walking every morning along the walls of the Tigris. Trying to get myself in some sort of shape so I'll be able to keep up with a young man.* Edith pictured him sitting in his café, sipping thick black coffee, books spread out before him, his white hair stirring under a slow fan. Glasses now, she thinks, and a plate of halva. She sees his plump hand hovering over it while he reads his Arabic newspaper, from right to left, from back to front. There is something immoveable about the way he sits, everything within his reach.

She liked to think of the way he would raise his head as the stranger comes into the café, of the gleam of recognition kindling in his eyes. Of the way he finds himself springing up as he reaches over the table to take this young man's hands in his.

'I thought you'd want to go,' Lawrence had said to her last night, as the three of them sat talking, the moths hitting the lamp. 'I thought you'd be on the first ship out.'

She shrugged. The shrug said what she didn't tell him, because that was their way with one another, that for her the great adventure now was to stay.

It was time for Jim to go. The air shook a little and everything turned unreal. Passport, ticket, money, notebook: he stood on the verandah and checked his pockets, already in the traveller's world.